D1264875

INCIDENT AT MUC WA

Books by Daniel Ford

NOW COMES THEODORA

INCIDENT AT MUC WA

INCIDENT AT MUC WA

DANIEL FORD

1967
DOUBLEDAY & COMPANY, INC.
GARDEN CITY, NEW YORK

Library of Congress Catalog Card Number 67–12876

Printed in the United States of America
First Edition

INCIDENT AT MUC WA

Readers who have never visited Southeast Asia will instantly recognize the locale of my story as the Vietnamese Central Highlands.

Those who have been there will know better. They will understand that the book is a fiction—places, people, and military units—and that it is not intended as a description of combat in South Vietnam.

It is dedicated nevertheless to the too-many-thousand men who joined that combat, who did what they were told, and who died.

One

"Could you direct me to the Raider School?" Rebecca asked.

"That's part of the Covert Warfare Center, Miss," the gate guard said, trying to look down the front of her dress.

"Covert Warfare? Where's that?"

"Just follow the signs, Miss."

Rebecca returned to her Volkswagen. She was a sweet little body, as she well knew, and the gate guard stared after her while she drove the car into the sprawling, sandy reaches of Fort Darby. She saw him in the rear-view mirror, leaning so far into the roadway that he almost fell out of the guardhouse. *I am Mata Hari,* she thought. *I dr-r-r-rive men wild and steal their secrets, the fools.* Rebecca was a reporter for the College Heights (N.C.) *Observer,* and was also a stringer for the *Liberal,* although that prestigious, low-paying magazine had yet to publish any of her articles. The arrangement was likely to continue, however. Rebecca was interested in the *Liberal* because it was prestigious, and the editor was interested in her because she was happy to work for nothing. She was twenty-three, and one year out of college, and her father owned a Cadillac-Oldsmobile dealership.

It was a bright day, and North Carolina was heavy with spring. As Rebecca drove along, following the signs which directed her toward the Covert Warfare Center, she passed bayonet ranges and assault courses where perfectly nice, ordinary young men were learning how to kill one another. They made barking noises while they plunged their bayonets into sawdust-filled dummies. Drill sergeants in broad-brimmed hats were urging them on. The cries reached Rebecca over the hum of the engine: "BLOOD! KILL! ARRRGH!" Rebecca felt close to tears. She wanted to wheel the Volkswagen around, drive home, and never come near Fort Darby again. But she didn't. *You have a job to do, Mata Hari,* she told herself.

Rebecca's reasons for doing anything were generally complex. She had entered Fort Darby on her press card from the College Heights *Observer*, intending, if she could see enough and hear enough, to write an article for the *Liberal*. But what she really wanted to do was make her peace with Private First Class Stephen Courcey, whose shins she had kicked the last time they met. Yes. She had been sitting happily in jail, soaking up material for an article about the treatment of civil-rights marchers, when the steel door swung open and there was Stephen Courcey, in a policeman's uniform that didn't belong to him, saying in a Southern drawl that didn't belong to him either: "Yawl go home now, hear?" Thinking she would be terribly pleased. Hah! She had kicked him, first in the right shin, then in the left. Then, while he was doubled over with surprise and pain, she had pounded his ugly, marvelous face with her fists. Yes. Damn him.

But now she was ready to make her peace with him. *I'll seduce him if I have to,* she thought. *He wants to devote himself to something; very well, he can devote himself to me. . . . Kiss me, fool!* Rebecca told him, wriggling her tail in the bucket seat. Except that Stephen had never been backward about kissing her. Such nice lips, too. And gentle, powerful hands. *Oh, I should have gone the distance with him, that time on the Cape,* she thought. *He would have been wonderful, I know. But of course I was engaged to be married, so it wouldn't have been right. He'll be glad he waited. I'll make him glad he waited.* She glowed like brandy in front of an open fire.

Rebecca had just been jilted by her fiancé, who worked for

a publishing house in New York City, and who had been responsible for introducing her to Petrel McMurphy, editor of the *Liberal.* Now Robert planned to marry a blonde, empty-headed, gentile bitch who would make him miserable, which would serve him exactly right. Rebecca didn't care. Not really. She was delighted, in fact, because now she could give herself in good conscience to Stephen Courcey.

Such were her reasons for visiting Fort Darby that day in spring, 1964, ten years after the French had been gallantly and thoroughly whipped in Southeast Asia, and less than a year before American combat troops were committed to that same interminable war.

After half an hour of driving across sandy hills and through groves of great, long-needled pines, Rebecca came upon a tall board fence which seemed to stretch for miles. The fence was about twelve feet high. There was a small door facing the roadway, and upon this door was a sign:

MOCK VILLAGE

Property of the Raider School

USARGA

Do Not Enter

From inside the fence came the sound of gunfire and strange, birdlike cries.

Well done, Mata Hari, Rebecca told herself. She parked the Volkswagen on the grass strip between the road and the fence. This was much better than going to the Covert Warfare Center, where she would be faced with a lot of surly questions. In her year as a reporter Rebecca had learned that the good people were never to be found in front offices. Humming contentedly, she walked to the door and opened it. *Good heavens!* she thought. She was standing at the edge of a primitive village, with bamboo huts set high on stilts, and pigs, chickens, and half-naked men running about. The men were shouting and firing rifles into the air. Most of them were very small and very Oriental, but there were a few Negro and white Americans among them. The Americans ran more slowly, shouted less, and generally did not seem to be enjoying themselves, perhaps because they were wearing boots. The Orientals were barefoot. Apart from that, they were all dressed alike, in olive-green waistcloths that came down to their knees. Each man was also carrying a cartridge belt, slung across his chest or buckled over his waistcloth.

Rebecca strolled uncertainly through the village, hoping to find Stephen Courcey in this mad carnival. A pig trotted up to her, grunting curiously. But none of the soldiers—she assumed they were soldiers—seemed to notice her.

The village, she found, was backed up against the board fence on only one side. The other three sides were fashioned from barbed wire and bamboo stakes. Beyond the village—but still inside the board fence—soldiers in green uniforms were advancing through the pines. They were shouting and firing rifles, too, but in a more orderly way.

"Hey!" cried a voice at Rebecca's feet. "Watch it, huh?" She jumped back: she had almost stepped through a bamboo grill. There were other grills nearby, each covering a hole in the ground, and weighted at the corners with rocks. Rebecca knelt to peer into the hole from which the voice had come.

"Hello there," she said.

"Yeah," the voice said. It belonged to a marvelous truck-driver type, paunchy, his face creased and battered. He was wearing a green fatigue uniform like the soldiers who were attacking the village. Too big for the pit, he was lying with his knees drawn up and his head propped at an uncomfortable angle against the far side. This gave him a perfect vantage point for staring up Rebecca's skirt, which he did with honest fascination. She tried to pull the skirt over her knees, but it was too short, so she hugged them with her arms instead. "You got a cigarette, lady?" the soldier asked. "Them damn gooks took mine."

"Oh . . . Yes." She lighted two cigarettes and passed one through the bamboo grill. "What's going on?" she asked. "Are you a prisoner?"

"You know it, lady," the soldier said, puffing on his cigarette.

"But what is this place?"

"It's all on account of the gooks," he said, waving the cigarette in a gesture which took in the entire village. "The Koreans," he explained. "We got a whole shitload—shipload—a couple months ago, for to train them as Raiders, only we ain't at war with Korea any more, so the Old Man he got the bright idea of building this place. See?"

"No."

"Well, it's a gook village, see, and one week we attack it, and the next week we're inside it and *they* attack it. Well, this is our week to attack it, only they set an ambush and I got captured."

"You must be terribly uncomfortable," Rebecca said.

"Nah. It's better than running around out there in the sun. Except when it rains. I was in here one time when it did that, and I like to drowned."

"Don't they call off the . . . the exercise when it rains?"

"Nah. We're Raiders," the prisoner said in an unenthusiastic voice. "We're the roughest, toughest, goddamnedest soldiers in the U. S. Army."

A whistle cut through the gunfire and the shouting. It seemed to be a man, whistling through his teeth, but the sound was amplified many times. It was followed by a voice from an invisible loudspeaker: "All right, you men in the Aggressor force! You're falling behind the scenario. You're supposed to be overrun at fifteen hundred hours, so get with it!"

"The Aggressor force," the prisoner said to Rebecca. "He means the gooks."

"But *you're* attacking *them*."

"Yeah, but they're the Aggressors, all right. We're the Friendly force, see?"

Now there was some hand-to-hand combat in the barbed-wire defenses of the village. It all seemed terribly unfair—the Koreans were so small, the Americans so large—but Rebecca was pleased to see that the Aggressors were doing very well for themselves. Sometimes an officer in a white helmet had to stop a fight and convince the Korean that he was dead.

But she would have to be quick, if she was to learn about Stephen Courcey from her friendly prisoner. "Sergeant?" she said.

"Me?" he said. "Lady, I'm just a buck-ass private."

"Well, do you happen to know Stephen Courcey, Private First Class Courcey?"

"Corporal Courcey. He got his second stripe last month."

"You *do* know him?"

"Yeah," the prisoner said. "College man."

"Is he here?"

"Nah. He shipped out. That's how come he made corporal, see: they gave him his second stripe and shipped him out."

"Where?" Rebecca said, remembering the old ballad she had heard at that fraternity party in College Heights, the night she had met Stephen Courcey: *If you will not when you may, you may not when you will, sir!*

"We ain't supposed to know," the prisoner said.

"But you do know?"

"Yeah, we know, all right."

"Well, *where?*"

"Same place we're all going, sooner or later," he told her, waving his cigarette at the bamboo grill which separated them. "Gooksville."

"Southeast Asia?"

"That's the name of the game, all right."

Rebecca stood up, awash with dismay. *Oh, Stephen!* she thought. *You're going to play this game for real.* The Aggressors were falling back toward the center of the village now, toward her, and the green-clad soldiers were inside the barbed wire and advancing remorselessly, firing their rifles from the hip. Sometimes an officer in a white helmet would run up to one of the soldiers and make a chalk mark on his uniform, whereupon the boy would stretch out and pretend to be dead. *Why?* Rebecca asked herself. *Why do men become soldiers? Stephen—oh! Have you been reading Hemingway again?*

One of the Koreans ran up to her, dipped his head politely, and pointed his rifle into the prison pit. "So, Private Hollis," he said. "You die now."

"*Pagh!*" said the prisoner. "If they's anything I hate, it's a sore loser."

A saintly smile spread across the Korean's face, and the rifle exploded with a frightful bang. "*Ooo!*" Rebecca said. But the cartridge was a blank, apparently, because the prisoner carefully butted his cigarette against the sole of his boot, then shredded it, scattering the tobacco and rolling the cigarette paper into a little ball. Then he wriggled around in the pit, found a comfortable position, and closed his eyes. The Korean carefully placed his rifle on the ground. Then he raised his arms above his head, still smiling his beatific smile.

The battle seemed to be over. The Aggressors were squatting on the ground with their hands folded behind their necks, looking terribly pathetic, while the American troops guarded them with rifles. Rebecca turned toward the board fence. She had an awful time locating the door, which was almost invisible from this side.

"Just a minute, Miss!" a white-helmeted officer said to her. "You can't go out that way."

"That's the way I came in," Rebecca said.

"You can't have. That's a no-entrance door."

"Well, I did, so why don't I just go out and you can pretend it never happened?"

"Who are you, anyway?" the officer said, looking at the clipboard in his left hand. "A nurse?"

"No," Rebecca told him. "I'm a spy."

"Are you in the scenario?" he asked, studying the clipboard.

"No, I'm a special problem."

"Damn them," the officer said. "They're always doing this to me." He wrote something on the clipboard, and Rebecca took the opportunity to open the door and step outside, where her Volkswagen was parked peaceably on the grass, and a little girl in a print dress was bicycling down the road. "Hey!" the officer shouted. "What'd you say your name was?"

"Mata Hari," Rebecca said, getting into the Volkswagen and starting the engine.

"Miss!" he shouted. "How do you spell that? Please—Miss!"

Rebecca drove back to College Heights in a mist of tears. She went straight to her little apartment, telephoned the *Observer* with the news that she was suddenly, vaguely ill, and threw herself across the bed, which was large enough for two, only now there was no one to share it with her. The mist had become an ocean, drowning her in bitter, easeful tears. *Twenty-three years old,* she thought, *and I've been jilted by one man and abandoned by another. Oh, oh, oh . . . DAMN! . . . And the worst part of it is, I can't send Robert's ring back to him. He never gave me one, the bastard.*

After a while she felt better. She lit a cigarette and smoked it, sitting on the bed, relaxed and sad. She kept the sadness at a comfortable weight by thinking, now and again, of Robert with his gentile girlfriend, and Stephen Courcey attacking innocent villages in Southeast Asia. Gradually Stephen's image began to drive out Robert's, which was strange, because he wasn't at all good-looking. He rather resembled a monkey, in fact. Long arms and a low, brooding forehead, yes, and *oh! he always ended by sitting on the floor with those long arms wrapped around his knees, remember? Brooding. Always brooding. He was the first intelligent man I ever met who didn't have one of those ridiculous high foreheads. Or wear glasses. I suppose that's why they drafted him—because he didn't wear glasses. But oh!—why did he have to join the Raiders, those killers, those storm troopers? Why did he have to go to Southeast Asia?*

Rebecca butted the cigarette and, only half-aware, folded her arms around her knees. She imagined a jungle: yellow-green and festooned with snakes, and shrieking parrots flying through it, and men locked in silent combat while leeches dropped from the trees. *Ecch!* But perhaps it wasn't like that, after all. Perhaps it was beautiful, with white and purple flowers that bloomed all the year around. . . .

I wonder what it's like over there, she thought. *I wonder what it's really like.*

Two

Captain Olivetti came off patrol at dawn, slept five hours, and bounded awake with a great sense of joy. What a ball! What a rinky-dink ball! He put on a clean set of jungle fatigues and went over to the officers' latrine. *You're a handsome bastard,* he told his reflection in the mirror. His face shone back at him like a great brass sun. *You'll make major before you're thirty, by God you will, thanks to this rinky-dink war.* Snorting joyfully, he scrubbed his face and scoured his teeth, while his ears told him that something very odd was transpiring behind the latrine. After taking a good healthy crap for himself, he went out back to see what it was.

Six or seven Raiders from last night's patrol were clustered around a water jug, a big clay job almost as tall as they were. A man's bare feet projected above the rim of the jug. One of the Raiders held each foot and watched with pleased expressions as the air bubbles formed and broke in the gray, scummy water. The others stood aside for Captain Olivetti, although there was really no need. Even on his knees, he was taller than any gook. "What's going on?" he asked Cowboy, the interpreter.

"This man," Cowboy said, indicating the bare feet, "same man you capture last night. Him say: he not know any Communist rebels. But we make him talk, sir."

"Pull him out, for Christ's sake," Captain Olivetti said. "He can't tell you anything if you drown him."

"Yes, sir!" Cowboy said, and spoke in fluting bird cries to the other Raiders, who pulled the prisoner out of the water jug and stretched him on the ground. He coughed and vomited water. Cowboy hunkered down and asked a question in some damned dialect or other. The prisoner only coughed. Cowboy grabbed the man's wet, stringy hair and pounded his head a couple times against the ground. This was an odd thing about Cowboy: he seemed to hate gooks, although he was half-gook himself. French father. An officer, or so Cowboy claimed. Anyhow, he spoke French and English and about seventy-eight mountain dialects. Handsome little bastard. Almost as handsome as Captain Olivetti himself. "No good, sir," he said at last.

"Well, keep after him," Captain Olivetti said. "And don't kill him unless you have to. We might want to ship him down to Thaitan."

Whistling, Captain Olivetti went over to the headquarters building, which had been a schoolhouse before the Raiders came to Penang. "Ackley, m'boy!" he roared, filling the orderly room with his huge, happy presence.

The clerk-typist had been working through the pimples on his right cheek, prodding and squeezing with an expert touch. Now, just as expertly, he pretended he had only been scratching his ear. "Yessir," he said.

"Ackley," the captain told him, "you can write me up for the CIB."

"The what?"

"The Combat! Infantryman's! Badge! Same as we tried to get for Lieutenant Arsenault that time, only we couldn't, because the guys who shot at him were his own troops. You'll find the correspondence in the files someplace. Just change the names around and throw it on the major's desk, okay?"

"Okay."

"*Sir.*"

"Sir," Ackley conceded.

Captain Olivetti searched through the mess on Ackley's desk. He found the daily distribution packet from Thaitan, tucked it under his arm, and went into Major Barker's office.

The major was studying his maps. The office was walled with maps. There was even a map stand in front of the window, to break the glare of the sun. Each map was protected by a sheet of plastic and a canvas drop cover marked CONFIDENTIAL, SECRET, or TOP SECRET. One of Captain Olivetti's duties as the Y Team executive officer was to roll up the top-secret maps every night and put them in the safe.

"Distribution, sir," he said.

"Sort it out for me, Al." The major stood straight as a fence post, causing Captain Olivetti to feel offensively tall and clumsy. Major Barker was five-foot-three. Because of his height, his future in the Army was not very bright. He probably wouldn't have made major, in fact, if it hadn't been for the scar on his face. The scar was the luckiest thing that had happened to the major since the Korean War. It slashed from his jawbone to the corner of his mouth, which was twisted into a permanent, mirthless smile. This smile now brightened a bit. "How was the patrol?" he asked.

"Terrific! Ackley's writing up a recommendation for the CIB right now. We set an ambush about six kilometers south of here, and Charlie walked right into it. What a ball! We captured two carbines and an automatic rifle. All American-made."

"You sure it wasn't a government patrol?"

"Positive, sir. They fought too hard."

"All right, I'll sign the recommendation," the major said. "Anybody hurt on our side?"

"No, sir. Killed a couple civilians, though." Captain Olivetti sat down and opened the distribution packet. He sorted its contents into two piles, one for Ackley and one for the major. When he was done, the major's pile contained two items. "Here's a new query about Muc Wa, sir," he said, holding up the first of these items.

"Muc Wa." The major's scar began to glow, like one of those neon signs on the road outside Fort Darby. "I thought we gave Thaitan a negative report on Muc Wa."

"That's right, sir."

"Well, *now* what do they want?"

"They want a complete position paper on it, sir."

"Shit."

"Yes, sir."

"I can't spare the men to reconnoiter Muc Wa, let alone garrison it."

"I know, sir."

"We've got too many static defense posts as it is. We should be out there—bang! bang!—hitting Charlie where he lives. That's what happened to the French. They got themselves tied down with static defense."

"Yes, sir. The X Team wants a report today."

"What do we know about Muc Wa?"

"Nothing, sir. It's thirty-some kilometers south-southeast of here. The French maps show it as a fair-sized town. But the road isn't passable any more, and none of the Raiders have ever heard of it."

Major Barker paced the length of the office, once, twice, his scar burning red. "All right," he said then. "Write them a position paper. Tell them Muc Wa has a population of two hundred Buru tribesmen, mostly women, children, and old men. Tell them that severe drought conditions—"

"It's near a river, sir."

"Oh. Well, tell 'em the soil is highly acid or alkaline or something, so the crops are poor. Inhabitants sickly. No sign of rebel activity in the area. In the opinion of this command, Muc Wa has no strategic significance whatsoever. . . . *You* know."

"Yes, sir. I'll take care of it."

"Good," the major said. "What else?"

Captain Olivetti held up the other item, a page of mimeographed movement orders with two names circled in red. "Here's the orders on two new men," he said. "Pipeline replacements from Fort Darby. Hamilton, R., second lieutenant—"

"Second lieutenant? Since when have we been taking second goddamned lieutenants into the Raiders?"

Captain Olivetti studied the long, unpunctuated lines, full of numerals and capital letters. "He volunteered, sir," he said.

"Damned fool," Major Barker said. "ROTC, I suppose?"

Captain Olivetti looked at his commanding officer. "I got my commission through the ROTC," he pointed out.

"Um," the major said. "I didn't mean—"

"Sure, the guys from West Point look down on us, but the training's not so bad."

"Of course it's not, Al." Major Barker had never been to college, let alone West Point. He had been field-commissioned in Korea. "Sorry about that," he said. "What else has Lieutenant Hamilton done?"

Satisfied, Captain Olivetti looked at the orders again. "Graduated from the Raider officer's course at Fort Darby," he said. "Went to Army language school. The usual crap."

"Doesn't sound very useful, does he?" Major Barker asked cautiously.

"No, sir."

"Well, we can always assign him to the mosquito patrol. Who's the other man?"

"Courcey, S., corporal. He's a demolitions expert."

"Demo! Tits on a bull! There isn't a factory or a bridge between here and the South China Sea; and if there was, Charlie Romeo would blow it up, not us. . . . I suppose Corporal Courcey is another volunteer?"

"Yes, sir."

"That's the trouble with this man's Army," Major Barker said. "There's too much volunteering. If *I* had my way, nobody under the rank of captain would be allowed to volunteer for *anything*."

"He's a draftee, though," Captain Olivetti said. "Took a six-month extension to come over here."

"God. Draftees and second lieutenants. What right have they got to volunteer for anything?" Major Barker sat down in the swivel chair behind his desk, a signal that Captain Olivetti should prepare to leave. "Well, send 'em in when they arrive," he said. "And take care of that Muc Wa business for me, will you, Al?"

"Yes, sir!" Captain Olivetti stood up, saluted, and took the rest of the distribution out to the orderly room, wishing he had said: *Major, you were an enlisted man once, and you'll be an enlisted man again before you're through. It's up or out in this man's Army*. But of course he couldn't have said that. Anyhow, the same spook was haunting Captain Olivetti. Up or out. And he wouldn't go up unless he made one hell of a splash in the next few years.

In the orderly room Ackley jumped and began to scratch his left ear. "Got that recommendation typed up?" the captain demanded.

"It's almost chowtime," the clerk-typist said. "I'll do it first thing this afternoon."

"Ackley, did you volunteer for duty in Southeast Asia?"

"What d'ya think, I'm crazy?"

"That's what I figured. Well, if that recommendation isn't typed up and signed and on the afternoon Caribou to Thaitan, I'm going to volunteer you for the loneliest goddamn outpost in the country. Boo Jum, maybe, or Mung Tau. How'd you like six months at Mung Tau?"

"I'll do it first thing this afternoon," Ackley promised. "Sir."

Captain Olivetti nodded. He dumped the distribution on the clerk-typist's desk, then went out to look for Sergeant Toffington, the Y Team radioman. Toffee was a bright lad. Between them, they should be able to dream up a first-rate position paper on Muc Wa.

Halfway to the communications shack, the captain spotted Cowboy and his little group of Raiders, heading for the main gate. Four of them were carrying the prisoner. Two more were carrying shovels. Cowboy brought up the rear, looking guilty as hell. *Stupid bastard,* Captain Olivetti thought. *We better ship him out of here before he puts us all in the soup. . . .* *Well,* he thought, *it's a good thing I didn't say anything about prisoners to the major. He'd court-martial me, the bastard, just to keep his own nose clean.*

Captain Olivetti sighed and looked south-southeast, in the general direction of Muc Wa. The sun blazed on his neck. The sky was soft and blue, with rain clouds just beginning to boil across the horizon. And the mountains rolled away from him—wave upon wave, like a frozen green sea. Muc Wa! The mountains were full of villages with names like Muc Wa, and each of them was more useless than the last.

The Commies can have Muc Wa, and the rest of the country with it, Captain Olivetti thought. *Just so long as I get my Combat Infantryman's Badge.*

Three

Sweating quietly, Stephen Courcey slouched in a steel-and-plastic armchair and wondered what the hell he was doing there. From time to time he blotted his face with the sleeve of his fatigue shirt, catching the olive-green fabric between his fingers and the heel of his hand, and using it to soak up the sweat. He did this for his own comfort, not from any hope that it might improve his appearance. Looks didn't count for much in the U. S. Army, except for the officers.

"Corporal, what patch are you wearing?"

Anyhow, Stephen's looks did not allow for much improvement. He was long in the body and squat in the face, with all his features jammed furiously together—black hair plastered to his forehead, beetling black eyebrows, hawk nose, hard mouth, and a belligerent, chopped-off jaw. . . . Jesus. Forget it. Very early, at fourteen or thereabouts, Stephen had learned to avoid mirrors, Prom queens, and any thought of selling life insurance as a career. He concentrated instead on the things he could do well. *To do one thing well,* he told himself, having read it in a book: *that makes all the difference.* The first thing he found to conquer was the mountains of New Hampshire. He climbed them in the summer and skied them in the winter, racing against himself, not against others, with the result that he soon became the best skier he knew. So he won an athletic scholarship, because the state university wanted some local talent to put beside the Norwegians it had imported.

"Corporal?"

But college turned out to be a Phi Kappa Phi sort of place, not a home for former Junior Alpine champions, so he let the athletic scholarship go. *Do it well,* he told himself. *Study.* He even studied in the winter, while the fresh white powder drifted across the campus, reminding him of how the dwarf pines looked, rimed with snow at the summit of Cannon Mountain; and he earned his Phi Kappa Phi key. It was in his duffel bag somewhere, for laughs.

"I'm talking to you, Corporal Courcey."

The Army grabbed him when he was a year out of college and working like hell to forget everything he had learned about steam engines—come to find out, engineers did not need to know about steam engines any more. But the Army was impressed. They put a Scientific and Professional hold on him, but Stephen had no intention of being a slide-rule soldier. *If you've got to do it,* he told himself, *do it all the way.* He volunteered for the Seventh Raider Group, Airborne, which boasted the roughest, toughest, goddamnedest soldiers in the U. S. Army.

"Corporal!"

So here he was, in a steamy corner of Thaitan Municipal Airport, waiting for the privilege of getting his well-educated ass shot off, as had hundreds of Americans and thousands of Frenchmen before him.

"CORP-*RAWL!*"

Stephen ramrodded to his feet. "Sir!" he said, because the short, angry officer in front of him was wearing a star upon his lapel. Stephen had never been this close to a general before. Neither had the other men, apparently, because the waiting room was a flowerbed of faces, dark and light, all turned numbly in his direction.

The general was built like a powder keg. He was absolutely bald, and had two smudges where his eyebrows should have been, as if he had blown up at least once before, burning all the hair from his head. He was Brigadier General Hardnetz, according to the nameplate stitched beneath the star.

"Corporal Courcey," said the general, "if it isn't too goddamned much trouble, would you tell me what patch you're wearing?"

"Seventh Raider Group, Airborne, sir!"

"What's that?"

"Sir, it's the roughest, toughest, goddamnedest outfit in the U. S. Army."

There was a groan from Lieutenant Hamilton, old reliable Ray Hamilton, who was standing near the soft-drink machine with his own Raider patch pressed to the wall.

"What did you say, Corporal?"

"Sir, I said—"

"I heard what you said. I don't care what kind of funnyman outfit you belonged to in the States, Corporal; that patch is not authorized in this command." The general slapped his own left shoulder. "You should be wearing the Military Advisory Command insignia, like this." When the general took his hand away, he revealed a multitude of stitch marks, but no unit insignia of any kind.

"Sir," Stephen said, "there is no patch on your shoulder."

The general swiveled his head around, like the turret of a tank, and glared at his shoulder. "*Brmm*," he said, swiveling back to Stephen. "They're hard to find in Thaitan. . . . That will be all, Corporal." He turned and marched toward the dispatch office, followed by a wedge of majors and captains and all-purpose ass-lickers.

When the general and his party were gone, Lieutenant Hamilton unstuck himself from the wall and came over to Stephen, carrying two sweating bottles of Moxie. He looked sad-eyed and subdued, the cause of it all. And well he might. Because it was Lieutenant Hamilton who, when Stephen was feeling sorry for himself over that business with Rebecca, had talked him into driving up to Washington, had gotten him drunk on bourbon-and-ginger in the Purple Tree, and had persuaded him that it was their patriotic duty to travel twelve thousand miles and fight in a war that had never been declared. Lieutenant Hamilton and his cow-brown eyes. He sat down with Stephen, and the plastic seat cushions whistled beneath them. The whole waiting room was filled with sighs and whistles, as fifty or sixty men settled back, relaxing now that the general was gone.

"The Army wouldn't be so bad if it weren't for the officers," Stephen said, accepting a bottle of Moxie from the lieutenant.

"Heck, Steve, somebody's got to give the orders."

"If you put all the possible orders in a hat, mixed 'em up, and pulled one out whenever you wanted to make a decision, you could run this Army better than General Hardnetz."

"Yes, but!" Lieutenant Hamilton's pink, corn-fed face bloomed with inspiration. "Officers are for wartime, Steve. Don't you see? When we get out there in a real fire fight, somebody has to give the orders. Otherwise—bang! Chaos."

"I'd trust chaos before I'd trust General Hardnetz," Stephen said.

"Anyhow, it isn't always easy, being an officer. You ought to try it sometime."

"No, thanks. I've got enough on my hands, just being a soldier."

Stephen drank off the bottle of Moxie, chucked it under his chair, and settled back like the others to doze and dream. *To hell with General Hardnetz,* he thought. *To hell with Lieutenant Hamilton and the whole race of officers. I'm going to think about Rebecca.*

He had not conquered Rebecca. Oh, no. She had kicked him black and blue, the last time they had met, and all because he had made the very natural mistake of assuming she didn't want to be in jail, and had therefore done the logical thing—busted her out of there. But logic never seemed to work with Rebecca. She was always throwing these curves at him, like saying *Why me?* when he told her that he loved her.

"Why me?" she said. "Why me, of all the people in the world?"

Now what kind of an answer was that? In his experience, women either believed a man or they didn't, or they did believe and pretended they didn't, or they didn't believe and pretended they did; and a man could build from there. But not with Rebecca.

That was the weekend on Cape Hatteras. The innocent weekend. They were driving down for the afternoon only, to picnic among the bleached skeletons of ships—but Stephen had a weekend pass in his pocket, just in case, and a bottle of moonshine in the glove compartment. Gay young PFC from Fort Darby. He wanted to share his discovery of the Cape with Rebecca, not knowing that her Poppa owned a fair-sized chunk of it, that she had spent summers there as long as she could remember. She was too nice to tell him.

So there he was, in his pale yellow '55 Pontiac with the flawless engine and the rusted-out body, heading for Cape Hatteras with that darling, sweet-breasted, saucy-tailed girl he had met at College Heights. Jesus, he was happy. He was king of the road, king of the sovereign state of North Carolina.

Rebecca was never going to see him again, that's what she had told him. That's what she was always telling him. The very first night they met (Lieutenant Hamilton was responsible for that, too, damn his cow-brown eyes) Rebecca had said: "I can't see you again."

"Why not?"

"Because I'm engaged to be married."

"Why don't you break your engagement?"

"Because I love him."

But she wasn't wearing a ring, and her boyfriend was not in evidence. If Stephen Courcey—New Hampshire Junior Alpine champion, Phi Kappa Phi, U. S. Army Raider—couldn't beat those odds, he might just as well become a monk. And he was doing pretty well, wasn't he? Because there she was—a beautiful bundle on the seat beside him.

Perhaps not beautiful. If Rebecca had been beautiful, that would have been the reason he loved her, but it wasn't. She was only pretty. Eyes of no particular color—hazel, he supposed. A noble Jewish nose, but not so noble that a small girl would feel uncomfortable wearing it; and anyhow, who was he to criticize noses? Small mouth. Full lips with little vertical lines in them, as if the lips had been designed for a slightly larger mouth, then switched to Rebecca's at the last minute. No, she wasn't the greatest beauty from Cape Hatteras to Casco Bay, but she was so warm and wonderful, so absolutely REBECCA, that it nearly broke his heart.

Now, if you tell a girl who isn't beautiful that she is, she'll say, "I'm not," and what do you say then? Because she isn't.

But she is.

Of course, it wasn't until sundown that they talked of such things. During the drive to the Cape, during the golden afternoon on the sand, they talked about civil rights and world peace and the existence of God and all the other things that bright young female college graduates like to talk about. Rebecca had an opinion on every one of them. Southeast Asia, for example:

"We're worse than the French," she said. "At least the French had history behind them; their only mistake was not getting out of there fast enough. But we! Oh! We just stepped in and took sides in a civil war that was none of our business."

"Some people call it a revolution," he pointed out.

"What if it is? Didn't the United States begin with a revolution?"

"Some people," he said, watching her dress perk up—God, it was marvelous, the way politics made Rebecca's breasts come alive—"some people say that the rebels are getting arms from China."

"I don't believe it," Rebecca said. "And anyhow—what if they are? American weapons are doing most of the killing. Jellied gasoline—oh!" she said, three outraged furrows in her brow, and her lips a lovely, outraged circle. "I hope every American in Southeast Asia is killed."

There is no more bloodthirsty creature on the face of the globe than a well-educated young woman with liberal convictions.

She was sitting against the rib of a long-dead sailing ship, and he was holding her feet in his lap. Rebecca had faulty plumbing, it seemed; her hands and feet were always cold. So he warmed them for her—the small, high-arched feet, callused at the toes and gritty with sand. "Here's a man," he said, pressing her feet against his belly. "I might be shipped over there before it's finished. Do you want me killed?"

"You shouldn't go."

"But I'm a soldier."

"You shouldn't be a soldier."

"But I am."

"Then . . . you should be killed."

So he said: "Who would warm your feet then, Rebecca?" And she slid away from that bleached rib she had been sitting against, and kissed him so eagerly that it seemed they were the last two people alive on earth, and Rebecca would die an old maid if she didn't overwhelm him then and there.

The sun was going down. They built a fire of driftwood, and necked. Stephen could do no more than cup his hands peaceably on her breasts. He tried—man, how he tried!—while the sunset flamed over North Carolina, but he couldn't unfasten the topmost button of her blouse, or rest his hands anywhere except peaceably on her breasts.

"Oh my God!" Rebecca cried. "The ferry!"

Yes, the ferry—hiccuping black smoke into the sunset, chuffing to the mainland for the last time that day. No matter, he said, congratulating himself on the weekend pass in his pocket. We can always sleep in the car, he told her, very offhand. Rebecca sifted sand through her fingers and pursed her small, rich mouth and finally came out with it: one of those fine old summer houses on the seaward beach belonged to Poppa. They were both embarrassed, for different reasons. But a man can live with that kind of embarrassment.

There was a fieldstone fireplace in the living room, and a couch in front of the fireplace, and a pitcher of orange juice, a Mason jar full of moonshine, two glasses—and them. Rebecca drank very cautiously, of course, being Jewish and on the defensive.

Her face was full of shadows. Soft shadows, female shadows. He told her that she was beautiful; she said she wasn't. But she was. Then he told her that he loved her, and she must have believed him, because she said: "Why me?" She asked it in a very small voice, but it seemed the largest question he had ever heard. Why her? Why Rebecca? Why this girl, of all the girls in the world?

He didn't know. He couldn't even make a guess, and therefore couldn't make Rebecca either, although she was no virgin, if he knew anything about women. She wanted him, too—he was damned if she didn't. But he was a traveler before the Sphinx, and he couldn't answer the question she had put to him.

It was two o'clock. The fire had collapsed long since, and black shadows were chasing across the coals. He kissed Rebecca one more time, stood up, and said, "Good night, sweetheart." But she pulled him down to the couch again, and pressed against him from forehead to toe.

"Don't leave me," she said.

So they slept there on the couch, fully dressed, as innocent as Hansel and Gretel in the woods, and all, he was convinced, because he couldn't answer the simple goddamned question she had put to him.

"Sergeant!" The general was marching through the waiting room again, like Sherman through Georgia. "What kind of a funny-man uniform is *that?*"

Stephen sat up, blinking, but the general had a new target

this time, hidden from Stephen by all those majors, captains, and ass-lickers.

"Sir!" said a gravelly, familiar voice.

"What kind of a soldier are you?" General Hardnetz insisted.

"Sir, I'm the roughest, toughest, god*damnedest* soldier in the U. S. Army."

Another groan from Lieutenant Hamilton. As soldiers and airmen hustled out of the way, Stephen finally spotted him: Sergeant Ski, good old Ski, who used to teach the hand-to-hand combat course at Fort Darby. He was wearing a broad-brimmed hat with one side pinned to the crown, like a bloody Australian, and tiger-stripe camouflage fatigues.

"What, what?" the general said. "Sergeant, what's your name?"

"Oleonowski, sir."

"Somebody write that down. Major? Write that down. . . . What kind of a name is that, Sergeant? Is it an American name?"

"Brooklyn, sir."

"I see. Well, Sergeant, the next time you visit Thaitan, make sure you're wearing regulation Army issue instead of those . . . those . . . those *Frenchified* jungle fatigues." The general turned on his heel, saw Stephen, and turned back to Sergeant Ski. "AND GET A SHOULDER PATCH!" he thundered. As he marched to the door, men turned their left shoulders to the wall, because most of them were in pipeline and were still wearing their Stateside insignia. The general was almost to the door when he turned again and shouted at Stephen: "What outfit did you say?"

Stephen stood tall. "Seventh Raider Group, Airborne," he said. "Sir."

"Major? Write that down." General Hardnetz pulled a baseball cap from his belt and put it on. There was a silver star on the front of the cap, too. "Raiders," he said. "Airborne Raiders. What's the Army coming to?"

When the general was gone Ski charged across the room toward Stephen, swinging his Awol bag to clear a path. "Hot damn!" he shouted. "If it ain't a pair of innocents from Fort Darby!" Then he pulled up short. "I know *you*, by Gor," he said. "I'd know that ugly mug anywheres. Ain't you . . . ain't you—"

Stephen introduced himself, then Lieutenant Hamilton.

"It's a pleasure to see you again, Sergeant Oleonowski," the lieutenant said. "I went through your course in—"

"Yeah," Ski said, sitting down on the other side of Stephen. "Where you headed, Steve?"

"Place called Penang."

"Number one! We'll be on the same plane," Ski said, sounding very pleased. Penang, he said, was the biggest town in the highlands, and the main military center; there was a Raider Y Team there, among other things. He had been there about a month, waiting for an assignment and running errands for Major Barker, the Y Team commander. This was Ski's second tour in the country. He had spent six months in the delta, last time around, but he didn't seem anxious to talk about that.

Ski still had his famous beer-belly, but over-all he looked twenty pounds lighter and ten years older. His jaw and cheekbones stuck out like the rump of a peddler's horse. Stephen remembered him as a roaring, ass-kicking tyrant, a year and a half ago; now he looked like a man who had just crossed the Pacific on a life raft.

Lieutenant Hamilton was eager to make friends. "Those jungle fatigues are great," he said, leaning past Stephen. "Where can I buy a set like that?"

"There's thirty, forty tailor shops in Penang," Ski told him. "There's more tailor shops than cathouses, I swear. They'll make you any kind of uniform you want. Also genuine tribal burial blankets, in case you're interested."

"Well, maybe for my fiancée," Lieutenant Hamilton said, looking uncertainly at Ski. The lieutenant never knew when somebody was pulling his leg, so he was always on the lookout for it.

"Sure. Tell you how it works: they put this blanket on top of you, and then they put you and the blanket on top of a good blazing fire, and then they put the ashes in a clay jug. Your fancy could keep the jug on her mantelpiece. She got a mantelpiece, Lieutenant?"

Lieutenant Hamilton laughed, but he didn't make a very convincing job of it.

Then a scrawny Air Force corporal came in and called off half a dozen names, among them: "Courcey!"

"Here," Stephen said.

"Hamilton!"

"*Lieutenant* Hamilton . . . Here."

"Ol . . . Oleo . . ."

"Sergeant Ski, all present and accounted for!"

Stephen picked up his duffel bag, then the carbine that had been issued to him at five o'clock this morning—a brand-new carbine, still gleaming with cosmoline. Ski led them out to the bus. Lieutenant Hamilton staggered after him, sweat blackening his olive-green fatigues. It was noon, and the tropical sun was blazing on the asphalt. *Jesus,* Stephen thought. *What a place to fight a war!*

The dispatcher allowed three native troopers to join them on the bus.

"Are they soldiers?" Lieutenant Hamilton said. "They look like Boy Scouts."

Ski studied the troopers, small-boned and gentle, with skin like honey. "Oh, I'd say they're eighteen or nineteen," he said. "Maybe even twenty, although I swear to God I sometimes wonder if there's any twenty-year-olds left alive in this forsaken country. . . . Hell, if *they* look young, you ought to see Charlie Romeo."

"Who's he?" Lieutenant Hamilton asked.

"He's the guy we're fighting," Ski said. "When we can catch him."

The Air Force corporal drove them across the asphalt apron, past liaison planes and jet fighters and helicopters and old gooney-bird C-47s, to where a C-123 was squatting on its tricycle landing gear. "Happy landings," he said, grinning horribly. They piled out and stood in the shade of the C-123. The pilot was waiting for them, dressed in a faded flying suit and a well-oiled shoulder holster, which was empty. He gave them the usual lecture. Then he planted his fists on his hips and counted them. "Well," he said, "we don't have enough parachutes to go around, so we'll fly the coast as far north as we can, and if we have any trouble we'll ditch in the water."

"I can't swim," Lieutenant Hamilton said.

"Sorry about that," the pilot told him. "I think there's a life raft on board someplace."

They followed him into the dark, cargo-filled hold, where they strapped themselves into a row of canvas jump seats along one side. They were one seat short, so two of the native troops had to double up. The crew chief, trailing a long microphone cord, went aft and closed the cargo door. The engines revved up, causing Sergeant Ski's Awol bag to skate along the floor plates; the engines screamed, and then they were rushing down the runway and into the air. Stephen's ears popped. Through the porthole in the passenger door he saw the runways and hangars of Thaitan Municipal Airport, rapidly shrinking, then a pale green pattern of paddy fields and canals. They were climbing in a tight spiral over the airport. With each loop the earth became smaller, until finally the plane leveled out and the no-smoking sign went dark.

Ski unfastened his safety belt, lit a wilted cigarette, and inhaled deeply. He offered the pack to Stephen, who shook his head. Then Ski leaned close to him, surrounding him with cigarette smoke and the stink of day-old beer.

"What the hell you doing here, anyways?" he yelled.

"Damned if I know," Stephen said.

"What?"

"I said: I WISH I KNEW!"

Ski leaned back and demonstrated laughter, slapping his skinny thigh and rolling his head around. Then he cupped his hands beside his mouth and yelled: "SO DO I!"

But I'm here, Stephen thought, grinning at Ski, *and I'm going to make a damned good job of it.*

Four

The heat of afternoon was seeping through the thick clay walls of the schoolhouse, and Major Barker was sweating. He glared at a map, trying to wring some sense out of the green and yellow blotches, the contour lines, and the place names bristling with strange French doodles; then he wiped his face and moved on to the next map. Usually the major did his map work in the morning. It was cooler then. But today was a mess: the garrison at Mung Tau was under siege by a battalion of rebels, and three other Z Teams were mounting large patrols near the border. There wasn't much he could do for Mung Tau, except radio them a brave message every morning and request a flare ship to light the area at night. But the patrols were supposed to be under his direct command. Major Barker was charting their progress with red arrows and crosses, grease-penciled on the plastic; they crawled along the map like weary ants, radioing complaints about the scarcity of water, the hardships of the terrain, and the misery of the refugees they were collecting. The major ached to be out in the field with them, kicking ass. But he was forty-three years old. Those bright young lieutenants would walk him into the ground.

The Mung Tau quadrant was on the map stand screening the window. Major Barker moved it, since there was an off-chance that a breeze might be stirring outside. There wasn't, but the open window framed a hopeful sight: a red rooster tail of dust on the road from Penang. That would be Sergeant Toffington with the afternoon distribution packet.

Perhaps he was bringing permission to call U.S. aircraft to the aid of Mung Tau, or an offer from Major Minh, the local province chief, to loan a few companies in support of Major Barker's patrols, or . . . At worst, the distribution packet would give the major an excuse to forget his problems for an hour or so.

He sat down at his desk, laced his fingertips behind his head, and waited for Toffee's jeep to arrive.

Captain Olivetti brought the distribution in. He looked like a stallion who had just lost his favorite mare.

"What's wrong now?" Major Barker said, standing up. If there was no good news in the afternoon distribution, he might as well get back to his maps. "Have those damned fools at Mung Tau been overrun?"

"It's my recommendation for the CIB," Captain Olivetti said, pulling a sheaf of correspondence from the distribution envelope.

"Ah," the major said, sitting down again. "What about the CIB?"

"There's a new set of regulations on it, sir. My application was not favorably considered."

"Sorry about that," the major said.

"Thaitan now requires three days under hostile fire."

"Well, well," the major said, letting a grin struggle with the scar on his face. He had practiced this combination in front of the mirror in the officers' latrine, and he knew it was pretty awful. "It looks like you'll just have to go out into the field for a couple more days, doesn't it, Al?"

"Yessir," the exec said.

"What about jumping into Mung Tau? I'd like to have a firsthand report from that damned place."

"Well, sir," Captain Olivetti said, "if you don't mind, I'd just as soon have a couple days to study these regulations. I don't want to get caught short again." He stuffed the sheaf of correspondence back into the envelope.

"Nothing else in there?" the major asked.

"Just crap, sir. Ackley can take care of it."

"Oh." Major Barker climbed to his feet.

"By the way, sir," the captain said then, "the new men are here."

"What new men?"

"Lieutenant Hamilton and Corporal Courcey. We got orders on them a couple days ago."

"Ah—the volunteers. Outstanding! Send 'em in and I'll see what they're made of. And cover those damned maps for me, will you, Al?"

When the maps were secure, Captain Olivetti went out to the orderly room and spoke to somebody out of sight. A pink-cheeked second lieutenant immediately rushed in, breathless and saluting. "Lieutenant Hamilton reporting as requested, *sir!*" he said.

"Lieutenant," the major said without returning the salute, "how old are you?"

"Twenty-three, sir!"

"Twenty-three years old and still a shavetail?"

"Sir— I—"

"What the hell d'you expect us to do with you? We don't have any slots for second lieutenants in the Raiders."

"Send me out into the field, sir," Lieutenant Hamilton said, his right index finger still glued to his eyebrow. His brown eyes were fixed on a point just above the major's head. "I can kill Communists as well as any first lieutenant in the U. S. Army."

"You volunteered, didn't you?"

"Yes, *sir.*"

"How come?"

"Sir, I believe that every generation has its war. This is my war, and it's my duty to fight in it."

Oh, crap, Major Barker thought. "There's a garrison near the border, name of Mung Tau," he said, smiling a large, crooked smile for the lieutenant's benefit. "They've taken ten per cent casualties in the past three days. How'd you like to parachute in there and give 'em a hand?"

The lieutenant swallowed hard. "Yes, sir," he said. He swallowed again and added: "I haven't made my payday jump this month."

"You mightn't live to collect your money, Lieutenant. Charlie will be shooting at you all the way down."

"Yes, sir."

"Think you're ready for it?"

"Yes, sir."

"Well, let's not rush things," the major said. "Maybe we can find something that's not quite so hairy, just to start you off. . . . Now, why don't you stop saluting for a minute, and tell me how come you weren't promoted?"

Lieutenant Hamilton came to parade rest. He was blushing—actually blushing, by God, just like one of those Southern girls getting goosed for the first time. "Sir," he said, "I was passed over."

"I figured that out for myself, Lieutenant."

"Yes, sir. Well, I had a little trouble with the civilian authorities in North Carolina."

"What kind of trouble?"

"Yes, sir. There was this, uh, young lady. She was in jail."

"My God," the major said.

"Oh, it's not what you think, sir. She was a civil-rights demonstrator."

"She what?"

"Civil rights, sir."

"That's worse than what I was thinking."

"Sorry, sir. Anyway, a friend of mine was, you know, fond of this young lady, so we spirited her out of town, and the authorities were a bit upset. They hadn't booked her, you see."

"You busted this gal out of jail?"

"Well . . . yes, sir."

"Outstanding!"

"Sir?"

"Covert Warfare, Lieutenant! That's what we're here for. The Raiders *need* men who can break the rules."

"Why, thank you, sir."

"Just don't pull any damn-fool tricks like that while you're under *my* command."

"Yes, sir—no, sir!"

"Well, that's all for now," the major said. "Send Corporal Courcey in, will you?"

Lieutenant Hamilton nearly broke his arm saluting, and backed out of the office as fast as he had entered it. Major Barker sighed. The lieutenant was a weak sister, all right, but he might shape up. That kind often did. They were so anxious to prove they were men that they turned themselves into tigers.

Corporal Courcey was a different sort. He snapped off a perfect salute, waited five seconds for it to be returned, and went to parade rest when it wasn't. Major Barker fancied he saw a big FUCK YOU branded on the corporal's forehead. And what a forehead!—low and moody, and damned well hiding whatever went on behind it. *I know your type,* the major thought. *Always thinking. What the hell do you think about, Corporal?*

"Well, well," he said. "You're a college man, just like the lieutenant."

"Yessir," Corporal Courcey said.

"How come you joined the Raiders, if you're a college man?"

"Sir, if I had to be a soldier, I wanted to be in the roughest, toughest, goddamnedest outfit in the U. S. Army."

Which was exactly the answer they had taught him at Fort Darby. *Yes, I know your type,* the major thought. *You look down your nose at us twenty-year men, and then you try to be a better soldier than any one of us.* "You were drafted for two years, Corporal," he said. "You had to extend for six months, to come out here. Why did you do that?" Ah, there was a flicker! "Let's see now," the major said, feeling like Humphrey Bogart closing in for the kill. "Was it because of that girl you busted out of jail?"

Corporal Courcey gave him a look like a bayonet thrust. "Sir," he said, "I guess that's none of your damned business."

"Hah!" Major Barker cried. "I hit the nail on the head that time, didn't I?"

The corporal glared at him a moment longer, then he laughed. "Yessir, you did," he said.

"A woman," Major Barker said. "Well, there are worse reasons for fighting, Corporal. What matters is not *why* you fight, but how well."

"That's what I think, too, sir."

"Good. We'll find a job for you in a day or so." He nodded, and Corporal Courcey snapped to attention. "By the way," the major said, "just how did you and the lieutenant manage that jailbreak?"

"It was during maneuvers, sir. We were supposed to be guerrillas, operating behind the lines, and we kidnaped a couple state policemen with the idea of snarling up traffic."

"Kidnaped?"

"Yessir. Knocked 'em over the head and took their uniforms. We heard about the arrest on their car radio, so we just walked up to the county jail and turned the demonstrators loose. There was quite a fuss. They threw the Seventh Raider Group out of the maneuvers because of it."

"I don't wonder," Major Barker said. "Initiative is all very well in its place, Corporal, but there are limits, you know."

"Yessir. I'll try to remember that."

He saluted, turned on his heel, and left the office. A *tough guy*, the major thought. *Well, that's what we need.*

As soon as the corporal was gone, Captain Olivetti stuck his tanned face through the orderly-room door. "What d'you think, sir?" he said.

"Courcey's a hard-ass. The lieutenant . . . well! He's eager."

"Yessir. What'll we do with them? Put 'em on the mosquito patrol?"

Major Barker shrugged. "What else?" he said.

Five

Stephen enjoyed the mosquito patrol. The hours were good, and the work—his share of it, anyhow—was pleasant enough, far better than the jobs which usually fell to the new men in an outfit. "Relax, Ray," he told the lieutenant. "It could be worse. We could be out in the sun all day, filling sandbags or some damned thing. Do you know how I spent my first month at Fort Darby? I whitewashed all the coal-bins in the Covert Warfare Center."

"But I want to fight," Lieutenant Hamilton said.

"You have to get acclimated first."

"Acclimated?"

"Sure. You'd pass out from the heat if you went into combat this soon."

"I never thought of that," the lieutenant said. "Do you suppose that's why Major Barker gave me the mosquito patrol?"

"Sure it is," Stephen said. "One thing at a time."

"Well, that's all right, then. I thought maybe he just didn't like me." He chewed it over for a while, then burst out: "But it's so undignified!"

The mosquito patrol took place at night. Stephen would walk over to the chow hall as soon as darkness had settled in, about seven-thirty; Lieutenant Hamilton would be there ahead of him, and Sergeant Ski and three or four others. Ski was usually bull-shitting about the Korean War. The lieutenant wanted to know about the Local Situation, but all

Ski would talk about was the retreat from the Yalu in December of nineteen-fifty.

"Do you think the Chinese will intervene in Southeast Asia?" the lieutenant asked, trying to bring him back to the present.

"Any American is worth ten Chinks!" Captain Olivetti shouted from the next table.

"Lotta fucking good *that* did us, in nineteen-fifty," Ski said, his bloodshot eyes bulging at the captain. "They outnumbered us twenty to one, thirty to one. Why, they had more Chinks than we had bullets . . . FIX BAY-ON-ETS!" he roared. Lieutenant Hamilton shuddered.

The chow hall, like all the hooches in the camp except the schoolhouse, was an airy building with a high-pitched tin roof, a concrete floor, and walls that were sandbagged to shoulder height. The walls were open above the sandbags, but there were wooden shutters which could be dropped when the monsoon came, or if Charlie Romeo attacked. Apparently Major Barker did not believe there was much chance of that. Light bulbs were strung through the rafters like Christmas-tree ornaments, flickering to the beat of the gasoline-powered generator behind the commo shack.

At eight o'clock, Lieutenant Hamilton sighed and said: "Well, I suppose . . ." He took his pistol belt from the table and buckled it around his waist. Stephen picked up his carbine. They walked over to the schoolhouse, where the charge-of-quarters issued a flashlight to Stephen and a clipboard to the lieutenant. The clipboard was marked: MOSQUITO CONTROL ROSTER—CONFIDENTIAL.

"The password is *baumi,*" the CQ told them.

"What's it mean?" Stephen asked.

"Thirteen."

"What's six?"

The CQ consulted his English-Buru dictionary. The cover was red with gold letters:

IN THE BEGINNING WAS THE WORD

WESLEY BIBLE TRANSLATORS

"*Choi,*" the CQ said.

Stephen repeated it a few times, to get the accent right, and then they went out into the night.

There were eight sentry holes around the perimeter of the camp, each containing a thirty-caliber machinegun and two native Raiders. Stephen and the lieutenant visited each hole in turn, creeping soft-footed across the dark, slippery clay, and shouting "*Choi!*" before the sentries could spot them. The password changed from night to night. The idea—it was Major Barker's idea—was to challenge a man with a smaller number, and he would answer with whatever number added up to the password. Since the Raiders did not speak English and the Americans did not speak Buru, the challenge was always the hairiest part of the mosquito patrol.

When it was safe to approach, Lieutenant Hamilton jumped into the sentry hole, sometimes splashing up to his knees in water. The Raiders thought this was very funny. They had been sitting in the water for hours, but when an American got wet they giggled like schoolgirls.

Stephen sat on the sandbagged rim. They were silent for five minutes or so, then the lieutenant said "Okay" and rolled back one sleeve of his new jungle fatigues. Stephen waited one more minute. Then he bent forward, switched on his flashlight, and counted the mosquitoes that were feasting on the lieutenant's arm. The tally usually ran between two and seven, but Stephen once counted twenty-three while Lieutenant Hamilton whimpered with disgust.

That done, the lieutenant marked the number on his clipboard, while Stephen gave cigarettes to the sentries. They were mountain tribesmen, tougher and darker than the troops he had seen in Thaitan, but not an inch taller. Major Barker must have liked that. Small and tough. They were mercenaries, of course, paid from bales of funny-money which the X Team sent up from Thaitan. Stephen did not know if he liked the idea of fighting beside men who were fighting for pay. When the shit hit the fan, they might decide to look for other employment.

"Well," the lieutenant said. "I suppose . . ." And they tiptoed to the next sentry hole.

After completing the circuit, they returned the flashlight and the clipboard to the charge-of-quarters. A courier from Penang would pick up the roster next day, and the night's count—an average of the mosquitoes which had attacked the lieutenant's arm in each sentry hole—would be entered on a master mosquito-control chart at sector headquarters.

"It may seem like a small thing," Major Barker had said when he briefed them, "but don't you believe it! The quartermaster people need this information. Otherwise, how would they establish priorities for mosquito netting, DDT bombs, insect repellent, all that crap?"

"I don't know, sir," Lieutenant Hamilton admitted.

"Well then! Go out and make a good job of it, and I'll see if I can't find a replacement for you in a week or so."

One night, after they had been on the mosquito patrol for almost two weeks, they met Toffee outside the commo shack. He refused to join them at the chow hall. "Got to find the major," he said, waving a radiogram form covered with neat block printing. "Big doings."

"What kind of doings?" Stephen said. "A job for us?"

"Hope not," said Toffee, who never said *I*. He was too modest. "See you after a while, maybe," he said, vanishing in the direction of the officers' hooch.

Stephen and the lieutenant walked on. It was eleven o'clock. Low on the horizon, a cargo plane droned unseen above some beleaguered outpost, dropping flares. The flares drifted to earth like dying stars. From time to time the sour *crump!* of a mortar came clearly across the night. "Poor guys," the lieutenant said, but not so sadly as he had said the same words last week. "Somebody's catching heck," he announced when they entered the chow hall. "Over to the west."

"Just so long as it ain't us," Ski said.

"That's the garrison at Mung Tau," Captain Olivetti said. "Happens every night. The Air Force is getting real sick of Mung Tau—they flew forty-three hours last week, keeping that place lit up."

Stephen went to the urn and drew two cups of coffee, black as tar and almost as thick. He lightened it with canned milk from the refrigerator. He was sitting down with the others when Toffee came in, holding his camouflage cap in his hand.

"Cap'n?" Toffee said. "The major wants to see you."

Captain Olivetti groaned, swung his feet to the floor, and left the chow hall. Toffee went over to the refrigerator and took a beet and six carrots from the vegetable tray.

"How come the officers are working nights?" Stephen asked.

"Shouldn't say," Toffee said. "Classified. You know." He went into the kitchen, returned with a fat chrome juicing machine, and plugged it into the extension cord that was draped around the coffee urn. He began to feed carrots through a trapdoor in the top of the machine. It whined like a big metal insect, and yellow juice dribbled from a spigot into a waiting cup. Then Toffee pushed the beet through the trapdoor and the whole mess turned purple. "Want some?" he asked.

"Gor!" Ski said, grabbing his neck and pretending to gag.

Toffee rinsed his juicing machine and put it away. Then he sat down with them at the table.

"Come on, Toffee," Stephen said. "What's up?"

The radioman squirmed in his chair. "It's about Muc Wa," he said at last.

"What about it?"

Toffee shook his head.

"Muc Wa," Ski said. "Never heard of it." He stared bug-eyed at the radioman. "We got any troops at Muc Wa?"

"Not yet," Toffee said.

Captain Olivetti knew he was in for a storm the minute he walked into the major's office. Major Barker was sitting down, and the scar on his cheek was purple. "I thought I told you to take care of that Muc Wa business," he said in a very flat and unfriendly voice.

"Yes, sir." Captain Olivetti decided to remain standing. *Boy oh boy,* he thought. *The sooner I get my CIB and get out of here, the better I'll like it.* "Toffee sent off a signal that same afternoon," he said. "It sounded like a good one to me."

The major pushed a radiogram across the desk. "How does that sound?" he asked. Captain Olivetti picked up the form. Toffee always printed his signals in block letters, to look like they had just come off the Western Union wire:

—SECRET—

SUBJECT: MUC WA, ENGARRISONMENT OF

1. THE COMMANDER, Y TEAM (PENANG) USARGA, IS HEREBY DIRECTED TO ESTABLISH A Z TEAM GARRISON AT MUC WA, FOLLOWING APPLICABLE SOPS.

2. DUE TO LIMITED AIRLIFT CAPABILITY YOUR AREA, ENGARRISONMENT WILL BE ACCOMPLISHED BY SURFACE TRANSPORTATION.

3. ONE COMPANY NATIVE RAIDERS WILL BE DETACHED FOR DUTY THIS PROJECT. FURTHER COMBAT ELEMENTS WILL BE RECRUITED FROM THE INDIGENOUS POPULATION.

4. AMERICAN PERSONNEL WILL EXFILTRATE

THE GARRISON IN THE EVENT OF SUSTAINED ATTACK BY NUMERICALLY SUPERIOR HOSTILE FORCES.

FOR THE COMMANDER
X TEAM (THAITAN)
US ARMY RAIDER GROUP AIRBORNE

"Well?" the major said.

"Maybe I could go to Thaitan . . ."

"The last time you went to Thaitan, Al, was when the Cho Rhee Raiders were holding Lieutenant Arsenault for ransom."

"Yes, sir."

"I got a reprimand from Washington on that deal."

"Yes, sir."

"Where I ought to send you, Al, is to Muc Wa."

"But sir—"

"I know. The slot calls for a first lieutenant. We don't have one."

"Lieutenant Hamilton—"

"My God," the major said.

"Let me talk to some of my buddies in Thaitan. Maybe I can wangle a promotion for him."

"My God. Do you think he could find the place?"

"If he had Sergeant Oleonowski with him . . ."

The major's scar faded to a healthy pink. "Ski would make a first-class team sergeant," he agreed, "and he's no damned good to us here. He just drinks up all the GI gin we've got in the dispensary. . . . What else do we need?"

"A signalman-medic, sir."

"Who've we got?"

"Nobody, sir."

"Right. We'll have to send Sergeant Toffington, and request a replacement out of pipeline. What else?"

"A weapons specialist."

"Corporal Courcey."

"He's demolitions, sir."

"What the hell," Major Barker said. "He went through basic training, didn't he? He's a weapons specialist. Tell Ackley to make the change on his Form Twenty."

"Yessir."

"Now: we need a garrison. Weren't there two companies at Cho Rhee?"

"Yes, sir. Half of 'em ran away when we sent in the Marines to rescue Lieutenant Arsenault. The others are on a road-clearing detail somewhere."

"Pull 'em back, re-form 'em into one company, and give 'em to Lieutenant Hamilton."

"What if they mutiny again, sir?"

The major leaned back in his chair, and a happy, crooked smile spread across his face. "Well, there's always the Marines," he said.

Lieutenant Hamilton was afraid they had goofed the mosquito patrol. "Ackley told me yesterday that the count was way up," he said as they hurried after Captain Olivetti. "Heck, is it my fault if the mosquitoes like me?"

"Vitamin B-one, sir," Toffee said eagerly.

"What about it?"

"If you took vitamin B-one with your diet, the mosquitoes wouldn't touch you, sir. Got a catalog you can have. It's all natural organic stuff."

"*She*-it," Ski said.

"Honest," Toffee said. "If you get plenty of vitamin B-one, you give off a smell that mosquitoes don't like."

Ski sniffed at Toffee's ear. "Whew!" he said. "I don't much care for it, neither."

Stephen had his own idea about why they had been called to the major's office in the middle of the night, and everything clicked when he saw the map stand, with Major Barker proud as a pigeon beside it. He tried to signal his guess to Lieutenant Hamilton, but the lieutenant was busy saluting and reporting everybody present and accounted for.

"Good, good," Major Barker said, cutting him short. He began to tell them about Muc Wa. Lieutenant Hamilton looked puzzled, Ski looked bored, and Toffee . . . well, Stephen didn't like the expression on Toffee's face. He was the radioman, and he would *know*. . . . Muc Wa, the major said, was a French outpost which had been abandoned in 1953. Shortly after that the French had lost control of the highway from here to the sea. Penang came under siege. A relief convoy was ambushed and destroyed. Penang was lost with two thousand defenders. Disaster, and all because some blundering ass in the French colonial office had decided to abandon the garrison at Muc Wa. But the U. S. Military Advisory Command was not about to repeat the mistakes of the French. No, sir. Muc Wa would be reoccupied and regarrisoned.

"Yes, sir," Lieutenant Hamilton said, since it was clear he was supposed to say something. "Who's going to garrison it?"

"You are."

"Me, sir?"

"That is correct, Lieutenant."

"But sir, I'm only—"

"A shavetail. Yes. But I've had my eye on you these past two weeks, Lieutenant. I've tested your leadership ability on the mosquito patrol, and I'm convinced you're just the man for Muc Wa. I'm recommending you for promotion."

A sappy grin spread across the lieutenant's face. "Thank you, sir," he said. "*Thank* you."

"All right. Let's look at the map, gentlemen." Major Barker showed them the highway, a pale yellow worm wriggling through the mountains. "Muc Wa is *here*," he said, slapping his palm against the plastic map cover. His hand covered ten or fifteen square kilometers, but even so, it was clear that Muc Wa was nowhere near the highway it was supposed to defend. "There's an improved road along here someplace," the major said. "It's impassable for vehicles, of course, after all this time. But you should be able to make it from the highway in one day's march."

"Sir?" Captain Olivetti said, stepping away from the wall.

"Yes, Al," Major Barker said. "It's all yours." He surrendered the map stand to the captain.

"I suggest we go in shooting," Captain Olivetti said, white teeth flashing in his handsome face. "Make a two-day sweep through those mountains. Give old Charlie Romeo something to think about."

"Just the four of us?" Lieutenant Hamilton said.

"You'll have a crack company of native Raiders," Major Barker said. "They were blooded at Cho Rhee, which we lost to Charlie, unfortunately; but they've kept fit since then."

There was a choking sound from Toffee.

"Yeah, and there's a battalion of native Marines in Penang," Captain Olivetti said. "The American advisor is a buddy of mine. He's willing to provide a couple platoons for a heliborne assault if we can give him a good target."

"What do you think, Lieutenant?" Major Barker asked. "It's your operation."

"Your ass, he means," Ski whispered.

"Well, sir," Lieutenant Hamilton said. "I've never led a combat patrol before."

"We discussed that, Lieutenant, and Captain Olivetti has volunteered to go along with you."

"In that case—"

"Fine," the major said. "It's all settled, then." He nodded to Captain Olivetti, who flipped the canvas drop cover over the map. Then the major looked expectantly at Lieutenant Hamilton. This was the lieutenant's clue to salute and get the hell out of there. But he didn't. He stepped forward and said:

"Sir? I just want to say . . . thank you."

They all stared at him, embarrassed.

"I think I've got a fine team here," Lieutenant Hamilton

went on. Ski looked at the ceiling, his lips thrust out, as if he were whistling Dixie to himself. Toffee looked at the floor. Stephen caught the major's eye and stared him down. *Ray is my friend, after all,* he thought. *I'm responsible for him.* But the lieutenant wasn't done yet: "We'll do our best, sir," he promised. "I just want you to know that we appreciate this chance to fight for . . . you know. Our country."

"Well said, Lieutenant," Major Barker told him in a tired voice.

Six

The convoy moved out on Thursday. Major Barker watched them go—six trucks crammed with Raiders—then hurried back to his office to follow their progress on the map. With a grease pencil he printed OPERATION BLAZE across the map cover. Then he brought out the hatpins he had swiped from Madame What's-her-name, that French belly dancer in Thaitan, during the last Commander's Conference. He made two red flags which he labeled OLIVETTI and OLEONOWSKI, and a green flag labeled MARINES. These he taped to the hatpins.

At nine hundred hours the clerk-typist, who was now doubling as radioman, reported that the convoy had passed Checkpoint Alpha. The major planted his two red flags. A French regimental combat team had been cut to pieces there, ten years ago. It made a handy checkpoint.

"Well, Ackley," he said to the clerk-typist, "it's all downhill now. Don't you wish you were out there?"

"Nossir."

"Why didn't you tell me you were a signalman-medic? I might of assigned you to Muc Wa, instead of Toffee."

"Fact is," Ackley said, scratching his cheek, "they dropped me from the medic course. Couldn't stand the sight of blood. Made me sick to my stomach."

"Oh," the major said.

"So they sent me to language school instead."

"Outstanding! Ackley, you're full of surprises. Which dialect d'you speak? Buru? Mao?"

"Nossir. Arabic."

"Oh, for Pete's sake," the major said. "Get your ass back to the commo shack."

The convoy reached Checkpoint Bravo at eleven hundred hours. This was the detrucking area, and Major Barker planted his red flags on the footpath leading south, one flag a bit behind the other. Then he went to lunch. With Olivetti out in the field, there was nobody in the Raider compound worth talking to, so the major drove down to the officers' club in Penang. He came back at three o'clock, found that Olivetti's Raiders had already forded the river at Checkpoint Charlie, and moved his flags accordingly. It was a long afternoon after that. He read the *Infantry Journal* for a while, wishing he could find the time to write articles. Then he sent Ackley over to the chow hall for coffee. At six o'clock he sent Ackley out again for sandwiches, which they ate in the darkened commo shack. It was seven-thirty before the signal came in. Major Barker took the microphone and said:

"Hello, Blaze! This is Thunderhead, Thunderhead. How do you read me, over?"

"Whoo-*ah*-Blaze brak-brak umber five eee-*hoo*, over."

The major looked at Ackley. "What the hell's he saying?" he asked.

"You're not coming in very clear," Ackley said.

"This is Thunderhead," the major said into the microphone. "I don't read you so good, either. What is your present position, Blaze? I repeat: what is your present position? Over."

"Whew-*oo*-haw, betta—pete betta, over."

"They're at Checkpoint Delta," Ackley translated.

"This is Thunderhead," Major Barker said. "Keep up the good work, Blaze. We'll expect your next transmission at oh-eight-hundred hours from Checkpoint Echo. Understood?"

"Hoo-*hah* eeeeee," the radio moaned.

"Over and out," the major said, and hung the microphone

in its cradle. Then he went back to the schoolhouse and moved his flags. The Raiders were now camped for the night, and only a small ridge separated them from the rebel stronghold they would attack at dawn tomorrow. Operation Blaze was looking good.

Stones rolled beneath their feet. Brambles and thorn trees slashed them when they fell, and mosquitoes came down in clouds to drink their blood. On the map, their route was no longer than Stephen's thumbnail, with a contour line every millimeter or so. He pushed the Raiders as hard as he dared, up this invisible ladder of contour lines; two hours later they lay panting on the height-of-land, sucking water from their canteens.

"We're bang on schedule," he said when Ski caught up.

"Ooff!" Ski said. "We're so pooped . . . we couldn't . . . take . . . the old ladies' home." He collapsed beside Stephen. "Got some refugees," he said after a while.

One of the Raiders brought up a family of mountaineers, wild and dark, driving them in front of him with his carbine. There was a boy who seemed almost old enough for combat, so Stephen marched him along the ridge line to Captain Olivetti's section.

The captain had set up a command post near a tree. A Raider was up in the tree, searching the valley through binoculars and calling down information to Cowboy, the interpreter. Toffee was trying to contact somebody on the radio. Lieutenant Hamilton was sitting against a rock with his eyes closed, his face pale and greasy.

"What you got, Courcey?" Captain Olivetti cried, grinning like a man who has just scored the winning touchdown. "A live one? . . . Hey, Cowboy!"

The interpreter came over to where they were standing. He looked at the refugee boy, said something to him, then slapped him across the face. The young man fell. Cowboy knelt and began firing questions at him.

Stephen heard a droning, fluttering noise beyond the trees. He looked at his watch: eight o'clock. The Marines were on schedule, too.

"Sir!" Cowboy said. "This man he say: he never hear of any Communist rebels."

"Ask him how many people in that village yonder."

"Sir, he say: he never go to that village."

"Oh, for Christ's sake," Captain Olivetti said.

Toffee switched frequencies and began calling: "Marine aircraft, Marine aircraft, this is Blaze, Blaze. Do you have any traffic for this station, over?"

"Hello, Blaze!" the radio replied. "This is Black Knight Four; I read you loud and clear. What is your present position, over?"

"Is he lying?" Captain Olivetti said to Cowboy.

"Yes, sir," Cowboy said, kicking the refugee in the kidneys.

"Take it easy," Stephen told him.

"This is Blaze," Toffee said. "We are at Checkpoint Echo. Will you relay that to Thunderhead, over?"

"This is Black Knight Four. Understand that you are now at Checkpoint Echo. We'll try not to drop any ordnance on you, buddy."

Rockets whooshed and thundered beyond the trees. Fifty-caliber guns chattered like air hammers. The Raiders grinned uneasily and fingered their carbines, looking at the Americans for comfort.

"Sir," Cowboy said, "this man he say: maybe ten, fifteen families in that village. No Communist rebels."

"Is he lying?"

"Yes, sir."

"To hell with it," Captain Olivetti said. "We don't have time to fool with him."

Quick as a cat, Cowboy whipped his bayonet from its scabbard and plunged it up to the hilt in the refugee's chest. The boy looked at Cowboy and tried to grab the blade. But he went dead before he reached it. Cowboy removed the bayonet and wiped it on the young man's loincloth.

"You son of a bitch," Stephen said. "You—"

"Forget it, Courcey," Captain Olivetti said. "We've got work to do."

"Killing prisoners? Killing kids?"

"I said *forget it,* Corporal."

Stephen turned and walked back to his own section. Behind him, he heard Lieutenant Hamilton vomiting into the bushes. "Okay!" Stephen yelled. "Let's go!" The Raiders stood up and began fussing with their packs, like dark-skinned Boy Scouts wishing they had stayed at home. *Hurry!* Stephen thought. *Hurry! Let's get down there and do some honest fighting.* Ski was asleep behind a rock. Stephen turned the refugee family loose, then went over and shook Ski awake. "That son-of-a-bitching Cowboy killed the kid," he said.

"Good," Ski said, yawning. "One less rebel to shoot me in the back." He didn't seem to notice that the other refugees were gone.

The armed helicopters—the Black Knights—were pounding the valley with rockets and machinegun fire. Stephen hustled his Raiders down the slope, into a rocky gully bristling with thorn trees. They were jumpy. The flanking squads kept edging close to the main column, and the column was breaking into two clusters, one around Stephen and the other around Ski. "Get away from me!" Ski roared. "Spread out—scram!" The Raiders seemed comforted by the yelling, and they pressed in closer.

Stephen heard the crackle of small-arms fire ahead, sharp and near, much nearer than the helicopters, and he broke into the open with his carbine pointing. But there was no battle that he could see, no village, no people. He waved the Raiders on. They crossed a small hill, and then he saw Captain Olivetti's section, fifty meters to the left. The mortarmen were folding their tripod. Beyond them was a lonesome bamboo hut with flames shooting through its walls. Stephen and Ski went over to say hello.

"Where's the action?" Stephen asked.

"Some people ran out of that hut yonder," Captain Olivetti said. "So we zapped 'em."

"Guerrillas?" Stephen said.

The captain shrugged. "Who knows?" he said. "But I hope somebody puts up a fight. Otherwise we'll just have to cross over and scrap with the Marines."

The Black Knights stopped shooting. Like dragonflies, they danced above the valley, about two kilometers away. Stephen could see the rocket pods slung from their bellies. Then the troop-carrying helicopters swept down, vanished briefly behind the hills, and rose again with daylight showing through their open doors.

"That's sure the easy way to go to war, ain't it?" Ski said.

"Getting there is half the fun," Captain Olivetti told him. "Wahoo!" he shouted, waving his carbine like a swagger stick. "Let's go, you little mothers!"

Stephen and Ski went back to their Raiders, who were just standing around, goggling at the helicopters. Ski ran through them like an angry sheepdog. When they were straightened out, Stephen took the point and led them across the valley. It was ten o'clock, and his plastic water bag was dry, and still no sign of battle. *Where the hell is Charlie Romeo?* he thought. *Where the hell is the war?* He signaled the Raiders to bear left, toward the low ground where they might find water. After half an hour they met Captain Olivetti again in a dry riverbed. A few gray pools of water showed here and there among the rocks, with a circle of Raiders around each pool. They looked beat. Stephen dropped four iodine tablets into his water bag and joined the nearest circle. Toffee was there, too, draining a water bag into his uptilted mouth.

"How about a drink of that?" Stephen said. He would be dry for another ten minutes, while the iodine tablets did their job. Toffee passed the water bag across the pool. Stephen tilted it to his lips, squeezing it like a wineskin, and a warm, thick, yellow-tasting fluid poured into his mouth. "Carrot juice!" he said.

"Sure," Toffee said. He took back the water bag and sank it in the pool. Air bubbles rose and broke in the gray surface slime. "Hate those C-rations," Toffee said. "Trouble is, the juice won't stay fresh in this heat."

"You should have brought your juicing machine," Stephen said. Silence from Toffee. "No," Stephen said. "You didn't. Did you?"

"Well, what if it was on a helicopter, and the helicopter crashed?"

"You're carrying that monster in your pack?"

"It only weighs fifteen pounds," Toffee said.

Stephen shook his head. He filled his own water bag and went over to where Ski was hunkering in the shade of an umbrella tree. "Guess what Toffee's carrying in his pack?" he said.

"A woman."

"His juicing machine."

"Gor," Ski said.

"Why does he drink that stuff, anyway?"

"His old man had a heart attack or something when Toffee was a kid, and Toffee don't want it to happen to him. Funny, ain't it?"

"Or sad," Stephen said.

"Sometimes I think they're pretty much the same thing," Ski told him, trying to find a more comfortable spot in the shade.

Crack! of a rifle beyond the hill.

"What the hell?" Ski said, jumping up. "*That's* no carbine."

They grabbed their weapons and ran to the top of the hill. Captain Olivetti was there first, but Stephen was right at his heels; they stood breathless on the high ground and stared at a small, determined man who was trudging toward them with a pig across his shoulders. An infantry rifle was slung from his neck. "Well," said Captain Olivetti. "I'll be a dirty . . ." He raised his carbine and fired. The man stopped, looked at them, and dropped his pig as if he were suddenly sick of carrying it. Then he turned and ran the other way, holding the rifle in front of him. He was wearing sandals and floppy black pajamas. It didn't seem fair to kill him, somehow, but all the evidence was against him, so Stephen snapped up his carbine and squeezed off the round that was in the chamber. He missed. Captain Olivetti was missing, too, and cursing himself for it.

Then the Raiders swept across the hill. The mortarmen set up their tube, dropped a round into it, and ran on without waiting to see where the shell exploded. Stephen and the captain were sucked into the race. They charged across the rolling valley floor like hounds after a fox, while mortar shells exploded in front of them and carbine shots rattled beside them. But the little man had gone to earth. The hunt broke up and became a matter of poking through bushes and groves of trees, until Captain Olivetti called it off.

They sent a runner after the Marines, and Captain Jellison, the U.S. advisor, came over to join them. "Commander Khan sends his regrets," Captain Jellison said, "but he's taking a nap."

The Raiders scattered in groups of two and three to cook their rice, while the Americans roasted the pig. Toffee gave his share to Cowboy. Stephen would have preferred to eat with the Raiders, too, but the meat smelled like paradise, and he sat down with Ski and the officers.

"Looks like the major landed us in the wrong valley," Captain Olivetti said. He tore into the roast pork with flashing teeth, and juice ran through the stubble on his jaw. "What a fizzle!"

"Sorry about that," Captain Jellison said.

"Hey, Cowboy," Captain Olivetti said, throwing his empty water bag at the interpreter. "Fill that, huh?" Cowboy went over to the nearest group of Raiders and gave the water bag to one of them.

"Christ," Captain Jellison said. "You guys don't know how lucky you are. You just say SHIT, and two hundred Raiders squat in the dust. But me—I tell Commander Khan he ought to do something, and he wants me to show it to him in a book. So I do, and then he wants to think about it for a while. Then he has to make some changes, you know, to save face, and by that time Charlie is over the hill and far away. . . . I'm telling you, Al, we're not going to win this war until we bring in the U. S. Marines."

Captain Olivetti looked up. "Think there's a chance of that?" he asked.

"Just wait till the elections are over. The Marines'll be landing inside of a week, once the elections are over."

"And the Army."

"Well, maybe the Air Cavalry. But the Marines'll be first, and then it's good-by to this advisor crap for me. I'll have a company of my own, and watch 'em jump!"

"The Air Cav," Captain Olivetti said. "By God, Jelly, I think you're right. *That's* the outfit with a future." He went back to his chunk of pork, chewing thoughtfully.

Ski winked at Stephen, then rolled his eyes toward the soft blue dome of the sky.

Major Barker had given them until twelve hundred hours to defeat the rebels and move out, sweeping south through the valley. They kept to the schedule, leaving the bones of the pig to mark their passage. The Marines took the east wall, Captain Olivetti's section took the west wall, and Ski and Stephen went straight down the middle. They would all link up again tomorrow at Muc Wa.

Stephen and Ski were the last to leave the riverbed. They arranged their Raiders in good marching order, with two squads flanking the main column, and moved out with the sun flaming upon their necks. Then—WHUNK! A high-explosive shell crashed down upon the riverbed, showering them with gravel. Stephen's head rang with the noise. It was Ski who kept the Raiders on the march.

"Eighty-one-millimeter mortar, that was," Ski said after a while. "Good thing we didn't stick around for dessert."

Stephen nodded, still unable to speak. *Now I know where Charlie is,* he thought. *Up in the hills. Watching us . . . You see, Rebecca? There really is a war.*

They marched through the valley all afternoon. The Raiders seemed to enjoy the work, which consisted of destroying every hooch they could find. There was one old warrior, especially, who searched out huts where Stephen could see nothing but the rain forest. He was a bandy-legged little man with earlobes that drooped down to his shoulders, and no front teeth. Stephen gave him a handful of matches and turned him loose. The old man gathered six or seven Raiders into an incendiary squad; they looted the huts, stuffed their packs with tobacco and rice, and set fire to what remained. The crackle of burning bamboo followed them across the valley.

"Let's promote that guy," Stephen said. He tore the chevrons from his left sleeve, called a halt, and presented the stripes to the old Raider. "You—Corporal!" Stephen announced. "You, me, same-same." The old man turned the chevrons this way and that. "Yes," Stephen said, "you're a corporal now, same as me." The old man stepped back and saluted, grinning toothlessly.

"Oh-*kay!*" he said.

"Corporal Old Man," Ski cackled. "Well, dang me, Steve, but I think you've made a friend."

Corporal Old Man produced a safety pin from his pack and fastened the chevrons to his breast pocket, upside-down in the local manner. Then he appointed a runner. He stuck close to Stephen and Ski, trying to guess what they wanted, and sent the runner out to see that it was done. The column moved much more smartly after that, and they reached the end of the valley by four o'clock.

The heat was stifling here. The blood burned in Stephen's cheeks, and his mouth felt as if it had been stuffed with cotton all day. Ski was just as badly off, by the look of him, sucking on his canteen as he marched, his bulging eyes peering from side to side.

Finally the valley turned into a forested, waterless ravine. Stephen called a break as soon as the entire column was under cover. Then he found the most comfortable spot in creation, slouched with his back against a cushion of roots.

"Is every operation like this?" he asked.

Ski nodded. "Most every one," he said. "You go out fifty times and don't see nothing. Then comes number fifty-one and Charlie jumps you, pow! I'm telling you, Steve, there ain't no fighter like Charlie in the world, once he gets his hind leg planted."

Beyond them the ravine became a gully, then a slash in the mountainside. The trail seemed to cross the gully about a hundred meters from where they were sitting. From there it climbed steeply until it reached a little plateau, dotted with boulders *and two men eating lunch, by God!* Stephen pointed them out to Ski. Then he studied them through his binoculars: young fellows with wild black hair and bony faces, scooping rice with their fingers from a china bowl. They were wearing black pajamas, like the little guy who had shot the pig. Stephen gave the binoculars to Ski.

"What d'you think?" he said.

"Send out a flanking squad," Ski said.

Corporal Old Man took the flanking squad into the ravine. Twigs snapped, dead vines rustled.

"Shit-a-goddamn," Ski said, squinting through the binoculars. "They hear him. Should we take 'em from here? What do you say?"

Stephen thought of the mortar shell that had almost landed on top of them, back at the riverbed. "Yes," he said. "I'll take the guy on the left." He adjusted the carbine's rear sight, then spitted the small black figure with the front sight, a knife larger than its victim. "Ready?" he said. *I'm ready,* he thought. *Ready to kill a man. If he is a man, and not some damned little kid.* "Now!" He squeezed the trigger, and the carbine coughed and bucked against his shoulder. He didn't hear Ski's shot; they must have fired at the same instant. The young men had vanished. "Let's go!" Stephen yelled, slinging his pack. *I think we missed,* he thought. *Now it's their turn, if they want to take it.* He ran up the trail, driving six or seven Raiders in front of him; he crossed the gully and scrambled up the open slope, heart thumping, back itching, waiting for the bullets to smash into him. *There! Home safe, by God!* The little shelf of land was empty. There was an open-walled hooch on the side nearest the trail, just large enough to shelter two sleeping men, and a smoldering fire in the middle and two white scars on the rocks. The bullets had struck about two feet low.

Stephen assembled a squad of Raiders and sent them out to search the mountainside. He did the same with the next group that straggled up the trail. Then, with a third squad, he searched the hut and the shelf of land, finding nothing except a large wooden fork, a few scraps of cloth, and a notebook that seemed to contain penmanship exercises, the same sentence written again and again.

Ski finally came puffing up the trail. "Look what I found," he said. He was leading a bare-breasted native girl, his hand clamped securely around her wrist. Eyes like licorice drops. Skin the color of walnuts. Breasts like grapefruit halves, so high and wide apart that she could have been no more than fifteen years old. A black cloth was wound around her hips, down to her calves. She was carrying a tall wicker basket, which was fitted with shoulder straps like a knapsack, and a clay water jug in her free arm.

"What are you planning to do with her?" Stephen asked.

"Well, boy, if you don't know I can't tell you," Ski said.

"But don't our orders say to pick up all refugees and their gear, and take 'em to Muc Wa?"

"That's right," Stephen said.

"Well, then! This little butterfly is going to Muc Wa as my own personal prisoner of war."

"*Jus primae noctis,*" Stephen said.

"Just what?"

Stephen told him about the Law of the First Night.

"Just Prime Nooky, *I* calls it," Ski said.

The rest of the family came into sight then, an old woman with fallen breasts and a wrinkled belly, and a girl-child carrying a baby on her back. Stephen guessed that the two young men had belonged to this same family. But he wouldn't know until they reached Muc Wa and Cowboy questioned the women.

He showed the notebook to Ski. "What d'you think?" he asked. "Were we shooting at a couple of school kids?"

"Where would they find a school, out here in the puckerbrush? Anyhow, they's no reason why a school kid can't be a guerrilla, too."

The sun was going down. The Raiders built fires to cook their dinner rice, and the refugee family cooked up a pot of leaves and roots. The Americans ate cold C-rations. After dinner Stephen took out the little tin of peaches he had been saving in the bottom of his pack. The girl-child crept over to watch him open it. When Stephen looked at her, she covered her eyes.

"She's afraid you'll eat her eyeballs," Ski told him. "That's what Charlie tells 'em—Americans eat babies' eyeballs. *Pagh!*"

Stephen gave the peaches to the little girl. She crammed them into her mouth with dark, dirty fingers, then threw away the juice, which he had been thirsting for all day. Afterward she would not go back to her mother, or grandmother, or whatever the old woman was.

"Well, she's a bit young for my taste," Ski said. "But leastways she ain't had a chance to pick up no bad habits."

Stephen scooped up the little girl and carried her back to the old woman. *Just my luck,* he thought. *Ski gets the ripe one, and I get the child.*

Corporal Old Man posted the guards and sent a detail down into the ravine to look for water, and Ski tried to contact Toffee on the small backpack radio, without luck. Then it was dark. Stephen tucked the notebook into his pack, which he then used for a pillow. They slept in the hut with Ski's girl between them. The old woman seemed happy enough with the arrangement, and settled down with the rest of the family a few yards away.

"Hey, Steve?" Ski said out of the dark.

"What?"

"You want to knock off a piece of that Just Prime Nooky?"

"No, thanks," Stephen said. "I'm too tired." Although he really wasn't.

"Me too," Ski said. "Besides, I want Toffee to have a look at her first. You never can tell, with this native meat. It might be a bit spoiled."

Stephen kept waking through the night. He was fiercely thirsty, and worried that Charlie might drop a mortar shell on them, and very, very conscious of the young woman who was sleeping beside him, breathing comfortably through her mouth.

Major Barker did not sleep well, either. Operation Blaze was not going as smoothly as he had hoped: the Marines were furious because one of their helicopters had crashed on the way back to Penang, the rebels had somehow slipped out of the trap Major Barker had set for them, and now Sergeant Oleonowski's section could not be located. The major knotted his sheets and sweated through his pajamas. If only he could be out there, kicking ass! Things would be different then.

Next morning he was in his office at seven hundred hours. The map assured him that he had planned the operation perfectly: two sections of Raiders penetrating the target area on D-Day minus one, the Marines leapfrogging them by helicopter, the three-pronged sweep through the valley . . . but not one lousy Communist casualty to forward to Thaitan.

New reports came in at eight hundred, ten hundred, and twelve hundred hours. Major Barker moved his hatpins, and marked the intervening space with a red grease pencil. Captain Olivetti was averaging one kilometer an hour. The Marines were doing a bit less. Then, at fourteen hundred hours, Toffee relayed a signal from Sergeant Ski, and the major filled in the missing prong. The red lines were beginning to converge upon Muc Wa—but slowly, so goddamned slowly. At sixteen hundred hours he went over to the commo shack and waited for Ackley to decipher the blips and beeps that Toffee was transmitting across the mountains. They were too far away now for voice transmission.

"Never mind that," the major said. "Ask him: What the hell is keeping you?"

Ackley crouched over the telegraph key and pecked out the message. "The ter . . . the t-e-r-r-a-i-n is more difficult than anti . . . anticipated," he recited, sweating over the loudspeaker. "Request permission to make camp here and contain . . . continue . . . to continue on to Checkpoint Tango tomorrow morning, over."

"Negative," Major Barker said, and Ackley pecked it out.

"We have no water," Ackley said slowly. He paused to wipe his mouth with his hand. "Refugees in poor physical condition, over."

"Tell him to shoot the refugees if they can't keep up," Major Barker said. "Request denied." While Ackley was transmitting the message, the major took a radiogram form and wrote:

—SECRET—

SUBJECT: MUC WA, ENGARRISONMENT OF

1. MUC WA HAS BEEN GARRISONED AS PER YOUR DIRECTIVE OF 14 MAY. OPERATION WAS CARRIED OUT WITH DISPATCH AND INITIATIVE BY ALL ELEMENTS INVOLVED.

2. A FULL REPORT FOLLOWS BY COURIER.

FOR THE COMMANDER
Y TEAM (PENANG)
US ARMY RAIDER GROUP AIRBORNE

"Send this down to Thaitan," he told Ackley. "If you need me for anything tonight, I'll be at the officers' club in Penang."

Seven

Muc Wa did not exist. Where the village should have been, they found only a river, a few acres of grass and scattered trees, and the ghost of a road. Even these landmarks soon vanished in the night.

"We must be in the wrong place," Captain Olivetti said.

Captain Jellison, the Marine advisor, huddled beneath his poncho with a flashlight and a map. "Nope," he said, emerging. "This is Muc Wa, and you're welcome to it."

"But the map—"

"The map is ten years old," Captain Jellison said. "A lot can happen in ten years."

Lieutenant Hamilton hunkered on the grass with his head in his hands. "You mean I'm supposed to build a garrison from this?" he said. "From nothing?"

"Sorry about that," Captain Jellison said.

The helicopters came in at nine hundred hours next morning, a bottle-green swarm, to unload the Raiders' class-A supplies in untidy heaps on the grass. The pilots seemed puzzled by the notion of dumping all that gear in the middle of nowhere. They did not shut down their engines, but stood grimly beneath the whirling rotor blades, hands on hips, waiting for the Raiders to get on with it. Then they loaded the Marines and took off. Captain Olivetti scrambled into the last chopper. "See you in six months!" he yelled above the rotor blast, and the helicopter danced on the grass.

"If we're lucky," Ski said to Stephen.

"So long, sir!" Toffee yelled. "Hope you get that CIB!"

"The hard way," Ski added.

Muc Wa was deadly silent when the helicopters were gone. A breeze stirred the grass, and the crushed blades began to spring upright again; clouds marched swiftly across the soft blue sky. The Raiders squatted beside the supplies they had unloaded, waiting for somebody to tell them what to do.

"Well," Stephen said, hoping to prod Lieutenant Hamilton into action. "Why don't I take a squad and find a spot for the command post?"

"Yes," the lieutenant said. "Yes, why don't you?" Stephen left him staring hopelessly at the grass.

He had a pretty good idea where the command post should go, and he led Corporal Old Man and his incendiary squad to a grassy knoll, sheltered by six or seven tall hardwood trees. The knoll was only a hundred meters from the river, and a comfortable distance from the rain forest. It was the ideal center for a fortified camp.

Somebody else had thought so, too. Corporal Old Man dropped to his knees in a mossy depression and pretended to fire his carbine. "Boo-*boom!*" he said, very pleased with himself. He was right: the depression was an old fighting hole, and there were others spaced around the knoll. One of the Raiders turned up an empty cartridge case. Another touched Stephen's arm and pointed to the north, where, two or three hundred meters distant, there was another small grove of trees. Stephen inspected it through his binoculars. A large stone cross leapt into sight, a tombstone, with the peak and each arm ending in a fat trefoil design. There was an inscription of some kind. *Go, stranger, and tell the Spartans that we lie here in obedience to their laws.* . . . The idea didn't thrill him as much as it had done in college. *What good is Greek history to an engineer?* he thought. *I should have stuck to Hemingway.*

He lowered the binoculars and went back to tell the others that they had found the old French garrison of Muc Wa.

Ski was lecturing Toffee, whose face was burning beet-red.

"Why can't you?" Ski insisted. "You went to the medic school for six months, didn't you?"

"Yes, but—"

"The Army spent all that money to cross-train you, didn't it?"

"But, Ski—"

"Then how come you can't do a little thing like tell me if Butterfly's got the clap?"

"Ski!" Toffee wailed, sweat rolling down his face.

They both turned to Stephen, but Ski got there first. "Tell him, Steve," he said, jerking his bony thumb at Toffee. "Tell him Butterfly ain't got nothing down there to bite him with."

"Don't know if ladies *get* chancres," Toffee said. "Wouldn't know where to *look*."

"You could give her a shot of penicillin, even so," Stephen said. "You do that from the back end, don't you?"

Toffee nodded.

"And it can't do her any harm, can it?"

Toffee shook his head.

Ski snapped his fingers and went off to collect Butterfly from the little band of refugees. She seemed to accept the idea that she was under his particular orders. Ski brought her back, unfastened her body cloth at the waist, and dropped it. Butterfly's skin glowed in the sun like oiled walnut. "Well, looky there!" Ski said, his eyes nearly popping out of their sockets. "Ain't she a beauty? By Gor!"

Stephen looked away. "Where's the lieutenant?" he asked.

"He's behind a tree someplace," Ski said. "He's got the runs. . . . Never mind!" he said, grabbing the throwaway plastic syrette from Toffee. "*I'll* do it." He stooped over and swabbed Butterfly's fine rump with alcohol, shaking his head in admiration.

Stephen saw Lieutenant Hamilton walking toward them, tucking in the tail of his tiger-stripe fatigue shirt, and he went over to head him off.

"You were right about the mosquito patrol, Steve," the lieutenant said.

"How's that?"

"About getting acclimated. I feel terrible."

"Ski said you had the runs."

"I just hope it isn't dysentery," the lieutenant said. "What are Ski and Toffee doing over there?"

"They're giving the refugees a health check."

"Oh, good," the lieutenant said. He went along with Stephen to inspect the knoll. "Yes, it's perfect," he agreed, sweeping the field with his binoculars. "It's the very spot. We'd better move our stuff up here right away." Stephen decided to treat this statement as an order, just to get things off to a good start.

"Yes, sir," he said. Lieutenant Hamilton stared at him. "I'll put a platoon on the job," Stephen went on. "We'd better have another platoon on guard duty, don't you think? The rest of the men can start building their hooches."

"Uh, yes," the lieutenant said. "Yes, do it that way . . . Corporal." Then he pointed down the slope. "What's that?" he said.

"French graves, sir."

"Graves?"

"Yes, sir."

"Oh," Lieutenant Hamilton said.

Ski trudged up the knoll to join them. Butterfly was right behind him, balancing his duffel bag on her head with one hand. With the other, she was rubbing her butt. "Well, well," Ski said. "So this is home, huh? . . . Just drop it anywhere, honey." Butterfly carefully placed the duffel bag beneath a tree.

Lieutenant Hamilton looked at Butterfly's fine chest, then at the ground. "Sergeant Oleonowski," he said, "who is that?"

"Her? Oh, that's just Butterfly."

"Yes, but who is she? Why is she carrying your gear?"

"Why, she's one of the refugees, Lieutenant."

"Yes, but—"

"Didn't you take that psychological warfare course at Fort Darby?" Ski said, rolling his eyes. "Don't you remember what they told us, about how we should win the hearts and the minds of the people?"

"Yes, but—"

"Well, then!" Ski said. "I figure each one of us ought to adopt himself a refugee, so's we can practice that psychological warfare at firsthand."

"Corporal Courcey," the lieutenant said. "Do you think . . ."

"Oh, the corporal's got one, too," Ski said.

"Steve?"

Sure enough, Butterfly's kid sister was legging it up the slope, making for Stephen. She halted a few feet away and peeped at him through her fingers. Stephen scooped her up. This time, instead of drooping like a puppy, she locked her arms around his neck and her legs around his waist, smiling all over her dark, delicate face.

"Yes," Lieutenant Hamilton said, with a sudden, cheery, officer's laugh. "Well! I'll just have to leave this matter to your discretion, men."

Ski got down on his knees, grunting, and opened his duffel bag. "You do that, Lieutenant," he said, pulling out a wrinkled *Playgirl* calendar. He straightened the pages, then hung the calendar from a branch. Butterfly looked at the model for June—a soft-breasted blonde in a hammock. She ran her palms across her own breasts, and seemed happy with the comparison. Ski was also studying the calendar. "Well, well," he said, "I wonder how many of them little sweethearts we'll see before old Charlie runs us out of here?"

"Nobody's going to run us out of here, Sergeant," Lieutenant Hamilton said, squaring his shoulders. "We have a full company of men and a good tactical position, and—"

"We got a hundred-fifty deadbeats, Lieutenant, that's what we've got. A hundred-fifty mutineers. And even if they was the U. S. Marines, old Charlie could still run us off." Ski stood up and dusted the knees of his jungle fatigues. "So we've got a hundred-fifty men? *She*-it. Charlie sends in three hundred. We got three hundred? He sends in six hundred. There ain't no way around it, Lieutenant: we'll last here as long as old Charlie leaves us alone, and not a minute longer."

Stephen put the little girl down, pointed her toward the main group of Raiders, and gave her a pat on the tail to start her off. Then he slung his carbine and walked down the slope in the other direction. The grass was knee-high, and crickets leapt out at him as he walked. Behind him, Lieutenant Hamilton was still arguing with his team sergeant.

The French gravesite was as handsome as it had seemed in the binoculars. The cross was as tall as Stephen's shoulder. It was made from granite, or something very much like it, and there were four small blocks of the same stone to mark the borders of the grave. The inscription had nothing to do with Thermopylae, after all. It only said:

H. Laporte

R. Plevin H. Girondeau

Stephen heard the whisper of grass behind him. He turned: Corporal Old Man had followed him down. The old Raider stopped and grinned at Stephen, showing the blackened roots of his teeth. He seemed afraid to come any closer to the grave.

"The lieutenant says we have a company of men and a good tactical position," Stephen told him.

"Okay!"

"We also have four mortars, four machineguns, and a radio."

"A-okay," said Corporal Old Man, who had learned the names of all their weapons. He nodded briskly, causing his earlobes to flap.

Stephen turned back to the French gravesite. "I wonder how many men Charlie has?" he said.

Eight

They set an ambush on the ghost road that night, and later in the week they ventured into the rain forest, on trails which the refugees pointed out to them. Mostly the ambushes were just a matter of trying to stay awake. They crouched on the dry forest floor, aching from their labor on the camp, and gently brushed the mosquitoes from their faces; at dawn they marched back to Muc Wa and joined the work force again.

"Charlie never heard of this place," Ski said disgustedly after his second night in the rain forest. "Why the hell we got to be patrolling? We got enough work to do, building a garrison out of nothing."

"The SOPs call for an ambush every night," Lieutenant Hamilton said. Stephen backed him up, because he was pleased to see the lieutenant acting like an officer.

The next night, though, he wished that he had kept his mouth shut. He drew the ambush, and it was a live one.

The Raiders were staked out about three kilometers north of Muc Wa, where a well-trodden trail crossed the river. There was a sandbar at the crossing, and a few huts which smelled of fish and human dung. Charlie's men came down the trail just after two o'clock. They were talking and laughing, right up to the moment when the Raiders cut loose. Carbines coughed along the trail; shouts answered them, and then the hammer blows of old French army rifles; the forest winked with muzzle flashes. It was not at all like the night-firing exercises at Fort Darby. Stephen couldn't locate his own

Raiders, never mind Charlie's men; he just fired blind in the general direction of the river. His throat was dry, and he was having a bit of trouble with his breathing. *Now I know what it means to have a tiger by the tail,* he thought. *How the hell do we let go?* Charlie took care of that, luckily. After a few minutes the only sound was the flat, stupid barking of the Raiders' carbines, and they were able to creep out on the trail and search for bodies, finding none.

They swaggered along the trail next morning, grinning whenever Stephen looked at them. He grinned right back. They carried their carbines muzzle-down, and their dark, wild faces glowed in the sun: the toughest goddamn troopers since Attila was a pup. It no longer seemed important that they were only five feet tall.

"They fought like Raiders," Stephen reported when they reached camp.

"You see?" Lieutenant Hamilton cried, reaching for the mustache he was cultivating on his upper lip. It was still too short for him to get a grip on it, however. "Don't believe those stories about what happened at Cho Rhee," he said. "That must have been some kind of misunderstanding. They're good boys; I knew it."

"They was too scared to run, that's all," Ski said, and detailed the ambush squad to cut brush down by the river.

"Give 'em the morning off," Stephen said. "They've earned it."

"We got a camp to build, Steve."

"I'll cut the brush, then, but I want my boys to have the morning off."

"*Your* boys?" Ski stared popeyed at him. "Well, shit-a-goddamn." He slapped his belly and went off to work on the wall, swearing to himself.

Stephen went up to the command post and changed his socks. Then he fried four eggs on the little gasoline stove which had been air-dropped to them, together with bales of barbed wire and other class-B supplies. Refugee hens had provided the eggs. Stephen was scraping them out of the pan with a spoon when Toffee came in.

"Here's a signal from the chaplain's office in Penang," Toffee said. "Poly-unsaturated fat," he said, frowning at the fried eggs. "They're healthier if you eat 'em raw."

Stephen shook his head and unfolded the radiogram, which read:

> CHAPLAIN'S FLIGHT SCHEDULED YOUR AREA NEXT WEEK. PLEASE INDICATE YOUR PRIORITY CATHOLIC PROTESTANT JEWISH.

"Give it to Ski," Stephen said. "He's the team sergeant."

"He said to give it to you," Toffee said.

"All right, I'll take care of it," Stephen said, finishing the eggs. If he didn't look at them, they tasted just like the eggs he had devoured at midnight or two A.M., in college long ago. It seemed a long time ago, anyhow, in the years when John Wayne had done all the night fighting the U. S. Army required.

Then he went to work with a squad of Raiders, clearing a good field of fire on the east bank of the river, across from the camp. Every once in a while he stopped and looked at his pitch-stained machete. *I fought like a Raider, too,* he thought. *It may not be the noblest profession in the world, but I'm trained for it, and I came through all right. . . . I wonder if I hit anybody, banging away in the dark like that?*

Butterfly's kid sister had followed him out and was gathering up the brush as he cut it. "Hello, angel," he said. She ran away, but crept in close again when he went back to work. *Angel's brother could have been in that column,* Stephen thought. *I might have killed him. Or her father.*

Across the river, the Raiders were singing mournfully as Muc Wa took shape beneath their shovels. Ski was the foreman. Every night he sat up with a sketch map, inventing attacks and ways to beat them; daytimes, he built these defenses into his fortress. It would be shaped like a fat, four-pointed star, with a machinegun emplacement at each tip and a gate halfway between, at each inside angle.

"Four gates," Lieutenant Hamilton complained at lunch, which they ate from C-ration cans in the command post. "Aren't you giving Charlie Romeo too many ways to break in?" He rubbed the smudge on his upper lip. He still felt uncomfortable about giving the enemy his GI nickname.

"Them gates is for us," Ski said. "So's we can get out of here when the time comes. You don't have to worry about old Charlie, Lieutenant. He'll come over the wall like a forest fire."

"Over the barbed wire?"

"You bet your sweet ass," Ski said.

The Raiders were digging a deep trench along the star-shaped line Ski had marked for them. They packed the dirt in a chest-high rampart just inside the trench. Next they would string barbed wire along the rampart and fill the trench with bamboo stakes, which the refugees were sharpening at the rate of one thousand per day. That was the quota, anyhow.

Ski's only breaks from this labor were long walks with Butterfly, from which he returned red-faced and yawning. "I'm trying to teach her English," he said that afternoon, when Stephen and the brush-clearing squad routed them out of a grove of trees. "She don't learn very fast. All she's got so far is *chocolate* and *make-love*. I sure hope she picks up some more words in a hurry, because I'm damned near out of chocolate bars." He walked slowly back to the camp, with Butterfly rubbing against his leg like a cat.

By chowtime, Toffee had another signal from the chaplain's office. He offered it to Lieutenant Hamilton, who rubbed his mustache and looked at Ski, who looked at Stephen.

"All right," Stephen said, "we'll take a poll. Ski? Do you want to see the chaplain?"

"I ain't been to Mass since I was seventeen," Ski said.

"Neither have I," Stephen said. "What about you, Lieutenant?"

"I'm a Unitarian," Lieutenant Hamilton said. "I don't think the Army has any Unitarian chaplains."

"Toffee?"

The radioman looked into his canteen cup, which was filled with a bright green liquid. "Like to try some?" he said, offering the cup to Stephen. It had a bitter, grassy taste.

"What is it?" Stephen asked.

"Grass."

"Grass?"

"Cows live on grass," Toffee said. "We don't have many fresh vegetables, and it'll be a month before the garden produces anything." He had planted beets, carrots, and green peppers behind the commo shack.

"Well, I've tasted worse," Stephen said, giving the canteen cup back to Toffee. "What kind of chaplain did you say?"

Toffee hid behind his cup of grass juice. "Christian Scientist," he said.

Ski rolled his bulging eyes toward the canvas roof of the command post. "My poor ass," he mourned. "Here I am, thirty-five kilometers in the puckerbrush, with a Christian Scientist for a medic. Hoo boy! I'm gonna take a bullet through the gut piece and old Toffee is gonna lean over me and say, *Pray, you bastard, pray!*"

Stephen turned the radiogram form over and printed:

THIS IS A NONDENOMINATIONAL CAMP.

"Maybe that'll keep 'em quiet for a while," he said, but it didn't. Two days later Toffee brought him another signal:

REQUEST CLARIFICATION YOUR LAST MESSAGE. NONDENOMINATIONAL IS NOT A DENOMINATION. DO YOU MEAN INTERDENOMINATIONAL

IN WHICH CASE YOU SHOULD SPECIFY QUOTE PROTESTANT UNQUOTE?

"Did you show this to the lieutenant?" Stephen asked.

"Yes. He said to give it to you."

"Ski?"

"He said the same."

Stephen wadded the radiogram and threw it into the trench, which was already beginning to fill up with brown, slimy water.

"No answer?" Toffee said, mildly disapproving.

"No," Stephen said.

They had more important things to think about, anyhow. Next morning the ambush squad was bushwhacked as it straggled down the ghost road to Muc Wa. Ski was in charge, so the Raiders held together pretty well, and they made it back to camp with only one man missing. They found the absent Raider the same afternoon, hanging by his heels from a tree, with a faded French tricolor pinned to his fatigue shirt. His throat had been cut.

Captain Olivetti devoured the after-action report. He could feel the carbine against his shoulder, could hear the rattle of gunfire, could smell the sweat and the powder, just as he had once been able to live through football games by reading about them in the papers. "They're sure having fun at Muc Wa," he said to Ackley.

"Yeah."

"Wish to hell I was down there," he added, with a feeling that Lieutenant Hamilton had cheated him, somehow. "Don't you?"

"Nossir," Ackley said.

The captain's latest recommendation for the CIB had come back from Thaitan. Not favorably considered. Thaitan now required three consecutive days under enemy fire, and Operation Blaze had only counted for two. Captain Olivetti saw the rest of his tour in Southeast Asia as a ladder up which he must endlessly climb—one day, three days, three consecutive days—while those clerks in Thaitan snatched the prize one rung higher, endlessly.

He took the after-action report and the morning distribution into Major Barker's office. "They've had another scrap at Muc Wa, sir," he said.

"That's the second in a week, isn't it? Any casualties?"

"One native Raider KIA."

Major Barker shook his head, and his scar darkened. "That's no good," he said. "Send Lieutenant Hamilton a message. Tell him that from now on he'll have to inflict two casualties for every one sustained by friendly forces."

"Yes, sir," Captain Olivetti said, making a note on the back of the distribution envelope.

"That's not a bad idea, is it? Maybe you'd better have Ackley send a copy to all the Z Team commanders."

Captain Olivetti made another note.

"Now!" the major said. "About Muc Wa—d'you realize that it's the first Z Team to be established in this command for more than a year?"

"Yes, sir, and a good thing, too. Static defense—"

"It's the first Z Team since I took over here, as a matter of fact."

"Static defense—"

"Never mind *that*," the major said, standing up and pacing the length of the office. Captain Olivetti sat down in the chair facing the desk. "Nobody in Thaitan is going to remember that I was against Muc Wa from the beginning," Major Barker said, halting in front of the map stand marked OPERATION BLAZE. "It's my camp now, goddammit. If something goes wrong down there, it'll be my ass, not Lieutenant Hamilton's."

"Yessir. We'll have to keep an eye on it."

Major Barker nodded and returned to his desk. "Anything in distribution this morning, Al?" he asked.

Captain Olivetti shuffled the distribution into two piles. "Here's a complaint from the chaplain's office," he said. "Our garrisons are not properly receptive to the idea of regularly scheduled chaplain's flights. . . ."

"File it."

Captain Olivetti transferred the letter to Ackley's pile. "Well," he said, picking up the other item in the major's pile, "Thaitan is sending up two VIPs. A brigadier general and a correspondent, plus party of five. Request rations, quarters, and all normal courtesies."

"All normal courtesies," Major Barker said. "That means we'll have to find a woman for the general. Who is he?"

"Hardnetz, S."

"Sam Hardnetz? I've heard of him. Runs that crazy little outfit, what d'you call it, where they change regiments into battle groups, then back into regiments again?"

"Effectiveness Analysis Research," Captain Olivetti said. A *general and a correspondent*, he thought. *Wow!*

"That's it," the major said. "He probably wants the Raiders to start carrying skin-diving gear, something like that. What about the correspondent?"

"Shaw, R."

"Who's he work for? *Life* magazine?"

"Nossir. Something called the *Liberal*."

"What's that?"

"Never heard of it, sir."

Major Barker gazed thoughtfully at the Muc Wa quadrant. "Al," he said, "this could be a golden opportunity for us."

"Sir?" Captain Olivetti said. *My God*, he thought. *The son of a bitch can read my mind.*

"A correspondent and a general," the major said. "This is our chance to get Covert Warfare before the public, Al. Why should the Marines get all the glory? The Raiders—the U. S. Army Raiders—THE RAIDERS GO TO WAR," he said in a booming voice, picking out the words in the air.

"You're absolutely right, sir," Captain Olivetti said.

"A correspondent and a general," the major said. Then he nodded. "Get me a sand table," he said.

"Sir?"

"A sand table. You know, like the ones they have in Advanced Infantry School. Some toy soldiers, too. Rocks. Trees. Barbed-wire entanglements. You'll find it all in the Quartermaster catalog under Military Equipment, Miniature. . . . And see if there's any traffic going down to Muc Wa this week. I want some aerial photographs of the place." Major Barker returned to his trance for a while. "Oh, and Al?" he said then.

"Sir?"

"See if you can scrounge a copy of that *Liberal* thing," the major said. "See if it's a picture magazine, or what."

The dead Raider was cremated in full uniform, and the stink of scorched boot rubber and human flesh hung over Muc Wa all afternoon. The ashes, in a clay jug, were placed in a little thatched hut, behind the row of longhouses where the Raiders slept.

"Right," Lieutenant Hamilton said, wrinkling his nose. "Now we know the kind of guy we're fighting. Killing prisoners—God!"

"We killed a prisoner on the way down here," Stephen said.

Lieutenant Hamilton thought about it, while the Raiders made a great ceremony of getting drunk on a brew of roots and insects. "You're right, Steve," he said. "We'll have to get rid of Cowboy."

"*What?*"

"We'll send him back to Penang on the first helicopter that stops here."

"For God's sake, Ray! You can't do that—we need him."

"I don't want murderers fighting under my command."

"What do you want? Boy Scouts?"

"There are good wars and bad wars," Lieutenant Hamilton said, looking clean and bright and sure of himself. "I want my war to be a good one."

He's turning into an officer, all right, Stephen thought. *And what an officer! An idealist.* "That stuff went out with World War One, Ray," he said. "Or with the Spanish Civil War," he added, thinking of old Robert Jordan holding off the Fascists. "Wars are fought by professionals now."

"The guys we're fighting aren't professionals," the lieutenant pointed out.

"Maybe not, but they kill prisoners, as you saw."

The lieutenant looked at the little thatched hut, which was decorated with silhouettes of animals and men, cut from C-ration cans. "I always wondered what the Raiders did with those cans," he said.

"Look, Ray," Stephen said. "You've got to take the good with the bad, and Cowboy is a good interpreter. I don't want an amateur in a job like that. At least, with Cowboy, we know what side he's on—he's on our side, because we've got the money and the firepower. Give him another chance."

Lieutenant Hamilton was still studying the burial hut. "All right!" he said. "Cowboy can stay. But he's your responsibility, Steve."

"Yessir," Stephen said, and almost saluted. But he caught himself in time.

Ski watched the drinking ceremony in a red, popeyed rage. He was furious at the loss of a perfectly good pair of jungle boots, and all those precious hours. Ski's latest plan was to lay a second string of barbed wire around the camp, ten meters out from the main line of defense. They would fill this no man's land with broken glass, noisemakers, and trip wires.

"Why can't they hurry up?" he moaned. "There's a hole so big in the north wall, old Charlie could march a regiment through it."

"Let the boy have his funeral," Stephen said.

"What's he need a funeral for? He's dead, ain't he?"

"It might have been mine," Stephen said.

"*She*-it! I could bury you in fifteen minutes, Steve, and I wouldn't need no hundred-fifty men to help me, neither."

"It might have been yours."

"Then I wouldn't have nothing to worry about, would I? But I'm alive, goddammit, and I'm worried."

"Relax," Stephen told him. "They'll be back at work in the morning."

But they weren't.

After work call next morning, Stephen went to the commo bunker with Toffee, to sort out a log jam of messages from Major Barker. The major suddenly wanted to know everything there was to know about the camp. There was also another plea from the chaplain's office, giving them one more chance at an interdenominational service. Stephen sat on the lowest step, with the sun warming his back, and dictated answers to each of these messages. Beyond Toffee, almost invisible in the darkness of the bunker, a young Raider pedaled furiously on a bicycle. The bicycle was mounted on a wooden frame. Its rear tire had been removed and a V belt installed in its place; the belt was connected to the generator which powered the radio and, at other times, Toffee's juicing machine.

"A company street connects the east and west gates," Stephen said, and Toffee's telegraph key went *tick-tick* in the darkness. "South of the street, there is a parade ground and four longhouses for the native Raiders. . . . Am I going too fast for you?"

"Nope."

"North of the street, we're building a supply room and a chow hall with concrete floors and wooden superstructure. . . . Is that the right word?"

"Sounds all right," Toffee said, and ticked it off. His assistant panted upon the bicycle.

"The command post and the commo bunker are located—"

"Mutiny!" cried a hoarse voice behind him. Stephen jumped out of the way. Ski plunged down the steps into the bunker, waving his carbine and yelling: "Mutiny!"

"What?" Stephen said.

"Mutiny," Ski insisted. "By Gor! I *told* the lieutenant; I told him those little buggers would mutiny first chance they got."

Stephen picked up his carbine. "You stay here," he told Toffee. "Keep the radio warmed up." He followed Ski outside, and they ran down the slope toward the north gate. "What happened?" Stephen asked, squinting against the glare of the sun.

"Was working—on the machinegun post—over there," Ski said, puffing and grunting. "Woof! Little buggers—they walked off the job. Booted a couple—in the ass—but they wouldn't move."

The Raiders were scattered along the perimeter of the camp, looking sullen. The north wall was still without barbed wire for most of its length.

Stephen rounded up Cowboy and Corporal Old Man. "All right," he said. "What's this all about?" Old Man went into a long, singsong explanation, pulling at the loop of flesh that was his left earlobe. He studied the ground while he talked. "What's he saying, Cowboy?" Stephen asked.

"Sir, him say: this place haunted," the interpreter said, looking scornfully at the old Raider. "Him say: ghosts of Frenchmen walk this ground, sir. You must move this camp, sir, far from here."

"Mutiny!" Ski roared. "Tell the bastard to hand in his stripes."

Stephen shut him up. "There's a hundred and fifty of them and only four of us," he said. "If they believe it's haunted, then it is haunted."

"This ain't no democracy. This is the Army."

"Cowboy," Stephen said, "do you believe in ghosts?"

The interpreter tried to sneer, but it came out as a twitch.

"No, sir," he said doubtfully, looking toward the trees where the French cross glowed in the sun.

Ghosts, Stephen thought. *That's a job for the chaplain, isn't it?* "What religion do the Raiders belong to?" he asked.

"Oh, sir, some of them very stupid. They think god is hiding everywhere—trees, stones, rivers. Not scientific, sir. But smart ones worship in the French way."

"The French way? You mean Catholic?"

"Yes, sir. Cath'lic."

"Are you a Catholic, Cowboy?"

"Oh, yes, sir!"

"Okay," Stephen said. "We're going to be very scientific about this, Cowboy. Tell the men they can work on the other side of camp for a few days, until we get rid of the ghosts in a scientific way."

"Yes, sir, very good, sir."

"And tell them: if they're not back at work in fifteen minutes, we'll shoot them all."

"Yes, *sir!*" Cowboy said, baring his teeth in a handsome smile, exactly like Captain Olivetti's.

Stephen and Ski went back to the commo bunker. Stephen, who went down the steps first, almost castrated himself on the muzzle of Toffee's carbine. "Everything all right?" Toffee said, lowering the weapon.

"You still on the air?" Stephen asked.

"Yep."

"Well, tell your boy to start pedaling," Stephen said, "because we've got to mend our fences with the chaplain's office."

Nine

"No," the lieutenant said, searching his mustache until he found a few strands long enough to tug. "I won't allow it."

"Why not?" Stephen said.

"It's not right. It's not ethical."

"It's not a matter of ethics," Stephen said. *You dumb-headed, corn-fed innocent,* he thought. *You really believe all the stuff they told you in that Unitarian Sunday School, back home in whatever it was, Wisconsin or Minnesota or some damn place.* "It's a matter of finishing this camp," he said.

"Not dignified, either," the lieutenant said. "There must be another way."

"Well, there's one," Stephen told him.

"What?"

"Put the Raiders in a row, take every tenth man out, and shoot him. Keep doing that until they start listening to reason. That was Ski's suggestion."

"You're kidding. Aren't you?"

"Not a bit. We can't move the camp because Major Barker won't let us. We can't convince the Raiders that the camp isn't haunted. So we've got two alternatives: either we drive the ghosts away or we make the Raiders more afraid of us than they are of the ghosts."

The lieutenant chewed at his lower lip. After a month under the blazing sun of Muc Wa, he was starting to lose the pink glow he had brought from Fort Darby. Maybe next he would lose some of those Rover Boy ideals.

"All right," he said then. "What shall I do?"

"Stand when I stand, kneel when I kneel," Stephen told him.

"All right, but I still don't like it. You're a cynic, Steve, and nothing good can come out of cynicism."

"Oh, hell!" Stephen said, and went off to look for Corporal Old Man.

The chaplain's flight was laid on for Friday. Stephen declared a festival until then, to impress the Raiders with the big deal he was arranging for them. "You're crazy," Ski told him, "but go ahead. It's your baby. Sober me off when it's over." Stephen managed to keep one platoon at work, guarding the camp and building a packing-case altar near the French graves. The rest of the Raiders celebrated. They brewed grain and roots and small insects in the ten-gallon cook pot and drank the result, all night, every night. In the mornings Stephen and Toffee rounded up a platoon and marched the men through the river for a while, until they were sober enough to relieve the guards. Ski got drunk with the Raiders. Lieutenant Hamilton remained in the command post and wrestled with his conscience.

The chaplain's flight, two green dragonflies, came over the horizon at ten o'clock Friday morning. Stephen ignited a yellow smoke grenade in the camp's northwest sector, which had been cleared for a landing pad. One of the helicopters settled to earth. The other continued to circle the camp, while a photographer leaned madly from the doorway and aimed his camera at each building in turn.

The chaplain was a burly, crewcut major with deep creases in his face. He wore jump boots and a silver airborne pin.

"Good morning, sir," Stephen said, saluting him. "Did you bring—"

"Call me Father," the chaplain said.

"Yes, Father. Did you bring a cassock and so on?"

"No, no, Corporal Courcey. We don't stand on ceremony in the Chaplains' Corps, y'know."

Lieutenant Hamilton came up to them. "Welcome to Muc Wa, sir," he said, also saluting.

"Call me Father," the chaplain said.

"Sir?"

"Oh, you're not a Catholic," the chaplain said, looking at the lieutenant's nameplate. "Well, you can call me Padre."

"Very good, uh, Padre."

But the chaplain seemed determined to soften him up. "You're pretty darned thin, for a Raider," he said, dropping his thick arm upon the lieutenant's shoulder. "Got a touch of the dysentery, m'boy?"

Lieutenant Hamilton stood to attention. "No, sir," he said. "I mean, I did have the runs, but I'm much better now, thank you, sir . . . Padre."

"I've got some polymagna in my kit."

"Oh, I'm over it now, thank you."

"You never get over it," the chaplain said. "It's this darned country. I haven't dared to fart since I got here." He brayed with laughter, thumping the lieutenant's thin shoulder.

Stephen moved between them, and Lieutenant Hamilton gave him a grateful look. "Sir?" Stephen said to the chaplain.

"Father."

"Yes, sir. Father, I'm told that most of the Raiders are Catholics, too, and I think they'd be pleased if you dressed more like a priest."

"Well, well, I'll see what I can do," the chaplain said. "I think there's a stole in my kit somewhere."

The other helicopter landed then. Stephen talked to the photographer, who had been sent down by Major Barker to take pictures of the camp. It seemed that the major was building a scale model of Muc Wa.

"So that's why he wanted all those measurements," Stephen said. "What's he planning to do with the model—stick pins in it?"

"Pins?" the photographer said. "What pins?"

Stephen could find out no more, because Ski wobbled

across the field at that moment, escorted by Butterfly, and the photographer ran over to aim his camera at her handsome, glowing chest. The helicopter pilots whistled. The chaplain looked at the sky and said, "Yes, yes, *hmmm.*" Ski was too drunk to notice the flap he had caused, so Stephen took off his own fatigue shirt and gave it to Butterfly. She had to turn up the cuffs, but the shirt fitted very nicely across the chest. Low-voiced, the chaplain asked Stephen: "Is Sergeant Oleonowski a Catholic?"

"Yes, Father, I believe he is."

"Hmmm," the chaplain said.

Butterfly had designed the altar cloth. It was a funeral blanket, actually, like the one she had woven for the murdered Raider. It was made from threads of parachute silk which Butterfly had dyed gold, crimson, and purple; it told the story of three white-skinned warriors who had traveled many miles, defeated many enemies, and died at last by this river in the mountains.

"Handsome," the chaplain said. "Pagan, of course, but a very nice piece of goods."

"What's he saying?" Ski mumbled. "I'll zap him, talking like that."

"He's a priest, Ski," Stephen said.

"Priest, huh? Well, that's all right, then." Ski thrust his head toward the chaplain and gave him a drunken wink. "Still," he said to Stephen, "priest or no priest, he shouldn't talk about my girlfriend like that."

With a great rumble, the chaplain cleared his throat. "Ah, Sergeant Oleonowski?" he said, draping the stole across his bull-like shoulders. "Would you like to assist?"

Ski stared wildly at him, then at Stephen. Finding no mercy on either side, he lurched forward and took his place as the altar boy.

The altar was directly in line with the French gravesite, so that it would seem to the Raiders that the chaplain was hurling his prayers, like mortar shells, across the funeral blanket and into the gravesite beyond. Stephen stood near the altar. The Raiders were drawn up in company formation, on the gentle slope between the gravesite and the camp. Cowboy had told them to watch Stephen, who had planned to watch the chaplain's assistant. It was a bit more difficult with Ski up there. Stephen had not been to Mass since he was a freshman in college, but gradually the old ritual came back to him. He even began to feel homesick, hearing the fat Latin phrases after six years . . . *mea culpa, mea culpa.* . . . Ski knelt, ringing his little bell; Stephen knelt; the massed company of Raiders knelt.

Then there was a stir in the company ranks, and Cowboy walked up with his hands folded, ready to receive Communion. Six or seven Raiders followed him. The chaplain hesitated, then blessed Cowboy and slipped a Communion wafer between the interpreter's white rows of teeth. The bayonet swung gently from Cowboy's belt. The chaplain then served Communion wafers to the other Raiders, while the ranks behind Stephen shifted and broke, and the entire company pressed forward to join in the white man's magic. The chaplain beckoned to Stephen.

"Are these men in a state of grace?" he whispered.

"Well, Father, they're soldiers."

"That's what worries me."

"Can't you give them some kind of conditional absolution?"

"I suppose so," the chaplain said, the creases on his face growing deeper. He began to break the remaining Communion wafers into smaller pieces. "Corporal?" he said then, looking sharply at Stephen. "Aren't you planning to receive Communion?"

"Well, Father . . ."

"Hmmm?"

"I'm not in a state of grace, either."

"That's all right," the chaplain said. "I absolve you."

Stephen nodded, seeing that he had been outfoxed, and

took his place in line. *For this is My Body . . . this is My Blood . . . do this in remembrance of Me. . . .* Stephen looked into the vast blue gulf of the sky, half expecting a thunderbolt to strike him down. *The things I do for Muc Wa,* he thought.

After Mass, the Raiders brought their cook pot down to the altar. The brew was covered by a thick mat of leaves, which helped contain the odor; a long, curved reed stuck through the center of the mat.

"Remarkable," the chaplain said. He folded his stole and tucked it into his pocket, then allowed Ski to coax him into taking the first drink. The Raiders pressed around. Private Bung, the company clown, poured water from a canteen cup onto the leaves, to measure how much the chaplain was drinking. "Enough," the chaplain said, pushing the curved reed away. His eyes were watering.

"No, sir!" Cowboy said, seizing the canteen cup from Bung, to see how much water remained. "Half enough, Father, sir!"

Stephen signaled to Corporal Old Man. They stripped the funeral blanket from the altar and carried it—gently, like a flag—to the French gravesite. Stephen touched a match to the blanket, then stepped back with Old Man to watch it burn. The flames were less brilliant than the cloth. *Not a bad idea,* Stephen thought. *If life is brighter than death, it really doesn't matter that death wins out in the end.*

"No more ghosts," he said when Butterfly's tapestry had burned to ash. "Everybody work tomorrow. Okay?"

"Okay, okay," Old Man said, grinning all over his round, mahogany face, like a happy newel post.

They went back to the party, where Cowboy and the chaplain were arguing about adultery. Cowboy claimed that, since soldiers were expected to break one of the Commandments, they ought to be excused from the others, too. "This only fair, sir," he said. He translated his argument for the Raiders, who nodded vigorously at the chaplain.

"No, no," the chaplain said. "Nobody is excused from the Commandments. As an individual, that is. Thou Shalt Not Kill; Thou Shalt Not Commit Adultery. *Thou,* Cowboy. If you kill a man in the line of duty, you're not acting as a private individual. You're acting on behalf of your country. Yes, that's it." He wiped the sweat from his forehead, using his index finger as a squeegee. "But adultery is always a private act."

Butterfly, who had been standing at the edge of the argument, began to lecture the chaplain in her musical voice, smiling and rubbing her belly beneath Stephen's fatigue shirt.

"Father, sir," Cowboy translated, "she say: make-love no sin if babies come."

"What?" the chaplain said, sitting up straight.

"Sir, she say—"

"Cowboy, is that young woman pregnant?"

"She try very hard, Father, sir."

"SAR-*JANT!*" the chaplain roared, suddenly turning into a major. Ski emerged from the circle around the cook pot. "Sergeant Oleonowski, have you got this young woman in the family way?" the chaplain demanded. Ski blinked at him with his bulging, pale-blue eyes. "Well?" the chaplain said.

"Well . . ." Ski said. He scratched his temple.

Butterfly made a singsong protest.

"Everything okay," Cowboy explained. "She say: they make marriage when sergeant take her home with him to the U.S. of A."

"Sergeant Oleonowski, did you seduce this child with a promise of marriage?"

"Well, nossir," Ski said, moving on to scratch the bald spot at the back of his head. "That's not exactly the way it happened."

Butterfly spoke again, her loving, licorice-drop eyes fixed upon Ski.

"Everything okay," Cowboy said. "She say: they can make marriage now if you want."

"Well, Sergeant?" the chaplain said.

"Nossir, that ain't exactly the way I remember it."

"It wouldn't be an officially recognized marriage, of course."

"The way *I* remember it . . ."

"You'd have to go through a lot of paper work at the Embassy in Thaitan."

". . . that marriage bit more or less came up *afterward*. It don't make sense, do it, sir, that I promised to marry her *before?* Heck, she can't talk English and I can't talk Buru."

"You would, however, be married in the eyes of God," the chaplain concluded. "And surely that is what matters." He was sounding like a priest again, deep-throated and kindly.

"Huh?" Ski said.

"You would be married in the eyes of God, but not in the eyes of the U. S. Army."

Ski quit scratching his head. He studied the chaplain with half-closed eyes. "Well, well," he said at last. "If that's what Butterfly wants, I guess we'd better do it, huh?"

"Marriage is a very serious affair," the chaplain told him.

"Oh, it sure is, Father. Very serious. That's why I put it off so long."

"You'll be faced with a lot of paper work before this ceremony is officially recognized."

"I know that, Father. A lot of paper work. Yessir."

"Very well, then," the chaplain said.

The Raiders, guessing that another entertainment was in store, formed a large, happy circle around them. Cowboy stood beside the chaplain, to translate. Stephen was best man. Lieutenant Hamilton, looking somewhat dazed, gave the bride away, since Butterfly's mother was too busy moaning and banging her head against the ground.

"Old woman very happy, sir," Cowboy explained.

Angel, the kid sister, was the flower girl. Afterward she ran off with the other refugee children to organize a make-believe wedding of her own.

I wanted to marry Rebecca, Stephen thought. *But I didn't tell her, and perhaps she never knew.* He kissed the bride, who was still wearing his tiger-stripe fatigue shirt. Butterfly's tongue dutifully came out and tickled his lips. *Rebecca!* he thought. *Your skin was lighter, your breasts were smaller, and your eyes were rounder—but you kissed the same.* Then he made way for Lieutenant Hamilton.

"Hey, Corporal," one of the helicopter pilots said, tapping Stephen on the shoulder. "Is it safe to kiss the little gook?" He was a cheerful, putty-faced warrant officer, just out of flight school by the look of him.

"Safe?" Stephen said.

"Yeah. You know. Is she clean?"

Stephen thought of kicking him, but there were too many witnesses. "Sure," he said instead. "Are you?"

"Listen, Corporal, don't wise-ass *me*."

Stephen moved away and shook Ski's hand. "You'd better tell Butterfly about social kissing," he said. "She hasn't quite got the hang of it yet."

"What? You mean she's French-kissing you bastards?" Ski charged over to rescue Butterfly from Major Barker's photographer. "All *right!*" he roared. "That's enough, break it up!"

The wedding party was drifting toward the camp, where more liquor was ready. Stephen remained at the gravesite. Corporal Old Man wanted to stay, too, but Stephen slapped him on the shoulder and told him to join the party. "Okay, okay," the old Raider said doubtfully. He squinted at Stephen's carbine, to make sure it was loaded. Then he hurried bowlegged up the hill.

Stephen walked through the tall grass toward the gravesite, thinking of Rebecca, who had also kissed with her tongue.

"You get a Sunday paper and I'll make breakfast," she had said, and he went out to the bright, sea-washed morning with a heart full of love, determined to marry her. Yes. He had set out to screw her, and had ended by falling in love. But later she said: "I'm not going to see you again. You're a menace." So perhaps she did not know.

Would things have happened any differently, if she had known?

Stephen found a likely tree and sat down with his back against it, the carbine cradled in his lap, a comfortable weight. The stone cross was at his right. The river was in front of him, running black and soundless between its banks. But . . . SOMETHING WAS MOVING OVER THERE! He whipped the carbine to his shoulder. Then a tiny deer broke out of the grass and ran across the field, barking like a dog. Stephen relaxed, and began to defend himself from Rebecca's scorn.

"Look at you!" he heard her say, in her husky, excited voice. "A killer. How could I have married you?"

"Somebody might have bushwhacked me from across the river."

"You shouldn't be here," Rebecca told him.

"I'm a soldier. This is my job."

"You're a killer," Rebecca said, "and a liar and a cheat. You told the Raiders that the chaplain was here to banish the ghosts, and you told the chaplain that the Raiders wanted to hear Mass. How could I ever marry a man like you?"

"I'm here," Stephen told her. "This is my job. I have to do my job the best way I know how."

"To do one thing well . . ."

"Yes."

"Hemingway!" she said in a voice full of scorn, as she had said it that morning on Cape Hatteras, when he had first told her his philosophy. But this time he had an answer ready. *I always have an answer when it's too late,* he thought. "Fascist!" Rebecca said. "That's what the guards thought, in Hitler's concentration camps. They were doing their job the best way they knew how."

"This is different," Stephen told her. "What I did this morning hasn't hurt anybody. In fact, everybody feels safer because of it, safer and more secure."

Even me, he thought.

He was too far from camp to hear the noise of Ski's wedding party. The heat of noon was a blanket, weighing him down, shutting out all sound. The gravesite was asleep. Even the French ghosts were at peace, sleeping beneath their cross with the trefoil arms. *What do you think of that, Rebecca? The white man's magic really worked.* Stephen yawned until the bones cracked in his jaw. He shook his head, then balanced the carbine on his knees to keep himself awake. *I came out here to forget her,* he thought, *and all I did was find the perfect spot for remembering.* A cricket chirruped in the grass beside him. *Yes, I wanted to marry Rebecca. I began by chasing her tail, and I ended by loving her. That sea-washed morning on Cape Hatteras, after our Hansel-and-Gretel night, I wanted nothing more than to buy the Sunday paper while she made breakfast, to the end of our lives.*

His scalp prickled. WHAT? A man was watching him from across the river. A buck-toothed man with high cheekbones and gleaming olive skin and straight black hair CHARLIE ROMEO his head and shoulders projecting above a stone JESUS!

Stephen threw himself sideways, and rolled and scrambled until he was behind the tree, his carbine pointing across the river. Charlie had vanished. But there was the stone, and there was a dry reed trembling. The rebel was lying doggo in the grass. Slowly the fright bumps dissolved on Stephen's scalp, and he began to sweat. *Jesus!* he thought. *I saw the deer, and I never asked myself what spooked it. That's what I get for daydreaming. That's what I get for not doing my job.*

No sign of Charlie. But Stephen could still see the face—

the homely, buck-toothed face—imprinted on the back of his mind. It was a friendly face. Stephen felt sure that he could just stand up and walk toward the river, and nothing would happen. Maybe Charlie would stand up, too. They would meet at the river, two ugly men on opposite banks, and grin at each other.

But he didn't try it. Instead, he jumped up and ran toward camp, crouched over, zigzagging, just as they had taught him at Fort Darby, North Carolina.

Ten

"Why didn't you shoot?" Ski wanted to know.

"Why didn't he?" Stephen said.

Ski stared at him, popeyed and unbelieving. "Gor!" he said. "What's that got to do with it? You should of thanked your lucky star and blasted the hell out of him."

"I didn't have a good fix on his position," Stephen said, although this was not strictly true. But he couldn't very well say that he had taken a liking to the rebel.

"Ski?" Lieutenant Hamilton said, searching nervously for his mustache. "Why didn't Charlie take a shot at Steve?"

"He was a scout," Ski said. He nodded vigorously. "Yep," he said. "A scout. We're gonna get hit. Tonight. Some honeymoon!"

"Sorry about that," the helicopter pilots said, and told their crewmen to untie the rotor blades.

"God bless you, lads," the chaplain said.

The helicopters lifted off at twelve o'clock. They hovered briefly above the French gravesite while the photographer took a picture, then climbed until they were safe from small-arms fire, and vanished toward the north-northwest. Now Major Barker would be able to add a rebel scout to his model of Muc Wa.

Stephen took Corporal Old Man and a platoon of Raiders, except for five or six men who were too drunk to shoot straight, and led them across the river. The patrol was a very hairy business. Stephen made the men search every clump of brush, while the edge of the rain forest waited for them silently, like the jaws of a trap. Then they searched the forest, three squads abreast and one out front, finding nothing. Stephen brought them back to camp at five o'clock. A work crew, sweating and scared, was stringing barbed wire along the north wall. Ski ran among the laborers and cursed them, and now and then kicked a Raider with the instep of his boot. Stephen's men shouted insults at the work crew.

"How hard will Charlie hit us?" the lieutenant asked at chow, which they ate in the command post just before dark.

"Depends," Ski said, spooning cold beef-and-potatoes into his mouth. "Probably not too hard. He won't try to run us off, first crack of the bat; he just wants to see what we're made of." When he was finished with the beef-and-potatoes, Ski opened a can of peaches and gulped them down. Then he swallowed two vitamin pills and a salt tablet. Then he belched. "I was down in the delta my last tour," he said, settling back and rubbing his belly. "Place called Loc Gia—ever heard of it? No. Well, it's a bunch of nothing, just like Muc Wa. But old Charlie decided to run us off, and he hit us one night."

"What with?" Lieutenant Hamilton said, leaning forward with a pained expression, as if he might have to take a test on this material someday.

"Mortars—good old made-in-USA mortars. They plastered us from hell to breakfast, and they had a machinegun trap for the helicopters, and an ambush set on the road to Nang Tre. Wasn't *nobody* fool enough to relieve us. And them mortar shells came in, night after night. There wasn't a solid piece of ground in Loc Gia. It shook like jelly, Lieutenant." Ski rummaged through the C-rations until he found a can of fruitcake. He opened the can and shook the little cake into his palm. "Then Charlie came over," he said, breaking off sections of cake and cramming them into his mouth. "They came over in waves, just like in Korea. One little guy would run up and throw himself on the barbed wire, and another guy would run over him and lay down on the next line of wire, and pretty soon they swamped us that way. The lieutenant took a bullet in his crotch, and he was screaming like a horse. I never heard a human being make a noise like that. And him an officer, too."

Lieutenant Hamilton wiped the sweat from his mustache. "I don't think—" he said.

"We dragged him into the commo bunker," Ski went on, collecting the last crumbs of fruitcake and dropping them into his mouth. "And we stuck there for two days. Gor! Me and the commo sergeant and the lieutenant, who was dying. Bodies just heaped outside, stinking. Black flies all over. Nothing to drink. I got the runs, and there was no place to go, so I just had to dribble in my pants."

"What about your Raiders?" the lieutenant asked.

"Oh, twenty or thirty of them was dug in, here and there around the camp. The rest of 'em ran out on us, them that wasn't killed. . . . I got a Silver Star for that action," Ski concluded. "A battalion of native Marines finally punched through and hit Charlie from behind. I was the only American left alive, so they had to give the medal to me." Ski pulled a fat, soggy wallet from his hip pocket. "Look at that," he said, taking out a medal on a faded ribbon, bleached by sweat. "They gave me the Silver Star, and I spent most of them two days dribbling in my pants."

"What . . ." Toffee said, then paused to clear his throat. "What happened to the commo sergeant?" he asked.

"Oh, he went off his nut and tried to break out. We never did find his body, so maybe he made it." Ski cackled with laughter. "He ought to be halfway to Indjia by now," he said.

Toffee nodded. His mild brown eyes were looking at nothing at all, or maybe he was watching his counterpart from Loc Gia, trudging through the silent rain forest on the way to India. He seemed pleased by what he saw.

After chow Toffee sacked out in the commo bunker and Ski went to the hooch he had built for Butterfly, between the longhouses and the refugee huts. Stephen and Lieutenant Hamilton walked the perimeter. They were taking the watch from six to eight, and again from ten to midnight, two hours on and two hours off for the rest of the night.

"Ski doesn't like me," the lieutenant said, midway in their rounds.

"Sure he does," Stephen said.

"No. He's always putting me on, the way he did tonight."

"He was scared, that's all," Stephen said. "He was just getting the fright out of his system."

The lieutenant was silent for a while. "Steve?" he said then. "Are you scared?"

"Sure," Stephen said, but he wasn't. He was breathless and eager, just as he had been on his first date with Rebecca, but he wasn't scared. Not yet.

"I'm not afraid of dying," the lieutenant said after another silence. "I'm afraid I won't measure up."

"That's the way I feel, too."

"But you've already been in a fire fight, that night you ambushed the rebel patrol."

"Yes."

"How . . . how did you feel?"

"I was too busy to think," Stephen said.

The lieutenant laughed. "Well, that's a comfort, anyhow," he said.

From eight to ten, they tried to sleep on the floor of the command post, between the desk and the filing cabinets. But the lieutenant was restless. He kept thrashing around and lighting cigarettes; finally he stood up and began to pace the floor. When he tired of this, he said: "Steve?"

"What?"

"You awake?"

"Yes."

"Remember," the lieutenant said, tapping something in the darkness, "if the camp is overrun, one of us has to pull the pins on these grenades before we exfiltrate."

"Exfiltrate," Stephen said, realizing that the lieutenant was playing with one of the thermite grenades which were taped to the filing cabinets. "That's quite a word."

"It means—"

"I know what it means. It's a West Point word for bug-out."

"Well, I don't know where it came from."

"From West Point," Stephen said. "Those guys take their degrees in engineering, don't they? Only an engineer could have thought up a word like that."

The lieutenant wasn't listening. "Destroy the files," he said, "but take the radio with us. . . . Otherwise, you know, they'd deduct the price of it from my pay."

"An engineer is a man who knows when to quit," Stephen said. "That's why he succeeds so often."

He went off into a cottony, confused dream, in which he was carrying the big shortwave radio through the rain forest, on his way to India. Then it was time to go out on the perimeter again. Fresh from his nap on the command-post floor, Stephen was bewildered by small noises—*buzz, click, pop*—which began inside his head and then moved outside, to the river and the rain forest. He could not see the source of any of these sounds. The night was black, land and sky the same, except for the soft white flakes of stars that were pasted to the sky, almost close enough to touch. Stephen made his way along the perimeter by his sense of smell. Blindfolded, he would know a Raider anywhere in the world —the rotten-fish sauce which had flavored their dinner, the stale fat which slicked their hair, and the gun grease on their weapons.

Toward the end of his second watch, the night noises suddenly stopped, as if each toad and cricket had caught its breath in fright. *Here comes Charlie*, Stephen thought, and held his own breath.

The night filled up with a noise like a flight of partridges. Stephen dropped to his knees. CRUMP . . . THUNK! The ground retched beneath him, and shells flashed haphazardly around the camp, and in their wild light he saw Ski running toward him. Ski's mouth was open and yelling: "Put up (CRUMP!) put up flares, you dumb (THUNK!) bastards!" Somebody must have heard him. Star-shells went up and burst across the river, green-white and flickering. The Raiders on the east wall began to fire at the figures that were suddenly revealed—black, leaping shadows, like the warriors of legend—while the star-shells burned down from the sky. Fifty men, a hundred men. They had not yet reached the river. Tracer bullets sailed among them, struck trees and stones, and sailed away in graceful ricochets. *Is he out there,* Stephen thought, *that homely scout with the stringy hair?* The carbine bucked against his shoulder; the tracers flew in a flat arc across the river, and burned into a clump of brush where three of those leaping shadows had taken refuge. *Was Charlie one of them?*

"Hoo boy!" Ski roared, throwing himself down beside Stephen. "I bet old Charlie thinks he's got a dragon by the tail. I bet he's never seen so many tracer bullets in his life." The Raiders were now dropping explosive shells across the river. "I sure hope they knock out Charlie's mortar," Ski said.

They didn't. As soon as the flares had died, fresh mortar shells whirred into camp and crumped and flashed among the longhouses where the Raiders slept. And when more star-shells went up, they showed nothing. Charlie had gone to earth. Crouched over, Stephen and Ski ran along the perimeter until they found the lieutenant. Toffee and Cowboy were with him.

"We gotta take out that mortar," Ski said.

"Yes, but how?" the lieutenant said.

"Somebody's gotta go over there and grenade 'em. . . . What the hell's *that?*"

A powerful voice was calling to them from across the river. "Sir," Cowboy said, "him say: all we want is the white devils. Him say: give us the white devils and nobody hurt you."

"Well, shit-a-goddamn," Ski said. "Psychological warfare."

"Tell the men to shoot at the voice," Stephen said. "Tell them I've got a carton of cigarettes for the man who hits him." Cowboy gave the order. The Raiders were delighted: they fired, paused to listen and laugh, then fired again. Soon the voice stopped calling to them. "Sir, I'll take care of that mortar," Stephen said, his heart thumping in protest.

"No, I want you here," Lieutenant Hamilton said. "We'd better send . . . Toffee."

"Yes, sir," Toffee said, taking the magazine out of his carbine and pressing fresh cartridges into it.

"We can't afford to lose our radioman," Stephen said.

"Can't afford to lose nobody," Ski said.

"Yes, you'd better go," Lieutenant Hamilton told Toffee. "Take two squads, go out the west gate, and circle the camp to the south. Cross the river about two hundred meters downstream. . . . Does that sound right?"

"Right as rain," Ski said.

"Pick your men from Corporal Old Man's platoon," Stephen said to Toffee. "Take him, too. He's the best there is."

"All right," Toffee said, and moved away into the darkness.

What made him do it? Stephen thought. *Why didn't he just tell us to go to hell?*

"Gee, that wasn't too bad," Lieutenant Hamilton said. "I never thought I'd be able to send a man out like that."

"It gets easier with practice, Lieutenant," Ski told him.

They put up no more star-shells, for fear of betraying Toffee's counterattack. Instead they poured a blind, steady fire across the river, guiding on the firefly flashes from Charlie's weapons and the tracer bullets from their own. The Raiders seemed happy enough. They called to each other whenever a particularly bright ricochet went up, and bummed cigarettes from Stephen as he passed by. They knew they were the superior force, because of the tracers: Charlie could not possibly cross the river against that searing torrent of fire.

I wish I could believe it, too, Stephen thought.

Charlie's bullets were invisible. Stephen sometimes heard one singing past, and the skin of his face was tight as a drumhead as he walked the perimeter, slapping shoulders and handing out cigarettes. He had quit smoking at Fort Dix, during basic training; but he had gotten into the habit of carrying them again, to help him communicate with the Raiders.

They allowed Toffee fifteen minutes to move into position, then they ceased firing. So did Charlie. The silence was absolute, loaded with menace. Then a fire fight broke out across the river. The Raiders were uneasy, and every minute or so a few of them began shooting again, until Stephen or Ski ran over to stop them.

"I'm going across," Stephen said at last, meeting Ski at the east gate. "Toffee doesn't seem to be making much progress over there."

"It's your ass," Ski agreed. "Just make sure you cut your buttons off."

"Buttons?"

"Sure," Ski said, making a choking sound in the darkness. "Pretty thick, them GI buttons. I've known some guys who shaved the hair off their chests, so's they could get closer to the ground." Stephen aimed a punch at him, but Ski ducked out of the way. "Me," he said, "I don't hold with shaving my chest, but *buttons!* A guy's asking for trouble, going out there with all his buttons on."

Stephen picked a squad off the wall and led them through the gate. They went down to the riverbank. Steel scraped against stone as Ski closed the gate behind them. Stephen's hands began to sweat against the carbine. *What am I doing here?* he thought. At the river's edge he stopped, and the Raiders crowded against him, smelling of rotten fish and rancid fat. They could not understand him if he spoke. The night was too dark for arm signals. So he opened his mouth and yelled "YAR!" and ran into the river. Piss-warm water splashed up to his waist. "YAR YAR YAR!" The Raiders were right behind him, barking like dogs after a bitch, more terrified of being left alone in the dark than of charging blind into Charlie's lines.

The river had never seemed so wide. It was a nightmare river, pulling at his legs, sucking the strength from them. *Why doesn't Charlie shoot? Why don't I fall down dead?* "YAR YAR YAR!" *What in the name of all that's beautiful —moonlight and sunrise and Rebecca's breasts—what in the world am I doing here?*

He reached the far bank and pressed against it, blessedly safe from Charlie's bullets. But this was no good. He scrambled over the bank and ran forward, eyes popping into the darkness, water slurping in his boots. Something jumped to life in front of him. Stephen swung the butt of his carbine against it—dull, sodden contact—then brought the barrel down and fired, and a figure was spitted on the orange muzzle blast. He ran on. *I have killed a man,* he thought. Behind him the Raiders were running and shooting, too damned much shooting for comfort, but Stephen had a triumphant sense that they were sweeping men in front of them. *He's running. He really is. Charlie is running.*

"Toffee!" he yelled. "Where the hell are you?"

"Okay, okay!"—from the front and to the right. "This Old Man, okay!" Then they were linked with Toffee's patrol, and Stephen no longer felt quite so lonely. "Mortar, okay," Corporal Old Man said. Pressing close to Stephen, he made the motion of throwing a grenade. "Boo-*boom!*" he said. "Mortar, okay."

"Where's Sergeant Toffee?" Stephen asked.

"Oh, sir—him bad, bad." Old Man called into the darkness, and two Raiders came up, supporting a man between them. Stephen reached out and felt the bristle of a GI haircut. Then the head flopped to one side, and Stephen found a wet, sticky mass of pulp where Toffee's left ear should have been.

"All right," he said, wiping his hand on his trouser leg. His dinner was threatening to leap into his throat. "Let's get him back to camp."

Eleven

The mosquito patrol had dropped into Captain Olivetti's lap again, as it did whenever the Y Team ran short of lieutenants. He rewarded himself by sleeping through breakfast next morning. He meant to sleep till noon, but there was a hell of a commotion in the compound, with starter motors whining and Major Barker shouting orders, so at ten-thirty Captain Olivetti cursed the world and jumped out of bed. He pulled on last night's fatigue trousers, stuck his feet into a pair of shower clogs, grabbed his toilet kit and a towel, and walked over to the latrine.

The clerk-typist was blocking the door.

"Ackley," the captain said, "what the hell are you doing in the officers' latrine?"

"Guarding it," Ackley said, scratching his jaw.

Captain Olivetti halted on the bottom step. Ackley might bite his foot if he climbed any higher. "Who from?" he said.

"Nobody. I'm guarding it *for* somebody."

"Yeah?"

"I'm guarding it for Miss Shaw," Ackley said, like a man throwing the crust of his sandwich to the pigeons.

"A woman?"

"Yep."

"A round-eye?"

"Yep."

Captain Olivetti cupped a hand behind his ear. "Well, I'll be damned," he said, hearing a shower head spitting water and a sweet voice singing *All My Trials, Lord, Soon Be O-o-ver.*

"She's the correspondent," Ackley said, throwing him another crust. "There's a general around here someplace, too."

"Screw the general. Let's have a look at this lady correspondent."

"Can't. She's got a poncho hung up for a shower curtain."

"You already tried, huh?"

Ackley gave him a dirty grin, peeling his lips back so far that his gums were showing. "Oh, Cap'n!" he said then. "I got a signal from Muc Wa this morning."

"What d'they want?"

"I dunno. It's in the Buru dialect or something."

"Well, get somebody to translate it."

"Yessir."

The lady correspondent was now singing *Blowing in the Wind.* "So that's Shaw, R.," Captain Olivetti said. "What's the R. stand for?"

"Rebecca," Ackley said.

The correspondent left off singing. "Yes?" she called, and the poncho rattled against the shower stall. Captain Olivetti lunged up the steps. Ackley was too busy to argue; he was hanging to the doorframe and staring into the latrine. But Miss Shaw was only showing her head. Her hair was pulled back and tied with a ribbon, giving a nice naked look to her face, which was young, saucy, and sparkling with drops of water. *Yes!* Captain Olivetti thought. *Yes, by God!* "Did you want me?" Miss Shaw asked.

"Well, now that you mention it . . ." Captain Olivetti said, turning on the old charm.

"I was just telling the cap'n he can't come in," Ackley said.

"That's right, Cap'n," Miss Shaw said, raising her dark eyebrows at him. "You can't come in." Then she vanished behind the poncho, and the shower head began to spit water again.

"Well, well," Captain Olivetti said. "So that's Shaw, R. D'you figure she's spreading for the general?"

"Nah. He didn't hardly talk to her, all the way from the airstrip."

"She wearing an engagement ring?"

"Nah. What'd she be doing over here, if she's got a boyfriend?"

"Damned if I know," Captain Olivetti said. "But she must be laying for somebody."

"She ain't the type."

"They're all the type," Captain Olivetti said, and hurried over to shower and shave in the enlisted men's latrine. Then he went back to his hooch and changed into a freshly laundered set of jungle fatigues.

Major Barker did not dislike generals, exactly, but he had learned to avoid them whenever he could. In his experience a general was a man who demanded the impossible, refused to hear why it was impossible, then took all the credit when the job was done. Muc Wa was a perfect example. If the garrison at Muc Wa turned out well, it would not be Major Barker who received the commendations, but some damned general down in Thaitan. In addition to which, generals were offensively tall.

But not Brigadier General Hardnetz. He was scarcely two inches taller than the major, and if Hardnetz at five-foot-five could be a general, surely Barker at five-foot-three could still hope for his colonelcy.

"It's a pleasure to have you here, sir," the major said, happier than he had been since the Korean War. "What can we do for you?"

"You can tell me about the Raiders," General Hardnetz said.

"A pleasure, a real pleasure," the major said, and uncovered his maps and his model of the garrison at Muc Wa. The model was a little beauty. Every tree was in place, every hooch, everything except that damned French grave, which would have spoiled the garrison's tough, clean lines. Major Barker returned to his desk with a warm glow of pride. He only wished that Captain Olivetti had been here to remove the covers. The general had five officers to run errands for him—a major, a captain, and three grim first lieutenants. They had raised the temperature in the office to something like ninety-eight degrees. Sweating from his exercise, Major Barker sat down and cleared his throat. "The U. S. Army Raiders are counter-guerrilla specialists," he said. "The basic formation is a four-man Z Team which organizes, equips, and commands a Raider company from the indigenous population in the guerrilla's heartland."

"His what?" the general said.

"His own back yard," the major said. "I have eleven Z Teams under my command. There are four Y Teams like mine in the country, all under the command of the X Team in Thaitan."

"Alphabet soup," the general said. "Do all your men wear those Frenchified fatigues?"

"Sir?"

"Two or three months ago I met a sergeant at Thaitan airport, a man with a funny foreign name. What was his name?"

"Oleonowski, sir," one of his aides said.

"Yes. Oleo . . . that was the name. He was wearing a most irregular set of fatigues with camouflage stripes, and the pockets set every which way."

"Uh, yessir," Major Barker said. "Jungle fatigues."

"Strictly unauthorized in this command."

"Yessir. We've allowed the men a bit of freedom in dress, you know, for the sake of *esprit*."

"That's a French word," General Hardnetz said.

"Why, yessir, so it is."

"You're aware, Major, what happened to the French in this country?"

"Yessir."

"They got the shit kicked out of them."

"They certainly did, sir."

"That won't happen to the U. S. Army, by God."

"No, sir!"

"So let's hear no more about *esprit* and Frenchified uniforms. They don't belong in the U. S. Army. This is the greatest army in the world because every soldier is the same as every other soldier, except for the officers, of course."

"Of course."

"Marines," the general said. "Raiders. Rangers. Air Cavalry. Abolish them all, if I had my way. What's the Army coming to, anyway?"

Major Barker was saved by a knock on the door. "Come in!" he shouted. The door opened and Ackley's polka-dot face appeared in it.

"Here's Miss Shaw and Cap'n Olivetti," he said.

Major Barker let his scar burn red. "Send them in," he said, adding silently: *Say sir, you idiot, or I'll ship you to Boo Jum tomorrow. Or Mung Tau. Or . . .*

"Yessir," the clerk-typist said.

"Thank you, Ackley," the major said.

"Oh, and here's a signal from Muc Wa. I had to get one of the gooks to translate it, because it was in the Buru dialect or something . . . sir."

"Muc Wa?" the general said, lifting his great, bald head. "Is that one of your ABZ outfits?" He held out a meaty hand. One of the lieutenants took the radiogram from Ackley and gave it to the general. "You don't mind, Barker?"

"Of course not, sir . . . Ah, Miss Shaw!" Major Barker said, rising as the girl came in. Captain Olivetti was close behind her, his face lit up like a lantern—and of course the damned fool was wearing jungle fatigues. "It's a pleasure to have you with us, a real pleasure," the major said. He tried to turn off the scar, for Miss Shaw's benefit. She was the first American woman he had seen for six months, and a correspondent besides, who might make him famous. "Welcome to Penang," he said.

"Thank you, Colonel," the girl said.

"Major."

"Oh, I'm sorry," she said, taking a chair which one of the lieutenants pushed forward. The temperature had risen another two or three degrees. Miss Shaw was a cute little thing, all right, and so young that Major Barker felt guilty about admiring her figure, which was . . . *All right,* he told himself. *She could be your daughter.* Miss Shaw smiled at him. "I thought those funny leaves on your collar meant you were a colonel," she said.

"Gold leaves for a major," he said, hoping she would be able to spell his name correctly. "Silver leaves for a lieutenant colonel."

"Oh, I see. The Army values silver more highly than gold."

"Well, yes, I suppose you could look at it that way."

"We picked that up from the French," General Hardnetz told her. "Barker, are your signals always this irregular?"

"Irregular, sir?"

General Hardnetz held the radiogram in front of him and began to read:

"Hello from Muc Wa.

"Communist fellow come along here last night. Raider fellow scare him away, send three Communist fellow belong ancestors.

"Sergeant Toffee belong ancestors, too.

"One Raider fellow run away.

"Six Raider fellow hurt.

"One house fall down.

"Please sir you give Sergeant Toffee piece of paper for to tell ancestors him very brave.

"Good-by from Muc Wa."

There was a silence when the general had finished. "Well, sir," Major Barker said, putting his hand up to hide his scar.

"Ackley said it came over in Buru. Maybe it lost something in translation."

"Belong ancestors," General Hardnetz said. "That terminology is not authorized in this command."

"Excuse me, sir," Captain Olivetti said, squaring his shoulders and advancing to the major's desk. He dodged the general and his aides like a quarterback running the field. "In the circumstances, I'd say that Sergeant Toffington was killed while repelling a Communist probe, and his native assistant sent this message."

"What?" Major Barker said. "Toffee's dead?"

"Afraid so, sir."

"I knew we should have sent Ackley to Muc Wa."

"Yessir. Suggest we enter this message in the log as follows: 'Sergeant Toffington KIA, one native Raider MIA, six native Raiders WIA; recommend Sergeant Toffington be decorated for gallantry above and beyond the call of duty.'"

"Yes, that sounds first-class," Major Barker said.

"I like the other version better," Miss Shaw said, and they all turned to look at her.

"Young lady!" the general said. "Casualty figures are classified, so please don't use that information in your story." Miss Shaw looked at him with clear, innocent eyes, saying nothing. General Hardnetz shifted his weight. "*Brmm*," he said. "We'll be discussing other classified information, such as the strength and disposition of the major's what-do-you-call-them teams. Perhaps Captain Olivetti would take you on a tour of the camp."

"Certainly, sir!" the captain said, his nostrils flaring like a stallion's.

"The captain will want to change his uniform, in any event," the general added.

Captain Olivetti looked at Major Barker. "That's right, Al," the major told him. "Those jungle fatigues are no longer authorized in this command."

"They never were authorized," the general said.

"That's what I meant," Major Barker said. "You might have Ackley put an SOP on the bulletin board."

Captain Olivetti saluted, held the door for Miss Shaw, and followed her out to the orderly room. When they were gone, the general said: "Barker, I think I'd better warn you about that young woman."

"How's that, sir?"

"She's a left-winger," the general said.

"No!"

"Absolutely. Works for a magazine called the *Liberal.*"

"Yessir. I tried to get hold of a copy, but the Special Services library doesn't seem to have it."

"I should hope not," the general said. "It's one of those nasty little left-wing magazines that look like they were printed on toilet paper. . . . You're not Jewish, are you, Barker?"

"Oh, no, sir."

"Not that I'd give a damn. Some of my best friends are Jews."

"Same here, sir."

"But still, it all fits a pattern, doesn't it?"

"I'm not sure I follow, sir."

"Barker, who were the only Americans ever executed for treason in peacetime?"

"Let's see, now—"

"The Rosenblatts," General Hardnetz said triumphantly. "Or the Rosenthalls or some damned name like that. Jewish couple. Sold the hydrogen bomb to the Commies. It all hangs together, doesn't it?"

"Well, yessir," Major Barker said. "I suppose it does, in a way."

Rebecca hated to admit it, even to herself, but she was enjoying the whole thing tremendously. *Here I am!* she thought, while she walked across the dusty compound with Captain Olivetti. *Here I am! Twelve thousand miles from home, with a letter of introduction from Petrel McMurphy himself, and a great oaf of a captain to show me around. And sooner or later . . .*

"Well, Miss Shaw!" the captain said, as if he were shouting orders across a parade field. "How long are you planning to be in the area?"

Sooner or later, she thought, *I'm going to find Stephen Courcey and give him the surprise of his life.* "Two or three weeks," she said. "Then I'll write an article about what you do and what the people think of you."

"What people?"

"The people who live here."

"Oh, the gooks," he said. "You don't need two or three weeks for that. I'll tell you in a minute: what we do is try to make 'em fight, and what they think of it is—they don't want to."

"Do you blame them?" Rebecca said, as frostily as she could.

Captain Olivetti lifted his great shoulders. "Well, I don't much care," he said. "All I want from this stinking country is the CIB."

"The what?"

"The Combat Infantryman's Badge. The major was wearing one—silver rifle, blue background, silver wreath around it." He took her arm with a sudden, sure grip, just above the elbow. "It means you've been under enemy fire, and it's a big help when you're up for promotion. . . . Here's my jeep," he said. "Hop in." He released her arm before she thought to pull away, and she was left with nothing to do but climb obediently into the passenger's seat. Captain Olivetti walked around to the other side, whistling to himself. "Nossir!" he said, jumping into the driver's seat, with astonishing grace for a man so large. "You don't count for much in this man's Army unless you've got the CIB."

He put the jeep in gear and drove it across the compound, spraying gravel on the poor gate guard. The gate guard—a gentle, olive-skinned youngster—lifted the barrier with one hand and saluted madly with the other. Rebecca clung to the windshield. *Oaf!* she thought, while they bucketed down the twisty dirt road to the town.

"So you turn boys into killers!" she shouted.

"I didn't say that." Captain Olivetti grinned at her—a blond beast, his skin glowing like well-kept saddle leather. "I said we teach 'em how to fight, which is a hell of a lot harder. These pretty boys are born killers. Why, we had one guy here, an interpreter, who killed twenty-one prisoners before we shipped him out. Gooks *like* to kill. All we're doing is trying to make 'em kill the right people, and it's uphill work."

"It's despicable," Rebecca said.

"That's easy for you to say," Captain Olivetti told her. "You've got looks and brains and money, but all I've got is a strong back. What d'you want me to do? Coach football in some two-bit high school?" He laughed uproariously, steering the jeep with the flat of his hand. "No, thanks!" he shouted. "Life's a great big steamroller, Rebecca. I'd rather be riding it than standing in front of it."

Halfway down the hill they passed another jeep. It was crammed with American soldiers, and Rebecca's heart did a slow, sweet somersault. But none of the soldiers was wearing the face she hoped to see.

"Do you happen to know a corporal named Stephen Courcey?" she asked, her heart thumping madly.

"A corporal?"

"Yes. Corporal Courcey."

"Boyfriend of yours?"

"Well . . ."

"I dunno," Captain Olivetti said. "We've got more corporals in the Raiders than we know what to do with."

"What about Ray Hamilton?" she said. "Lieutenant Hamilton?"

"Another boyfriend?"

"No, just a friend. I met him at College Heights, at a fraternity party. It was a chapter of the same fraternity he belonged to in college, you know."

"Yeah, I know. Bunch of snobs." Captain Olivetti twisted his great stallion's face this way and that. "Sure," he said. "Ray Hamilton. He's that lah-de-dah lieutenant we sent down to Muc Wa."

"Then Stephen must be at Muc Wa, too," she said, holding the name like a jewel in her mind. It sounded wild and beautiful. "They're friends."

"What?"

"I said: Ray Hamilton and Stephen Courcey are friends."

Captain Olivetti laughed. "An officer and an enlisted man can't be friends," he said. "No more than a horse and a donkey. You know what happens when a horse gets friendly with a donkey?"

"No," Rebecca said.

"A mule!" Captain Olivetti shouted, slapping his thigh. "*That's* what happens."

Rebecca stared through the bug-splashed windshield, hating him. Then it came to her: "Muc Wa!" she cried. "Wasn't that where the radioman . . ."

"Got himself killed," Captain Olivetti said. "That was Muc Wa, all right."

"Oh, dear," Rebecca said. "I never thought of that—that he might be killed."

Twelve

"Steve?" the lieutenant said, coming out of the command post and collapsing in the shade of a tree, a healthy distance from Stephen. "What shall we do with . . . Toffee?"

"Bury him," Stephen said. While the sweat dripped from his forehead, he cupped a grenade in his left hand and gently, gently worked the point of his bayonet between the detonator and the fuse.

"No," Lieutenant Hamilton said. "It's so . . . heartless. What if the camp should be overrun? I'd hate to leave him here."

"If Muc Wa is overrun . . ." Stephen shifted the bayonet to his left hand. He removed the detonator, then the fuse. Then he blew the sweat from his face. "There!" he said, looking at the lieutenant. Ray seemed to have lost ten pounds overnight. His mustache was blooming, though, and Stephen fancied that the lost pounds had gone to feed the growth on the lieutenant's upper lip. He said: "If we're overrun, a lot of us will be staying here besides Toffee. It's the Raider tradition, remember? Bury a man where he falls."

"I never understood why."

"Logistics," Stephen said. "We're puckerbrush soldiers. It's hard enough to supply a live Raider, without worrying about the dead ones."

"Well, that's not good enough for me. I want Toffee flown back to the States."

Stephen shortened the fuse so that it would burn exactly one second after the pin was pulled. "All right," he said, sweating again, replacing the detonator and the fuse and the spring-loaded safety handle. "I just hope Cowboy . . . can understand the idea . . . of Arlington National Cemetery."

"Why does the message have to be in dialect?"

"Toffee's assistant can't read," Stephen said, tossing the grenade to Private Tam, who was hunkering nearby. Tam trotted off toward the east gate, holding the grenade in his two cupped hands, like a wounded bird. "He knows Morse code, but he can't read. So Cowboy has to dictate to him."

"I keep thinking," the lieutenant said. "Toffee is dead because of me. If I had sent you out to get that mortar, you'd be dead, not Toffee."

"Maybe not," Stephen said, taking another grenade from the crate at his feet.

"I don't want that kind of power."

"Somebody has to do it. That's what you told me at the airport, remember?—that's what officers are for."

"Then I don't want to be an officer. Not in this war."

Tam returned, grinning and waving his fists. Stephen laughed. That would be the word from Ski, demanding more grenades, which he was planting in the no man's land between the inner and outer rows of barbed wire. Having delivered the message, Tam sat down. He was afraid of the finished grenades, but he hunkered trustfully beside Stephen while the hairy work was going on.

"Steve?" the lieutenant said then. "Are you proud of what you're doing?"

"Damned right," Stephen said. "When a demolitions man . . . doesn't take pride in his work . . . he blows himself to hell."

"Oh, I don't mean the grenades. I mean . . . the whole business." He waved his hand at Muc Wa, which was still smoking from last night's attack. "Killing rebels. Leading your own men out, seeing them get shot and killed."

"There's a war on," Stephen said. "I didn't start it."

"Who did?"

"Damned if I know." He did his trick again, shifting the bayonet to his left hand while the tip separated the detonator and the fuse. "I'm a soldier, Ray. My job is to fight."

"Don't you ever worry about the morality of it?"

Stephen removed the fuse and shortened it. "I took an oath, back there at the Boston Army Base," he said. He replaced the fuse, covered it with the point of his bayonet, followed that with the detonator. . . . "I took an oath to serve for two years," he said. "I'll serve the best way I know how, for those two years . . . and the six months extra."

Lieutenant Hamilton winced. "Yes," he said. "I'm sorry about that, Steve. It's my fault you're here."

Stephen tossed the finished grenade to Tam. Then he stood up to stretch. "Don't worry about it," he said. "I was past the age of consent."

"God! You never bend, do you? You're made of iron."

Below them, on the parade field, Corporal Old Man was drilling an unhappy refugee boy—the first they had found who was old enough to join the Raiders. He was trying to make a left-face. Old Man patiently hunkered down and showed him how to move his feet, but when the big moment came, the boy tripped himself. *Before too long,* Stephen thought, *I'll be taking him out on a patrol. I hope he's handier with a carbine than he is with his feet.*

"I just try to do my job," he said, feeling as tired as the lieutenant looked.

Tam came trotting back from the perimeter, and Stephen sat down again, to make another booby trap for the defense of Muc Wa.

To do one thing well, he told himself, *that makes all the difference . . . doesn't it?*

Major Barker took his guests on a tour of the New Life Pig Farm that afternoon. This project, which had been built by his predecessor, was supposed to convince the Buru tribesmen that they'd be better off supporting Premier What's-his-name, down in Thaitan, instead of slipping rice to Charlie Romeo. Whether the farm did this or not, the major wasn't sure, but he found it very useful for impressing VIPs. "This is how we win the hearts and minds of the people," he told them. "This is the Other War in Southeast Asia." But the New Life Pig Farm had let him down that afternoon. General Hardnetz asked questions like a man rapping on the wall, in the hope of finding a skeleton; then he hardly listened to the answers. And Miss Shaw kept wandering off to question the New Lifers on her own—in French, so there was no telling what sort of misinformation she was picking up.

Finally, when they returned to the Raider compound, Ackley was waiting with another signal from Muc Wa.

"I told you about that," said Major Barker, who had promised to ship the clerk-typist to Boo Jum, if he produced any more of those garbled messages in front of General Hardnetz. But Ackley would not take the hint. He stood there, smirking, until Major Barker accepted the radiogram, which read:

HELLO FROM MUC WA.

PLEASE SIR YOU SEND ANGEL FOR TO CARRY SERGEANT TOFFEE TO HIS ANCESTORS.

GOOD-BY FROM MUC WA.

The general's meaty palm was extended, so Major Barker gave him the radiogram. The general read it and passed it to one of his aides. Then he cleared his throat. "Angel?" he said.

"It's code, sir," Major Barker said, his scar throbbing. "Ackley! Why didn't you decode this message?"

"Sir, there ain't no Angel in the codebook," Ackley said. "Sir." He was starting to look a bit worried.

Captain Olivetti strode to the major's side, where he should have been all the time, instead of lurking in the background with Miss Shaw. "What's the problem, sir?" he said.

"They want an Angel at Muc Wa," Major Barker told him. "What in the hell's an Angel?"

Captain Olivetti looked up at the sky, then at the ground. Then he looked proudly at Miss Shaw. "A helicopter, sir," he said.

"Right!" Major Barker said. "They want a helicopter. . . . Ackley?"

"Yessir?"

"Request denied. Tell them to bury Sergeant Toffington at Muc Wa, according to the SOPs."

"*Brmm,*" General Hardnetz said.

"Sir?"

"Bury your men in the field, do you?"

"Yes, sir. It's the Raider tradition."

"Why's that?"

"Well . . ."

"Psychology, sir," Captain Olivetti said. "It's supposed to make the ground more valuable. The men will fight harder, knowing their buddies are buried there."

General Hardnetz shook his head, and the sunlight gleamed from his skull, making it look like a large pink diamond. "Expensive," he said. "We did a nice bit of Effectiveness Analysis Research on that. . . . How did it go again?" he asked his aides.

"Sir!" said one of them, Lieutenant Schlitz by name. He stepped forward. "Sixty-seven per cent of field interments result in subsequent disinterment," he said. "Since disinterment must be accomplished by a certified graves registration team, the cost to the government of this method of interment is in excess of one thousand dollars on the average."

"Exactly," the general said. "We ran it through the computer. D'you know how much your field burials could cost Uncle Sam before this thing is over?"

"I—"

"Assuming U.S. combat troops are committed during fiscal 1965," Lieutenant Schlitz said in his schoolteacher's voice, "and assuming escalation does not pass the nuclear threshold . . ."

"And we don't get sold down the river by the pinkos at home," the general said, scowling at Miss Shaw.

". . . fifty thousand casualties will be required to stabilize Southeast Asia," Lieutenant Schlitz said. "Of that number, ten thousand will be line-of-duty killed, qualifying them for interment at government expense. Cost of field interment: in excess of ten million dollars. Cost of interment in a U.S. military cemetery, Class B: four million, seven hundred twenty thousand, five hundred thirty-five dollars, and fifty-five cents . . . sir," the lieutenant concluded, and dropped back to his place in line.

"You see, Barker?" the general said.

"Yessir," Major Barker said, studying Lieutenant Schlitz with a sorrowful heart. The lieutenant was young. He was educated. He was six-foot-two. Soon the Army would be commanded by men like Lieutenant Schlitz, who knew all about computers, and who regarded World War Two as something for the history books. "Yessir," he said again. "I'll write an SOP about it."

During the lieutenant's lecture, the other aides had been passing the radiogram from hand to hand, snickering as they read it. Now it reached Miss Shaw at the end of the line.

"Muc Wa!" the girl cried, so excited that she jumped up and down, setting her rich little bubs to dancing. "That's Lieutenant Hamilton's garrison, isn't it?" Major Barker nodded, trying not to look at the dancing bubs. "Oh, I want to visit Muc Wa," Miss Shaw said.

"Nonsense, young lady," Major Barker said. He dragged his eyes away and forced them to look at Captain Olivetti, who was scowling as if he had just received more bad news about his CIB. "It's much too dangerous."

"Dangerous?" the general said.

"Absolutely, sir," the major said. "Muc Wa has come under heavy attack these past few weeks."

"By God, Muc Wa might be just the place for . . . for another little project I'm working on," General Hardnetz said. "Why don't you line up a trip for us, Barker? You'll have to send a helicopter down there, anyway, to evacuate the radioman."

"Oh, please!" Miss Shaw said, still dancing on her toes. She gave Captain Olivetti a triumphant, female look. "They sound like such wonderful people at Muc Wa."

Something going on there, Major Barker thought. He looked at the general, whose skull was gleaming like a cannonball eager to be fired. *Something going on there, too.* Then he turned to the clerk-typist. "Ackley," he said, "I want to see you in my office."

Lieutenant Hamilton was very pleased with the major's decision. "You see," he said to Stephen when the message came in, "logistics isn't everything. This proves it."

"All it proves is that Major Barker didn't graduate from West Point."

"He has a heart. That's the important thing."

"Well, it bothers the hell out of me," Stephen said. "I can't understand why the major is willing to provide a helicopter, just to take out Toffee's body, when it would be so much more practical to bury him here."

"Practical!" Lieutenant Hamilton said, so forcefully that he began to cough. He coughed until the tears ran down his cheeks and glistened in his mustache. Finally he had to stagger back to the command post, still coughing miserably.

"Goddammit," Stephen said to himself, "I *like* the idea of burying a man on the spot, at the place he died to defend."

Which was no reason at all, of course, so he filled out another radiogram next morning, telling Major Barker to hurry up. He sent the same message the following day, and the day after that. Cowboy translated the message into Buru, and the native radioman sent it off, and every afternoon the same answer came back:

> NO ANGEL HERE TODAY. YOU WAIT FOR TOMORROW.

But Toffee would not wait. By Friday, Stephen could smell him even at the latrine—a pale green odor hanging in the air. The Raiders didn't like it. They gave Stephen accusing looks from the neighboring crappers, and forgot to scatter lime into the pits as he had taught them. Later, at the morning formation, they were surly and slow when he told them where they would be working that day. Stephen had to shoulder their unhappiness by himself. Ski was already working on the perimeter, Lieutenant Hamilton was feeling under the weather, and Toffee of course was dead, making a nuisance of himself as he had never done in life.

After the formation Stephen caught up with Ski near the north gate, where he was pounding bamboo stakes into the ground. "I think we'd better have a funeral this afternoon," Stephen said.

Ski looked up. "Whatever you say," he said.

"Whatever I say, hell! I'm not the team sergeant."

"Sure you are," Ski said, spitting on his callused palms. "You're the team sergeant *and* the team commander. You're the goddamn mayor of Muc Wa, ain't you noticed?" Then he picked up his sledge hammer and went back to work.

At the noon formation Stephen announced that Toffee would be buried at two o'clock. The Raiders were delighted. They had never seen a white man put into the ground before, and they cheered Stephen when he dismissed the formation.

"Didn't I tell you?" Ski said, on his way to the hooch he shared with Butterfly, and where he now took his meals. "His honor!" Ski shouted. "His honor, the goddamn mayor of Muc Wa!"

Stephen went over to the command post and broke the news to Lieutenant Hamilton.

"Are you sure we can't wait?" the lieutenant asked.

"Positive," Stephen said. "We'll have another mutiny on our hands."

"All right. Will you take care of the . . . the details?"

"I already have."

The lieutenant laughed, but cut it off when it threatened to break into a cough. "Yes," he said. "I should have known. . . . I'd better conduct the service, though, don't you think?"

"If you're strong enough."

"It's my duty," the lieutenant said. Then he got into a sweat because he couldn't find the SOP on field burials. "The manual must be around here someplace," he said, sitting forlornly at his desk in his underwear.

"Maybe Toffee threw it away," Stephen said. "He was a Christian Scientist, remember?"

"I have a Bible," the lieutenant said. "That'll have to do."

Lieutenant Hamilton wore a clean khaki uniform for the funeral service, which was held beside the trefoil cross. The Raiders were drawn up in company formation on the slope. Toffee's body had been wrapped in tent cloth, then covered by one of Butterfly's best funeral blankets. Lieutenant Hamilton read from his Bible in a shaky voice: "'All things have their season, and in their time all things pass under heaven. A time to be born and a time to die . . . A time to kill, and a time to heal . . . A time of love, and a time of hatred; a time of war, and a time of peace.'" Cowboy strained to follow every word. Then he stepped forward, held up his hand, and translated the passage into Buru. The Raiders applauded.

"Steve?" the lieutenant said then. "Will you finish up? I have to go to the latrine."

"Sure," Stephen said, and the lieutenant hurried off toward camp, his tail tucked in. Stephen signaled to the grave-diggers. They came over and lowered Toffee's body into the hole they had dug for him, then hesitated. *I wonder,* Stephen thought, *what epitaph would Rebecca have composed for you? Not even a twenty-three-year-old female college graduate with liberal convictions could make you out to be a killer, Toffee. But you were a soldier, and you killed two of Charlie's mortarmen with a grenade. . . .* "Okay!" he said. "Fill it in." Giggling self-consciously, the men began to shovel dirt into the grave, while the Raiders crowded forward for a closer look.

"Aaaaah!" they said, and applauded again.

"All right, all right!" Ski bellowed at them. "Back to work, you deadbeats, before Charlie puts us all into that hole."

While the Raiders trudged reluctantly back to camp, the gravediggers erected a small mahogany cross upon the mound of earth. Then they nailed one of Toffee's dog tags to the cross.

"Very nice, sir," Cowboy said to Stephen. "Very Cath'lic."

"Well, you'd better raise Penang on the radio and tell them about it," Stephen said. "Tell them we couldn't wait for the helicopter any longer, because Toffee was decomposing."

"Dee . . . come . . ."

"Rotting," Stephen said.

"Ohhh—yes, sir!" Cowboy said, and went off at a trot to the commo bunker.

Stephen unfolded the funeral blanket and touched a match to it. While it burned, he heard Rebecca's husky voice, whispering: "Don't you see? All values are arbitrary." Flames ran along the bright threads of silk. "Your nationality," Rebecca whispered, "your religion, your friends—they're all accidents of birth, so why should you fight for them?"

I didn't know what to say, Stephen thought. *So I kissed her.*

The funeral blanket burned to ash, but the pattern was still visible in black and gray. Stephen scuffed it into the grass. *Strange,* he thought, *how my mind dwells upon Rebecca. Everything at Muc Wa reminds me of her. I have transplanted her to this lonely outpost, my Jewish passion flower, and now she's growing everywhere. Soon she'll be growing on Toffee's grave.*

He slung his carbine and walked up to the north gate, where Ski had his work crew sweating again, completing the second line of barbed wire.

"When Charlie . . . comes again," Ski said, panting, "we'll damned well be ready for him."

"I hope so," Stephen said, and walked on.

Maybe, Rebecca, you'll soon be growing on all our graves—a lovelier monument than ever a soldier dreamed of having.

Thirteen

"Now that the camp is finished," Lieutenant Hamilton said, "we should be doing some aggressive patrolling. Major Barker is sure to ask about that." The signals from Penang seemed to indicate that the major was coming down for a personal inspection. "But I'm not going to tell either of you to go out there," the lieutenant said. He waved his walking stick at the field, and the green face of the rain forest beyond. "If you want to volunteer, fine. Otherwise I'll take the patrol out myself."

"Hell, Lieutenant," Ski said. "You're still sick."

"I can manage," the lieutenant said, looking at Stephen. "I've been practicing, taking walks around the perimeter."

"Why look at me?" Stephen asked, because Ski was doing it, too.

"Hell, you're the mayor, ain't you?" Ski said.

"It doesn't sound like you're planning to volunteer."

"Christ, no! I'm a twenty-year man, and we don't volunteer for nothing. Else we wouldn't live to collect that pension."

"Okay," Stephen said.

"You *tell* me to go," Ski said anxiously, "and I'll go, all right. But it's plumb against my principles to volunteer."

"Well, I don't have any principles," Stephen said, "so I guess it's up to me."

"You got principles, all right," Ski told him. "You got more principles than any corporal I ever heard of." He hawked and spat. "*Pagh!*" he said. "You got too many damn principles for your own good."

Old Man had led the ambush patrol last night—they had to use him, with Toffee dead and the lieutenant sick—so Stephen took the second platoon under Private Tam. They were planning to promote Tam to corporal, anyhow, so the patrol would be good practice for him.

They swept the rain forest east of camp. It was easy going, and they covered eight or ten kilometers before breaking for lunch. *Funny,* Stephen thought, scooping rice into his mouth. *How ordinary it all becomes, after a few months. I'm just like the other Raiders now. I hunker the same, I eat the same rations—hell, I probably even smell the same. I belong here in the rain forest. It almost seems that I never belonged anywhere else.*

After lunch they picked up a family of Buru nomads—no men, of course, and some of the women so weak from hunger that they could hardly walk. Stephen decided to abort the patrol and take the refugees back to Muc Wa.

Two or three kilometers from camp, Tam stopped the column. They were in a glade where elephant grass grew waist high. Tam sniffed around for a while, then, proud as a rooster, he showed Stephen where a man had slept in the grass overnight, had eaten a breakfast of cold cooked rice, had crapped and moved on—toward Muc Wa.

They followed the spoor until they emerged from the rain forest. It led straight across the field toward camp.

"All right, Tam," Stephen said. "He's your baby. Go get him."

It might have been the track of some dumb tribesman, wandering through the mountains on his own mysterious business. Or one of the Raiders, selling weapons or information to the rebels. Or Charlie himself—that homely, amiable scout—back for another look at Muc Wa.

Tam led a squad into the field, while Stephen waited at the edge of the rain forest with the rest of the patrol. But then—goddamn!—the afternoon came alive with the snarl of engines. Two stubby T-28s swept down from the north. They buzzed the camp at flagpole height, dipping their wings like the heroes of a World War Two movie. Then they climbed, turned in a graceful cloverleaf, and came back for another pass. Some of the refugees had been watering their cattle in the river, south of camp; now they stampeded, refugees and cattle alike, galloping across the field toward Tam. He glanced back wildly at Stephen. Then the stampede swallowed him, together with the trail he had been following.

Stephen took the patrol back to camp. The T-28s were now circling overhead, looking them over. Stephen went into the commo bunker and raised the flight commander on the radio. "U.S. aircraft, U.S. aircraft," he said into the microphone, as he had heard Toffee say, so many times. "This is Blaze, Blaze. Do you have any traffic for this station, over?"

The loudspeaker crackled. "Hello, Blaze!" the pilot said. "We're escorting a live drop for you, buddy. Put down some smoke, will you?"

Stephen took two yellow smoke grenades from the rack and went out to the blazing sunlight again. Raiders and refugees were pouring through the north gate, to watch the drop; even Lieutenant Hamilton was hobbling down the slope. Stephen ignited the grenades in the middle of the field. The Raiders hunkered down and marveled as the thick yellow smoke curled westward on the breeze. High overhead, a Caribou transport tacked through the sky, trying to find the best spot to drop its passenger. The parachutist was standing in the open cargo door. Then he dropped into space, and a great "*Aaaaah!*" went up from the Raiders. The breath caught in Stephen's throat. He remembered the incredible, empty moments when he had hung in the air above Fort Darby, North Carolina, proving he was tough enough for the U. S. Army Raiders.

The parachutist landed on the ghost road which ran past Muc Wa to the west. Stephen went over to meet him, falling in with Ski on the way.

"Well, shit-a-goddamn," Ski said, "if it ain't Ackley."

"Hi, Sarge," Ackley said, gathering the collapsed parachute beneath his arm. He was carrying a folding-stock carbine and a field pack. "I'm your new signalman," he said without enthusiasm.

"Hallelujah!" Ski said. "We've been reinforced, Steve. Why, it's Dienbienphu all over again, damned if it ain't! Heroes dropping out of the sky, dead men shoveled into the ground . . . You seen our little cemetery yet, Ackley?"

Ackley gave him a sly grin from beneath the olive-green baseball cap which he was wearing instead of the Raider hat. He was wearing regulation fatigues, too. "You ain't gonna put me in that boneyard," he said. "General Hardnetz don't believe in it, and he's coming down here personal to tell you so."

"Oh, God," Stephen said, remembering the little powder keg who had stormed through Thaitan airport. "When?"

"Day after tomorrow. It's gonna be a regular unannounced inspection. I've got orders for the lieutenant, telling him all about it." Ackley pulled an envelope from inside his fatigue shirt. "Sealed orders," he said.

"What do they say?" Stephen asked.

"You think I read 'em?"

"Yes."

"Well . . . You're getting these VIPs—the general and a lady reporter—and you can't wear them jungle fatigues because the general don't like 'em."

"Seems this general don't like a lot of things," Ski said. "Ain't he the guy we tangled ass holes with, at the airport?"

"The very same," Stephen said.

Ski looked sourly across the field, where the barbed-wire defenses of Muc Wa were glinting in the sun. "I bet he don't much care for my garrison, neither," he said. "I bet he thinks it ain't regulation." The Raiders and the refugees were straggling out to greet them. Among them Stephen saw Butterfly's kid sister, his pet, and he scooped her up.

"Hello, Angel," he said. She snuggled against his chest, warm and soft as a cat. "How do you like the airplanes?"

"Okay," the little girl said. This was the only English word she knew, so Stephen always had to be careful with his questions, to make the answer come out right.

"I bet the general thinks she ain't regulation, neither," Ski said.

While the T-28s flew ring-around-the-rosy above the camp, the Caribou was returning for another drop. The first two bundles were free falls. They landed near the gravesite, bounded into the air, and burst, spilling olive-green garments across the field. The next four were tethered to parachutes, which blossomed just before they hit the ground.

"What did Santa Claus send us?" Ski asked.

"A whole shitload of GI fatigues," Ackley told him. "You got to wear 'em while the general's here."

"Fatigues?" Ski said. "Six bales of fatigues? Gor! What's he expect us to do with 'em—leave a thousand pair in the puckerbrush for Charlie?"

"Oh, they ain't all fatigues."

"What else, then?"

"You'll find out," Ackley said, grinning triumphantly.

The T-28s buzzed the camp again, the pilots waving cheerfully from the greenhouse canopies. They were Americans. Behind each pilot was a small and terrified hostage from the local air force, who was there to satisfy the International Control Commission. If the plane crashed, his body would prove that the American had only been on a training flight, not on a live-fire mission against the rebels. The hostages did not wave.

While the planes flew away to the north-northwest, Ski took a work crew over to pick up the supplies. Ackley winked and said: "Old Ski's gonna shit a brick when he sees what else the major sent us."

"What did he send?" Stephen asked.

"Take a guess."

"I don't have to guess. I can go over and see for myself."

"Okay, okay," Ackley said, and licked his lips. "Coffins."

"Coffins?"

"Yeah! Four of 'em, so's you don't have to bury any of *us* in that boneyard, like you did to Toffee. The general had 'em flown up special from Thaitan."

"That was real thoughtful of the general," Stephen said.

Surrounded by admiring Raiders, they walked back to the camp. Ackley seemed impressed by all the attention he was getting. "The major wants us to put on a good show for the VIPs," he said. "He wants us to stimulate an attack while the general's here."

"Stimulate?"

"You know—make-believe."

"Oh," Stephen said. "And who'll be doing the stimulating?"

"You will," Ackley said. He hesitated, then added: "Steve."

Stephen laughed. "I hope the major knows what he's doing," he said. "Because if there's one guy in Southeast Asia who can take this garrison, it's me."

"Not while *I'm* inside it," Ackley said, picking at his cheek.

When they were inside the gate, Stephen untangled Angel and set her on the ground. "Go home, sweetheart," he told her. "I've got work to do, okay?"

"Okay," the little girl said, smiling all over her wild, dark face.

Stephen walked up the knoll, meaning to report to Lieutenant Hamilton. But the coffins drew him like magnets, and he found himself passing the command post and walking down the slope to the north gate. Corporal Old Man was also heading that way. They walked along together, Old Man making it pretty clear that Stephen had let him down by going out on a patrol without him. He had come to regard Stephen as his own personal American, not to be shared with Tam or anyone else.

Something strange at the gravesite. Stephen unslung his carbine. *Something white attached to Toffee's grave.*

"Hey, Old Man," he said, and hurried toward the gravesite,

where fatigue uniforms were scattered like the victims of some epic battle. The old Raider followed him.

It was Charlie, then, Stephen thought, remembering the track he had followed with Tam. *He must have come here this morning. Maybe he's still here, in his hidey-hole across the river. And he's been messing around with Toffee's grave.*

He searched the far bank of the river, and saw it: a flash of movement in the grass. He flicked carbine's fire-select lever to full automatic, pressed the stock against his hip, and fired—not aiming, just spraying the opposite bank with lead. The bullets whipped the grass like a gust of wind. *You won't, you little bastard. . . .* The bolt locked open on the last cartridge, and Stephen yanked the magazine out and turned it, inserting the spare magazine that was taped to it. *You won't run ME off, you won't!* Emptied the second magazine, too. Old Man was also shooting, and some of the Raiders from Ski's work crew.

Ski came running over. "What the hell?" he roared.

"Our buddy is back," Stephen said, his hands shaking.

"Who?"

"That rebel scout." He forced his fingers to reload the magazine, and they soon steadied down.

"C'mon, you mother-humpers!" Ski yelled at his Raiders. "This is what you get paid for!" He drove them across the river with his curses.

Stephen went over to the gravesite. He found a piece of notepaper on Toffee's cross, wedged beneath the dog tag, with a message penciled in rough block letters:

!YANKE YOU GO HOMB!

He took a deep breath. He was shivering and sweating, both, as if he had just walked a tightrope across Niagara Falls, and he felt the same crazy sense of triumph. Old Charlie had gotten his answer, all right. But, just in case he had missed the point, Stephen searched through his pockets until he found a ballpoint pen, then turned the message over and printed:

I AM HOME, CHARLIE.

He tucked the piece of paper beneath the dog tag, laughing to himself.

Then he went over to have a look at the coffins. Ski's work crew had already opened one of the crates, revealing an olive-green box which seemed to be made of Fiberglas. The lid was stenciled: CONTAINER, INTERMENT, HERMETICALLY SEALABLE, M21A. Stephen opened the lid. Inside, the coffin was quilted with olive-green plastic. An instruction manual was stapled to the pillow, together with a small cardboard box which probably held tools and sealant and maybe even a field embalming kit.

"Him bed?" Corporal Old Man said, coming up beside him.

"You might call it that," Stephen said.

Old Man rapped the Fiberglas with his knuckles. "Okay," he said, nodding so vigorously that his great earlobes flapped. "A-okay!"

Fourteen

This trip to Muc Wa would be the heart of Rebecca's first dispatch to the *Liberal.* The article would be a marvelously understated thing, she had decided: the U. S. Army Raiders were going to damn themselves in their own words. While Captain Olivetti boosted her into the helicopter, Rebecca was already composing her lead paragraph: *"All I want from this stinking country is the CIB," a dashing young Raider captain said to me. "Hell, lady, it's the only war we've got."* Wonderful! Except that *dashing* was a bit much. Captain Olivetti would be more than ever convinced that he was the Pentagon's gift to women, and that she was just panting to be taken into his mighty arms (thick as telephone poles, they seemed to be). *Sturdy* was better . . . *a sturdy young Raider captain said to me.*

"What?" Rebecca said.

"You'd be better off back here, with me," Captain Olivetti said, pitching his voice above the beat of the rotor blades and the whine of the jet-turbine engine. There was a row of canvas seats against the cabin's rear wall, and two more in the center, one facing each door. Captain Olivetti settled himself in back. He patted the seat beside him, but Rebecca smiled and took one of the outward-facing seats.

"I'll be quite comfortable here, thank you," she told him.

"What's that?"

She repeated the snub, but found that she could not make herself heard, darn it. Anyhow, Captain Olivetti was soon hemmed in by Major Barker, General Hardnetz, and two soldiers who seemed to belong to the helicopter, since they were wearing big crash helmets, like the pilots. The soldier nearest Rebecca was a Negro. She smiled prettily at him, to show him she didn't have a prejudice in the world.

When the helicopter lifted off, Rebecca realized that she had made a mistake. She was sitting in the doorway, practically, and the earth receded horribly between the toes of her new canvas jungle boots. *Oh, dear God,* she thought, while the earth wobbled like a run-down top. She clamped her eyes shut and seized the frail aluminum framework of the seat. *I wonder if Major Barker would change places with me?* But then she would have to unfasten her safety belt, and that she would never do.

At last the Negro crewman closed the door, and she could breathe again. One of the pilots, seated at her right shoulder, turned around and gave her a pair of earphones. "Now we're safe from ground fire," he told her when she had put them on. His lips moved against a little microphone which projected from his helmet; his voice exploded mechanically in Rebecca's ears. It was like talking on the telephone to somebody in the same telephone booth. "We keep the doors open until we're two thousand feet up, so the gunner and the crew chief can shoot back if they need to. . . . Huh, Chief?" The Negro looked up and gave Rebecca a gleaming, bloodthirsty smile, lifting the machinegun which was cradled in his lap. "Yeah," his voice said in Rebecca's earphones. She nodded. She did not know how to operate the microphone, and anyhow she was already revising her lead paragraph:

There are roads in this revolution-torn country, but for the U. S. Army Raiders the only safe avenue is the sky.

She worked at this version for half an hour, while the pilots talked about the weather, the terrain, and the native women. Then the white crewman told a story about an American soldier at one of these isolated outposts who had married a mountain girl, or had pretended to. Rebecca perked up, hearing that, but the pilots only seemed interested in the girl's measurements, and she learned nothing that might help her with the article. Then the pilot said: "Open the door!" Cold air and terror swept across Rebecca again. Between her toes she saw a star-shaped fort, lonely and brave beside a river. It was exactly like the model in Major Barker's office—barbed wire, shell holes, longhouses, even a scattering of toy soldiers —which gave her the hideous illusion that she was a fly on the major's wall. She clamped her eyes shut again.

Stephen Courcey's face immediately formed behind her eyelids—that fierce, brooding face, so ugly it was beautiful— and she felt her bones melting with happiness. *Oh dear,* she thought. *What shall I say to him?* The image was so clear that she expected Stephen to be standing in front of her when she opened her eyes. But he wasn't.

The helicopter settled to the ground. A ragged honor guard was drawn up at the edge of the landing area, the men grinning hugely, while their green baseball caps sailed away on the rotor blast. Three Americans were standing stiffly in front of them. Rebecca recognized Ackley, the pimply clerk from Penang, and there was a darling sergeant with a potbelly and bulging eyes, and a terribly serious, terribly thin young officer who looked a bit like . . . who *was* . . . "Ray Hamilton!" she cried, but of course the words were drowned by the rotor blast. And Stephen was not in view.

As soon as the helicopter was steady, Rebecca unbuckled her safety belt and jumped out, throwing her arms around Ray Hamilton and hugging him for all he was worth. Dear God, he was thin! "What?" he said. "Who?" Then he recognized her, and actually seemed pleased for a moment, until the general stepped down from the helicopter. "General Hardnetz, sir!" Ray said, struggling to free his right arm. "Welcome to Muc Wa, sir!" He managed to get his hand up for the inevitable salute, but Rebecca hung on to the rest of him, desperately happy to have found a friend from home.

"Lieutenant," the general said, "do you know this young woman?"

"Oh, we're old friends," Rebecca told him.

"That's correct, sir," Ray said, stiff as one of those rifles in the honor guard. "Long-time acquaintances, sir."

"*Brmm*," the general said.

Major Barker climbed down, too, and Captain Olivetti began to sling their baggage to the ground, a murderous look on his face. What bears they all were! "Ray," she said, to torment them a bit more, "is Stephen here?"

"Uh," he said. "Who?"

"Stephen Courcey."

"Oh—Steve." He looked at the general, then at the major. "Uh, no," he said then.

"He isn't?"

"No, he isn't."

"Oh," Rebecca said. She went over to rescue her typewriter from Captain Olivetti, hearing again the ballad she had heard with Stephen: *If you will not when you may, you may not when you will, sir!*

She was so disgusted with the world and the U. S. Army that she only said, "Yes, please," when Ackley volunteered to show her where she would sleep.

"You'll be staying with Butterfly," he told her.

"Who's Butterfly?"

Ackley just rolled his eyes.

Rebecca meekly followed him, and six or seven native children followed her. They were jay-naked, most of them, with skin that varied from honey brown to chocolate, and all with great liquid black eyes and glossy black hair. As they trotted along beside her, they made circles of their fingers and goggled at her. After a while Rebecca realized that they were mimicking her glasses. Of course! They had never seen anything like them before, because their own people were too poor to afford them, and the Americans they met were too healthy to need them. The dears. Rebecca held out her hand to one pretty girl-child, cleaner than the rest, and wearing a dress of bright orange, but she scampered away out of reach.

"Whose children are they?" she asked, already feeling better.

"Refugees," Ackley said.

"Refugees from what?"

Ackley gave her a tough-guy scowl. "When we go out on patrol," he said, "anybody that runs away from us is a Commie, and we zap him. If he stands still, he's a refugee, and we bring him back here and take care of him."

"Do the mountain people know about this rule of yours?"

Ackley shrugged. "You got a better way?" he asked.

"Yes," Rebecca said. "Don't go out on patrols."

"Civilians!" Ackley said. Then he added: "Women!"

They came to a small hut on stilts, with a cleated ramp leading up to the door. The walls were fashioned from bamboo slats, tied at the top and bottom; the roof was straw. "Is this where I'll stay?" Rebecca asked, thinking of bats and spiders lurking in the thatch.

"Yeah, and that's Butterfly," Ackley said, waving at a handsome native girl who was standing in the doorway. He hoisted the luggage up to her. Then he turned to Rebecca and winked, the worm. "You need anything, just gimme a call," he said, and shambled off. Rebecca cautiously climbed the ramp to meet Butterfly.

Really, she was beautiful, with a dark body cloth wound tightly around her breasts, waist, and hips, then falling free to her ankles. She was suspiciously plump at the belly, too. Whose child was she carrying? One of the Americans', Rebecca decided, feeling terribly pale and mannish.

But Butterfly was also enchanted. She touched Rebecca's face and hair, and giggled over the uniform she wore—the tiger-stripe jungle fatigues which General Hardnetz had recently banned, and which Rebecca had adopted for that very reason. "Me same-same," Butterfly said, drawing Rebecca into the hut. "Oh, very nice." She made a story with her hands: man, love, baby. Then she tugged at Rebecca's fatigue shirt. "You?" she asked. "Same-same?"

Rebecca shook her head, quite lost.

Butterfly pressed a finger to her dark lips. Then she squatted in front of a huge olive-green chest, gracefully sweeping the body cloth under her thighs so that it would not touch the floor. She opened the chest, which was about seven feet long and quilted inside, like a coffin. In fact, it *was* a coffin. Rebecca stepped back, half afraid that Butterfly's dead husband was inside. But the coffin was used only as a wardrobe, apparently, because Butterfly took out a folded garment and closed the lid. "Me," she said, and told the story again: man, love, baby. Then she unfolded the garment and put it on. It was a camouflage shirt exactly like Rebecca's, although faded from the sun and many washings. Above the pockets, now richly modeled upon Butterfly's breasts, were the regulation nameplates, one saying U. S. ARMY, the other saying COURCEY.

"*You?*" Rebecca cried.

"Me," Butterfly agreed.

Rebecca found herself outside the hut, striding toward the knoll which she assumed would be the site of camp headquarters. *Stephen Courcey*, she thought, *you son of a bitch.*

She passed General Hardnetz and refused to look at him. "How *many* patrols?" the general was asking—he was with that darling, potbellied sergeant. "Are you hurting Charlie or just nipping at his heels?" Rebecca hurried on, but the general's voice followed her up the slope: "Suppose you were running this war, Sergeant. What would you do? Scatter your men from hell to breakfast, a company here, a company there?"

"Well, sir," said the sergeant's gravelly voice. "I don't know as I ever—"

"Wouldn't you go for broke? Wouldn't you be operating with battalions, regiments, *divisions?* Wouldn't you get the job done and get the hell out of here?"

"Shucks, sir," the sergeant drawled, "if you know a way to get us out of here, we'd sure like to hear about it."

At the crest of the hill, Rebecca went into a tentlike building, sheltered by trees and a wall of sandbags. Major Barker and Ray Hamilton were there, drinking Coca-Cola from bottles dripping with moisture. She recognized the ice chest as one of the boxes which had come down with them from Penang.

"Yes, sir," Ray was saying, tugging at the ridiculous mustache he now wore, "it's good to have radio contact again, but you realize we're still without a medic, and—"

"We took care of that," Major Barker said. "I talked with Thaitan the other day, and they're going to cross-qualify Sergeant Oleonowski as a medic. It means taking away his rating as an intelligence specialist, but you can manage without that, can't you?"

"Yes, sir, but—"

"No buts about it, m'boy!" the major said. "You'll get the authorization in your next supply drop. . . . Ah!" he said, smiling like an ogre at Rebecca. "Would you like a Coke, Miss Shaw?"

"No . . . I . . . would . . . *not!*" she said, and turned to the lieutenant. "Ray," she said, planting her hands on her hips. "Is Stephen Courcey in this camp?"

"Well—"

"You needn't lie to me, Ray Hamilton, because I know he's here."

"I—"

"Corporal Courcey is *assigned* to this garrison," Major Barker said. "He just happens to be on a secret mission at the moment."

"Oh," Rebecca said.

"Lieutenant Hamilton wasn't *lying* to you, Miss Shaw. Please don't write that in your story. He just wasn't authorized to tell you."

"I see. . . . How long will Stephen be gone?"

Ray looked at the major, who said: "That's classified information, Miss Shaw. But I think I can tell you that American personnel are not authorized to spend more than five days in the field without returning to their base of operations."

"Five days," Rebecca said. "So I won't see him, after all."

"I'm sorry, Rebecca," Ray said. "If I'd known it was you, I would have sent somebody else on the mission."

"By the way, Miss Shaw," Major Barker said. "Perhaps you shouldn't mention Corporal Courcey's absence to the general."

"This secret mission," Rebecca said, thinking of commando raids behind enemy lines. "Is it dangerous?"

"It could be," the major said with a terrible expression, "if he doesn't keep his head down."

Rebecca went back to the hut, her heart fluttering as it had not done since she was a freshman at college. These brutal, foolish men! In spite of all that Stephen Courcey had told her about his training at Fort Darby, she had somehow never dreamed that his lips (so good to kiss, remember?) might actually give the order to kill, or that his hands (so warm upon her breasts, remember?) might carry a rifle through the forest. *Why?* she thought. *Why do men do it? Don't they realize that nothing is worth it, worth the fighting and the killing?*

Then she saw Butterfly—melon-breasted and beautiful and almost certainly pregnant—and her fury returned. *Damn you, Stephen Courcey,* she thought. *I hate you, I hate you, I . . . oh!* Tears swam into her eyes. She bit her tongue, but the tears flowed even faster. "Oh, Butterfly!" she cried, and the girl's warm dark arms went around Rebecca's neck. "I love him, too!"

While she wept, Rebecca could feel Butterfly's plump belly beneath her cheek. She wondered how long it would be before the baby would start moving around in there.

Every game becomes the truth at last, she thought.

Fifteen

Stephen slapped at a mosquito, and wished it had been Major Barker. The Raiders around him giggled. They thought it was a hell of a joke, hiding in the rain forest while the night came down, waiting to attack their own garrison.

"Yesterday we make war," Stephen said, and the Raiders fell respectfully silent. "Who did we fight yesterday?"

"Communist!" Old Man said.

"Why?"

"Communist number-ten fella," Old Man said, smiling with his broken teeth. He looked proudly at the other Raiders, inviting them to admire his command of the white man's language.

"Who are we fighting tonight?" Stephen asked.

"Muc Wa!"

"Why?"

Old Man looked around in the gathering dusk, and, finding no answer, he tugged at his earlobe. "Big noise by Muc Wa tonight," he said uneasily.

"Sure," Stephen said. "Big noise—big joke. Last week you defended it, this week you attack it. Muc Wa doesn't mean any more to you than it does to Major Barker."

Old Man tugged at his earlobe and was silent. Soon, in the swift, dissolving twilight, he was only a vague green shape among the trees.

Stephen tried to find the reason for his anger. There was a certain stupid risk in what they were doing—some of the garrison's bullets might fly low, or Charlie might spring an ambush on them—but that wasn't what was bugging him. Raiders were trained to take risks. Raiders were the roughest, toughest, goddamnedest soldiers in the U. S. Army, wasn't that it? Live off the country. Make the night your friend. Turn the enemy's weapons against him. *Be a professional.* . . . And what was the difference, to a professional, between attacking somebody else's garrison and attacking your own? None. It was a job like any other.

But it wasn't.

Corporal Old Man was getting restless. He pointed to the stars, soft flakes of light between the trees, and said: "Time."

"No," Stephen said.

"Time," Old Man insisted.

Stephen looked at the luminous dial of his watch. It was time, all right—high time. They should have been approaching Muc Wa at this moment, if they were to keep to Major Barker's scenario. "Not yet," Stephen said.

Old Man came over and put his hand on Stephen's shoulder, enveloping him with the familiar Raider smell of rancid oil, rotten fish, and U. S. Army gun grease. "Me fight by you," he said. "You fight—me fight."

"Well, that's a start, anyhow," Stephen said. He stood up, feeling a bit stiff. *The joke is on the U. S. Army Raiders,* he thought. *They shipped me over here—the best-trained, best-paid mercenary in the history of war—to teach Old Man to be a loyal defender of Muc Wa. But they trained me too well, the bastards. I spilled my guts into that garrison, and I taught myself to be loyal. Not to the U. S. Army Raiders, though. To Muc Wa* . . . "All right," he said. "Let's go."

He brought the patrol in from the east, following the scenario Major Barker had written. The night was dark as a closet. Moving through the rain forest, with his skin alive to the threat of branches and vines, Stephen found himself pushing the Raiders, so he slowed them down. *To hell with the major,* he thought. *Let him sweat for a while.* They emerged from the rain forest at twenty-one hundred hours. Stephen checked the time, then took off his wristwatch and put it in his pocket. Then he scooped up a handful of earth, moistened it with water from his canteen, and daubed it across his face. Officers were lousy shots, but General Hardnetz might be the exception.

Across the field, he saw a chink of light from the garrison. *Silly damn fool,* he thought. *If I were Charlie I'd put a mortar shell right on top of you.* Using the gleam of light as his polestar, Stephen advanced across the field. The Raiders were spread out behind him. Their boots whispered in the grass; uniforms rustled, rifles clinked, canteens gurgled; and the river flowed between its banks with a dark, oily sound, just ahead of them. . . . How could seventeen men make so much noise? Voices, too, although Corporal Old Man had promised to shoot the first man who said a word. But perhaps the voices were coming from the garrison. It was impossible to tell, with the dark sound of the river underlying everything.

SNICK.

His heart jumped. *What the ever-loving hell was THAT?* His boots touched soft earth—the edge of a shell hole. He held out both arms. *Stop, you bastards, stop!* The Raiders gave a sigh and froze where they were. His face tingling, Stephen searched the night—eyes, ears, nose, and skin—trying to pick out the sound he had heard. It had seemed to spring from the ground beneath him.

SNICK.

An old infantry rifle: bolt open, bolt closed, Snick-snick. But the Raiders were armed with carbines. Only Charlie would be using a rifle like that—a MAS-16, probably, captured from the French ten years ago.

Stephen dropped into the hole, his guts knotted with fright. The blood roared in his ears. He sensed a man—smelled him—and *the smell was wrong.* He raked the darkness. Ah! His fingers touched human hair, damp as seaweed. He yanked the head against his shoulder, clamped one hand over the open mouth, groped with the other hand for the man's weapon. He had to be sure. . . .

"MMPH!" the mouth cried against his hand.

They strained together, like lovers. Then they fell, crashing sideways against the lip of the shell hole. Stephen's fingers touched steel, slid along it, and found the knob of a bolt handle. Yes. Charlie. *Jesus!* he thought. *We've walked right into the middle of an attack.* He took the bayonet from his scabbard and drove it into Charlie's side. But it hit a bone or some damned thing, and the poor bastard twisted and kicked, tearing with his fingernails at Stephen's hand. *I'm sorry,* Stephen thought. *No shit—I'm sorry. But I can't stop now.* He pulled the bayonet free and used it to cut Charlie's throat. Blood pulsed across his hand, and the rifle exploded, blowing the night apart: CRASH! . . . CRACK-CRACK-CRACK!

A man loomed over him, shutting out the stars. Stephen shrank back. But no—it was Corporal Old Man. Stephen tried to move, but couldn't; he was crushed beneath the weight of Charlie's body.

Old Man dropped into the hole and groped until his hands found Stephen's face. "Okay?" he whispered. With the word, a whole torrent of noise swept through: crackle of small-arms fire, chatter of machineguns, cries of men. *Life goes on,* Stephen thought. *The war goes on.*

"Okay," he said, and together they rolled Charlie over and stripped him of his rifle, cartridge belt, and a snap-top purse they found in his pocket. Then they talked it over, communicating with their hands and the faith they had in each other. "Where are the Raiders?" Stephen asked.

"On their bellies."

"Does Charlie know we're here?"

"Not yet."

"Okay. We'll pull back, and a bit to the south. Then we'll start shooting."

Old Man nodded happily.

"Maybe we can sucker Charlie into coming after us," Stephen told him. "We'll take him into the rain forest and lose him."

"Okay," Old Man said.

When the shooting began, Butterfly switched off the battery lantern and ran away, leaving Rebecca alone. Dear God, the noise was frightful! In the sudden, total darkness, she covered her typewriter and put it against the wall. Then she picked her way down the ramp. At the bottom, a running man crashed into her and knocked her down; she stood up and walked into a tree. Then she burst into tears. She felt like a bird trapped inside a house, where every flight ended headlong against a windowpane, simply because it did not understand the logic of living in houses. Rebecca did not understand the logic of war. The noise—why was the noise so awful? The machineguns, especially. They pounded at her ears until they seemed to work their way inside, and each shot was a needle stabbing at her brain. And the dark night, and the shapes of running men, and the dazzling, green-white lights that suddenly blossomed in the sky . . . What in God's name was *happening*?

The first Americans she encountered were General Hardnetz and Ackley, who was shouting in a reedy, joyful voice: "Oh, give it to 'em, General, ram it to 'em!" She almost knelt down beside them, but they were firing a machinegun. It was a small weapon, and quiet enough to begin with, but the end of each burst was the same old needle, stabbing at her eardrums. She moved away into the darkness, wondering if perhaps she wasn't foolish to be walking upright when the others were huddled against the wall.

"Rebecca?" a strong voice said.

She dissolved. "Yes," she said. "Where are you?" And Captain Olivetti appeared in front of her, like a massive tree for her to lean on. She leaned—never mind what he thought! She had to lean against someone or die.

"Frightened?" he said.

"No, no—just confused."

"Poor girl," he said, trying to turn her on. But what did it matter? His arms were strong. "I'm going around, checking the defenses," he said, speaking in the intervals between machinegun bursts. "D'you want to come?"

"Oh, yes!" Rebecca cried, and immediately hated herself. "I mean . . . if you're sure I won't be in the way." They moved along the wall, in the direction from which she had come. Captain Olivetti held her very close, his arm like a backrest and his big hand pressing against her ribs, which gave her the usual problem of what to do with her own arm, so she put it around his waist. God. He was built like a horse—no waist at all, just one strong wall of muscle from his ribs to his hip. She searched for something businesslike to say. "I . . ." she began, then her earlier fear of bullets returned. "Should we be standing up like this?" she asked.

He laughed—a cheerful, neighing laugh. "A bullet won't hit you unless it's got your name written on it," he said. "Then it'll get you, wherever you are."

Rebecca did not find this very comforting, but she couldn't very well follow him on her hands and knees, so they continued their lovers' walk along the wall. Soon they came upon Ackley, who was still crying: "Oh, ram it to 'em, General!" But the general seemed to be having some kind of trouble. Puffing and swearing, he would yank at the machinegun and fire a few shots, then it would jam, thank God, and he swore and puffed some more.

"What the hell's that?" Captain Olivetti said, turning Rebecca loose.

The general looked up. "Ah, Captain!" he cried, beaming in the horrible, green-white light of a flare. "What did you say?"

"I said: handsome weapon you've got there, sir."

"It's a Eureka Twenty-Three," the general said. "I always bring along a new piece of gear when I'm in the field. You'd be surprised how differently weapons function in combat. . . . Men, too," he said, slapping Ackley's shoulder. "Must be a reinforced company out there," he added.

"Oh no, sir," Captain Olivetti said. "Not that many."

Ackley giggled. "Maybe it's only a couple of squads," he said. "Maybe they're just running back and forth. Huh, Cap'n?"

"At least a company," the general said. "What's the reaction time, if we need reinforcements?"

"We could get air support in half an hour," Captain Olivetti told him, and Rebecca relaxed somewhat. He seemed so *confident*.

"Air support? Who's talking about air support?" The general yanked at his machinegun again. "When you've seen as much combat as I have, Captain, you'll know that air support doesn't win battles. I'm talking about the infantry."

"Yes, sir."

"Well?" the general demanded. "How long would it take for your reserves to get here?"

"The Raiders don't have any reserves, sir," Captain Olivetti said, and Rebecca's heart did a slow, despairing slide into her boots.

"No reserves?"

"No, sir."

"How the hell—"

"We'd ask Major Minh for support, sir. He's the province chief."

"God!" the general said. "How long would that take?"

"Maybe two days, sir."

"God," the general said. "Don't you people ever read the field manuals? Dividing your forces—operating without reserves—giving the initiative to the enemy. . . . Why d'you think we write field manuals, anyway?"

"Well, sir," Captain Olivetti said, "the field manual for Covert Warfare operations—"

"Covert Warfare, hell! There's only one kind of warfare,

Captain—you have an enemy and you kill him. *That's* the only kind of warfare there is. . . . Damn!" he said in a milder voice. "These links are drier than a sandblaster's ass. . . . Beg your pardon, Miss Shaw."

"I'll find an oilcan, sir," Captain Olivetti said. Taking Rebecca's arm, he drew her away into the darkness. As soon as they were alone, his hand came up and cupped her breast. "Well, I guess our little operation backfired," he said cheerfully.

Rebecca wanted to ask him what he meant, but the big hand confused her, cupping her breast like that. She felt terribly mushy. They were walking up a slight rise, and the branches of trees were shutting out the stars. The noise was more bearable here. Rebecca put her hand on his, meaning to remove it, but instead she found herself pressing his fingers into the soft, tingling flesh. *Oh-oh,* she thought. *That was a mistake.* She felt that Captain Olivetti had cupped her entire body in his hand, and was gently squeezing her into a ball.

He stopped. They sank into the grass, which was wet with dew, and he grappled her like a schoolboy, all lips and hands.

"The oilcan—" she said.

"I've got it right here," Captain Olivetti said, with his whinnying laugh.

She beat at his face with her fists, while her mind filled up with the image of Stephen Courcey, making love to that beautiful refugee girl. *It's only fair,* she thought, and said: "No." *If Stephen can have his Butterfly, then I* . . . "No," she said. "Please don't." The captain's hands were inside her fatigue shirt, and his head soon followed them. She felt his great teeth nipping at the skin of her belly. *Dear God,* she thought. *Now I know how a mare feels—that smothering weight of muscle!* And she said: "No, no, no."

Suddenly Captain Olivetti sat up. "What the hell's going on?" he said.

Rebecca sat up, too. A great change had come over the night: it was warm, and soft, and blissfully quiet. Like the rumble of a passing storm, rifle fire still echoed in the distance, but here in the camp there was peace. "They've gone away," Rebecca said, and tucked in the tail of her fatigue shirt.

"Impossible," Captain Olivetti said. "It's not ten o'clock yet. . . . And what the hell are they shooting at, out there?"

Rebecca stood up. "Let's ask somebody," she said, bubbling with laughter. "Let's find Major Barker and ask him. Or the general. Or Ackley!" she said, and ran lightly down the hill, certain that she would no longer crash into things. *Serve him right*, she thought. *Serve him right, serve him right!*

Stephen let Charlie stay on his tail for two or three kilometers, just to keep him interested. Then he began to push. The Raiders had been loafing all day; they had trained hard and eaten well ever since coming to Muc Wa, and they should be at the top of their form.

Sure enough, the running fire fight became thinner and thinner, until it was only scattered shots in the distance. "We've lost them, Old Man," Stephen said. "They're shooting at shadows." He took the Raiders down an open valley, where the grass was short and sparse and would leave no trace of their passage. Then he let them collapse in a grove of umbrella trees. One man was wounded, his elbow smashed by a bullet. Two men were missing. Stephen squeezed a syrette of morphine into the wounded Raider, then smeared the poor bastard with mosquito repellent, to spare him *that* misery, at least. "Okay, Old Man," he said then. "Tell the men to pair off. Two-and-two. One man asleep, next man awake. Okay?"

"Okay," Old Man said, and did it.

Stephen took the first watch, sitting against a tree with the carbine balanced on his knees. The moon was up now, and he could see a fair distance down the valley. He entertained himself by thinking of Charlie's rage—the rage of a fox who is carried off by the chickens. *He must be sorry he ever messed with Muc Wa,* Stephen thought. *He must think we've got one hell of a camp, at Muc Wa.*

Time passed. When he judged that it was one o'clock—time to change places with Old Man—he took the wristwatch out of his pocket and found that it was only twelve-fifteen. He opened his pack, searched through it, and discovered a C-ration can of fruitcake. Marvelous! He hacked it open with the GI can opener that hung from his dog-tag chain. Eating slowly, sipping water from his canteen, he made a feast upon the sweet, moist cake. When he had eaten half of it, he went over to the wounded Raider, who was awake and staring at the moon, and gave him the remaining half. Time passed. Quarter of one.

Of course, he thought, *it was only dumb luck that we blundered into Charlie like that. Twenty minutes earlier, we would have been caught between the rebels and the camp. We would have been cut to pieces.*

Time passed. He fell asleep, jerked awake, and found that it was four minutes of one.

I'm only a man, he thought. *A bullet could smash my elbow. Or a bayonet—dear Jesus!—a bayonet could cut my throat.* . . . Three minutes to go.

What the hell! He shook Old Man awake, and they kept each other company for a while. Then Stephen lay down on his side, with his legs drawn up and his hands tucked between his thighs, to keep them warm and to protect them from the mosquitoes. His face was covered by the broad-brimmed Raider hat. All this would change as soon as he was asleep, of course, but somehow the mosquitoes did not trouble a sleeping man: they could suck away as much as they liked, and never leave a mark. It had something to do with relaxation. . . . *Four months to go,* he thought. *I wonder if I'll ever see Rebecca again?* She seemed very close to him. His hands were too heavy to move, so he turned his head and kissed her, and she was warm and alive beneath his lips. . . .

A hand was clamped on his shoulder, a finger pressed against his mouth. "Charlie come," Old Man said. "Many, many, many."

Stephen struggled awake. Around him, other men were stirring, invisible in pools of shadow. But out there!—a long column was marching through the moonlit valley, marching at an angle that would bring it within fifty meters of the umbrella trees. Stephen took a bottle of cough syrup from his pack and gave it to Old Man, who nodded. Then Stephen pantomimed closing his pack and getting his gear ready for a fight. Old Man moved away to see that it was done, and to tell the Raiders that cough syrup was available if they needed it. They had done this many times before, on ambushes. But then they had been trying to maintain surprise. Now they would be trying to save their necks.

Charlie's point squad went past—seven men. They were sloppy, carrying their rifles like shovels, like the Seven Dwarfs coming back from the mine. Stephen cleared his throat when they were safely past. The Raiders did the same, and the cough syrup went from hand to hand. Then the main column reached them, porters mixed with combat troops, a long single file that stretched across the valley, no end in sight. Stephen began to count. He counted men with his mind, mortars with the fingers of his right hand, and machineguns with his left. Then he ran out of fingers and had to drop those counts into his memory, too. Sweat ran down his face, and the mosquitoes lapped it up like meat sauce. Beside him, the soft rasp of Old Man's breathing. Out there in the valley, the shuffle of bare feet and sandals through the grass, and the *clink-clink-clink* of machinegun tripods and ammunition boxes. . . . *If one of us coughs, we'll all be dead.*

But there was the end, thank God.

Two hundred and thirty-five men, a full company, about one third of them porters who could probably fight if necessary; seven mortars, thirteen machineguns, and baskets and baskets of supplies.

The column was gone. The Raiders stirred, coughed, blew their noses into the air, and whispered apprehensively to one another.

"What are they saying?" Stephen asked.

"Many, many," Old Man said.

"Too damned many," Stephen agreed. "What else are they saying?"

"Charlie, him make big noise by Muc Wa," Old Man said.

"Maybe they'll go on past," Stephen told him. "Maybe they'll go on south, to fight in the delta." But he didn't really believe it.

Four months to go, he thought. *I wonder if I'll ever see Rebecca again?*

Sixteen

From the edge of the rain forest, Stephen watched the helicopter come and go, hauling the VIPs back to Penang. They were headed for the officers' club, no doubt. Major Barker and General Hardnetz would spend the afternoon in front of the electric fan, telling each other how brave the general had been, while the lady correspondent wrote it all down and Captain Olivetti laughed into his bottle of beer. And the funny thing was . . . the lies they told would be very near the truth.

There really was a fight, you sons of bitches, Stephen told the departing helicopter. *And one of my boys spent the night with a busted elbow, because of you.*

He took the Raiders across the field to Muc Wa. He stood them to attention, praised them more than they deserved, and gave them the morning off. Then he took the wounded Raider to the dispensary. Then he sent Corporal Old Man in search of Cowboy, to translate the papers they had taken from the dead rebel. Finally he went to the command post. Somebody had rigged a table from two sawhorses and a Fiberglas coffin lid, and his three comrades were sitting around it, drinking coffee.

"What?" Lieutenant Hamilton said, when Stephen had made his report. "That attack was real?"

"What?" Ski said. "*How* many men did you see?"

Then they told him about Rebecca, and it was Stephen's turn to say "What?" and lean for support against the cool green coffin lid.

Only Ackley was unsurprised. "Whatsa matter, Steve?" he said, spearing C-ration peaches with his bayonet. "You look like you seen a ghost."

"He did," Ski said. "He seen the reinforced company old Charlie is moving up."

"No," Stephen said. "It's the girl—Rebecca."

"That Miss Shaw?" Ackley said. "You know her?"

"I spent most of last year chasing her tail."

"Did you catch it?" Ski asked, popeyed.

"No."

"College girls!" Ski said. "They got no seams, I swear. They're just like them dummies you see in store windows—pretty as can be—but all they got is dimples where they ought to have seams."

I could walk over to Butterfly's hooch right now, Stephen thought. *Maybe I could find a strand of hair from Rebecca's comb, or even the scent of her warm little body. . . .* He wanted to howl, but he didn't know whether to howl with laughter or with sorrow. So he compromised. He did nothing. He just sat there under pressure, like an aerosol can without a label. . . . *Oh damn, damn! Oh sweet goddamn!*

"Sorry about that, Steve," Lieutenant Hamilton said. "About missing Rebecca, I mean."

"Yes," Stephen said.

"She asked for you."

"She did?"

"Yes. She seemed upset about something, I don't know what. I didn't really get a chance to talk to her. Major Barker was on my back all the time."

"Yes," Stephen said, scarcely able to get the word out, with the loneliness clamping at his throat.

Cowboy came into the tent then. He poured a cup of coffee from the pot, sweetened it with sugar and powdered cream, and sat down at the end of the table. "Look at him," Ski grumbled. "He thinks he's a white man." Cowboy had already changed back to his tailored jungle fatigues. From the breast pocket he now took a ballpoint pen, a piece of GI typing paper, and the notebook which had been in the dead rebel's purse.

"Sir," he said to Ski, "my father was from the city of Paris, France."

"Yeah?" Ski said. "What about your mammy?"

"Gook," Cowboy admitted.

"Well, half-gook is all-gook to me," Ski told him. "Anyhow, them Frenchies ain't white men, not really. Americans is white, and Britishers, and I guess even the Germans is white, but not Frenchmen. Hell, no!" Smiling brilliantly, Cowboy planted his elbows on the coffin lid and began to translate. But Ski kept after him. "I don't need no half-gook, half-Frenchman to tell me what's in that notebook," he said. "It says old Charlie is gonna knock us off."

Ackley farted with his lips. "Let 'em try!" he said. "Any American is worth ten gooks, any day."

"Well, well," Ski said gleefully. "Is that a fact? Ten for one, huh?"

"Goddamn right," Ackley said.

"Terrific. So we can handle the first forty men that come over the wall—you, me, Steve, and the lieutenant. Is that what you figure?"

"You bet your ass!"

"Forty men," Ski said. "But there's two hundred guerrillas out there in the puckerbrush, and last night Steve counted another two hundred and fifty coming up."

"We got the Raiders," Ackley said.

"They'll run," Ski said. "When the shit hits the fan, they'll run."

"No, they won't," Stephen said. "I've worked with Old Man for two months, and I trust him."

"Trust? Trust?" Ski twisted his long face, all knobs and splotches. "When you've seen as much war as me, you'll know you can't trust nobody."

"You're scared," Ackley said.

"Well," Stephen said, "I trust Old Man, all the same, and I trust *you,* you old rooster. If we don't trust each other, we might as well pick up our gear and walk away."

"That mightn't be such a bad idea," Ski said.

"You're *scared,*" Ackley said, a wild fright on his face.

Ski stared glumly at the coffin-lid table. "I'm getting old," he said. "I don't want to fight no more. I just want to go to bed with Butterfly and feel that belly of hers, with my kid growing inside. Jesus," he said, "they ain't no feeling in the world like that—your wife's belly with your kid inside."

Ackley slammed the butt of his bayonet against the table. "She ain't your wife!" he cried. "That ain't no marriage!"

"We was married by a priest, for crying out loud."

"But you ain't got no papers. You ain't married without papers, and the Army won't give you papers to marry a squaw woman."

Ski jumped up. So did Ackley.

"Men!" Lieutenant Hamilton said, hunching forward and pressing both hands against his stomach, which growled and squeaked. "Save the fighting for the rebels," he said, but they paid no attention to him. Ski stalked Ackley around the table. Ackley held the butt of the bayonet close to his ribs, just as they had taught him at Fort Darby. But still he backed away.

"Papers?" Ski said, plodding after him with his head lowered, like a weary bull. "What's papers got to do with it, I'd like to know? A marriage is two people living together," he said in a reasonable voice. "It ain't no goddamn scrap of paper . . . IS IT?"

Ackley hurled himself against the rear tent wall, which burst and let him through. Ski went after him, bellowing hoarse, strangled threats.

"Can't you stop them, Steve?" Lieutenant Hamilton said. He was doubled over now, his chin almost touching the coffin lid.

"Hell, let them get it out of their systems."

"But what's wrong with them?"

"Ackley's never been in combat. He's worried about how he'll stand up to it."

"I'm worried, too," the lieutenant said. "Especially with this darned stomach of mine. But that's no reason to shout and swear at people."

"If you shouted more, you mightn't have a bad stomach."

The lieutenant carefully straightened his back. His face was pale, with tiny drops of sweat standing out from the skin. "But what about Ski?" he said. "*He* can't be worried. Why, he . . . he has the Silver Star."

"Ski's in love."

"In love?"

"Yes," Stephen said. "He found a refugee girl along the trail—Just Prime Nooky, he called her—and now he's in love with her. Isn't it the damnedest thing?"

They sat in silence over their coffee cups, while Cowboy's pen squeaked across the paper. Lieutenant Hamilton tugged at his mustache. Finally he said: "Steve?"

"What?"

"If you want to go to Penang—to see Rebecca, I mean—I'll arrange it for you."

"I can't take leave while I'm on garrison duty," Stephen said, his heart pounding.

"No, but I'll arrange it. I'll tell Penang that you have vital information about the rebels, and that I want you to be debriefed by Major Barker himself. I'll ask them to send a helicopter down for you."

Stephen took a deep breath. "Can you spare me?" he asked.

"No," the lieutenant said. "I couldn't run the camp without you, not the way I'm feeling. I don't mean the stomach—I mean the way I feel about everything."

"Then I can't go, can I?" Stephen said, furious that the possibility had been dangled in front of him.

"As far as I'm concerned, you can go."

"And what happens to Muc Wa?"

"I'm not even sure that Muc Wa should exist. Why should I care what happens to it?"

"Well, *I* care," Stephen said.

"All right," the lieutenant said. "I'm glad you're staying, but I wanted to give you the choice."

"I made my choice," Stephen said. "I made my choice every day of the past two months."

Ski came back after a while, blowing hard. "I chased the little bastard into the commo bunker," he said. "Hoo boy! He sure can run. If he fights half as good as he runs, we ain't got a thing to worry about." He refilled his coffee cup and sat down at the table. "How you doing, Cowboy?" he asked.

"All done, sir!" Cowboy said, holding up the sheet of GI typing paper, which was now covered with the loops and flourishes of Cowboy's writing. "All speak in very good English."

"Let's have it, then," Ski said.

"Is there any hard intelligence?" Lieutenant Hamilton asked. "The name of his unit? Numbers? Officers?"

Cowboy pushed his broad-brimmed Raider hat to the back of his head, as he had seen Captain Olivetti do, and began to read in an important voice: "'Today I am named scout to see what the Yankee imperialists are doing by Muc Wa. I am a mouse in the field, seeing all but myself forgotten. Many atomic helicopters come and go. The imperialists are very rich, but they do not belong here in the mountains. With strong arms and brave hearts we will crush them. . . .' This is what he write here, sir," Cowboy said. "Very stupid."

"Atomic helicopters?" Lieutenant Hamilton said. "Why does he say that? Does he think we're violating the Geneva Accords?"

"Well?" Ski said. "Ain't we?"

"Not with atomic devices," the lieutenant told him.

Stephen saw himself as a guerrilla, barefoot and hungry,

hiding in the rain forest while the helicopters came down. He heard their banshee whine, like a high-speed dentist drill.

"He's talking about the jet turbine," Stephen said. "He knows it's different from a gasoline engine, so he thinks it must be powered by . . ." Then it hit him: *This was the man I saw that time, down by the gravesite. That homely scout. Charlie. It was Charlie I killed last night.* ". . . atomic energy," he said, picking up his carbine.

"Where are you going?" the lieutenant asked.

"I'm tired. I think I'll sack out for a while."

"But don't you want to hear this?"

"Later. I'll read it later."

I cut his throat with my bayonet. His blood gushed over my hand, warm as the water of the river.

"All right," the lieutenant said. "But first—would you assign the patrol for tonight?"

"Sure," Stephen said. "Two squads under Ackley. He needs the practice."

"Better make it three squads," Ski said.

"Three squads, then. I'll tell Ackley."

Lieutenant Hamilton nodded, wincing over the pain in his gut, and Stephen went outside. Cowboy's voice followed him through the open tent fly:

"A strange thing. Today I see the Yankees send one of their people to his ancestors. They place him in the ground and plant a stick above him, with another stick across, to keep his ghost from walking. . . ."

Charlie, Stephen thought. *I've killed Charlie. What a lousy rotten break.*

He went to the lister bag, slung from its tripod like a dead pig. There was a sign hanging from the spigot: DRINKING WATER ONLY. Stephen removed the sign and washed his hands. Without soap, the best he could do was push the grime around, but he felt better when it was done. Less bloody. He replaced the sign, climbed the hill again, and went into the commo bunker to see Ackley.

"You're leading the ambush tonight," he said. "Take Corporal Tam and three squads from the second platoon."

"I don't need no Tam," Ackley said.

"Take him anyway." When Stephen's eyes adjusted to the dark of the bunker, he saw that Ackley was drinking from a canteen cup. Toffee's juicing machine was sitting on the counter. "My God," Stephen said. "You too?"

"I just thought I'd give it a try," Ackley said, squirming in his canvas chair. "You know. I mean, shit, the juicer was just sitting there, and . . . You won't tell Ski?"

"I won't say a word," Stephen promised.

Ackley thrust his face close to Stephen's. "D'you notice any difference?" he said.

"Well . . ."

"The pimples—don't you think the pimples are a lot better?" Ackley rolled his eyes, trying to see for himself. "I found this book of Toffee's," he said. "*Add Years to Your Life and Life to Your Years*. It said that skin blemishes, which is pimples, is caused by impurities in—"

"It didn't work for Toffee," Stephen said.

"It didn't?"

"Well, he's dead."

"Yeah!" Ackley said triumphantly. "But he didn't have no pimples, did he?"

Stephen laughed and left the bunker. He walked through the north gate. Here, between the barbed wire and the open field, the refugees had planted a garden. Some of the refugee women were hoeing the ground with pointed sticks. They saluted Stephen with a gesture that was half a wave, half a bow, and he waved back.

He crossed the field to the gravesite. *I'm a damned fool to come here*, he thought. *What if Charlie's replacement is over there, across the river? He could pick me off like a duck in a shooting gallery*. Brambles were growing between the two crosses, Toffee's wooden one and the fine French job with the trefoil arms. Stephen grabbed the stems and uprooted them. Then he went over and sat beneath his accustomed tree, facing the river with his carbine across his knees. *But I love this place, that's the thing,* he thought. *It's the most peaceful place I've found in all of this green world—here where Toffee is buried, and the French soldiers from ten years ago.*

His hand was bleeding. He dug around with his fingernails and extracted a thorn.

Ray gave me a choice, he thought. *I could leave Muc Wa, I could see Rebecca . . . that was the choice Ray gave me. But you can't give a man a choice. He makes his own choices, and he makes them a long time back.*

A breeze came across the river, cooling his face. Clouds boiled above the horizon.

Not even an officer can give a man a choice, he thought.

He heard Ski's raucous voice, bullying the Raiders. They were coming down the slope, a squad of men, looking very alert. Stephen stood up and walked over to meet them.

"We got a pretty good idea where Charlie's hidey-hole is," Ski said when he was within range. "You're the demolitions expert. Whyn't you come along and help us booby-trap it?"

"All right," Stephen said, and turned and marched along with them. "Did that diary tell you anything else?"

"Yeah. Americans got big noses."

"What else?"

Ski hawked, spat, and wiped his mouth with the back of his hand. "That company you seen last night," he said. "That was part of the 507th Battalion."

"Who are they?"

"Well, if you travel from here to Penang by road, you'll see some French armored cars, all rusting and blown to hell, and a little stone marker by the road. They call it Ambush Alley now. A French convoy was coming down that road, a thousand men, and they got zapped by the 507th Battalion. Real tough boys. They ain't no farmers, like the rebels we been fighting up to now."

"So we're in for a siege?"

"That's right," Ski said. "That's ab-so-lutely right. I tell you, Steve, it's gonna be Loc Gia all over again. Some damned little gook major, in a tunnel someplace, just pointed to Muc Wa on the map and said: Zap 'em. So we're gonna get zapped."

"Maybe."

"No maybes. Nothing stops old Charlie Romeo once he gets his hind leg planted. He'll knock us off if it costs him every man of the 507th. And I don't want to get knocked off, Steve. I'm a married man now."

"I'm sorry, Ski."

"Yeah," Ski said. "Sorry about that! It's the story of my life—up to the Yalu, down to Pusan—sorry about that, Sergeant Oleonowski. But I was a young soldier then. I was full of piss and vinegar, just like you."

Just like me, Stephen thought.

They crossed the river and began to beat the tall grass on the other side, looking for Charlie's hidey-hole.

I couldn't leave Ski, Stephen thought, *or Ray or Corporal Old Man. I couldn't leave Muc Wa. Not now. Not after I have killed for it.*

Seventeen

The general flew back to Thaitan on Thursday, taking his five aides and Miss Shaw with him, and leaving behind him the Incident-Flow Priority Indicator.

"Sir?" said the new clerk-typist, Ackley's replacement, peering earnestly through his glasses. "Where do you want it, sir?"

"On the wall," Major Barker said. "Where the hell else would I want it?"

"Sir, there's no room on the wall."

"Well, make room," the major told him.

So the clerk-typist mounted his Priority Indicator above the door, which turned out to be the worst spot in the office. Whenever Major Barker laced his fingers behind his neck, planted his boots on the desk, and *leaned* back—ahhh!—to relax for a minute, there it was, that goddamned Incident-Flow Priority Indicator, reminding him of the outposts that needed his attention. And it was the last thing he saw when he closed the office at seventeen hundred hours. The names of the beleaguered outposts haunted Major Barker at the officers' club, and followed him into his dreams at night.

The Priority Indicator had been invented by Lieutenant Schlitz or somebody, while the senior officers were at Muc Wa. It contained three square panels, painted glossy shades of red, orange, and yellow, which caught the light and reflected it into Major Barker's eyes. Each panel was equipped with a pair of metal brackets. The clerk-typist, who had been briefed by Lieutenant Schlitz or whoever it was, inserted the names of three outposts into these brackets. But that wasn't the end of it. From time to time, smiling like a girl with a new engagement ring, the clerk-typist came in and switched the names around, or replaced one of them with a new one.

"The Incident-Flow ratio at Mung Tau is up to thirty-nine point six," he said, or something similar.

"Oh, clear off," the major said.

The new clerk-typist was a tall, thin private first class with a triangular face and a gigantic pair of spectacles, the kind with brown-black frames and little silver doohickeys beside the hinges. Fruit glasses, the major called them.

"Whoever heard of a Raider wearing glasses?" he complained to Captain Olivetti. "What's this Army coming to, anyway?"

"He's a psychological warfare specialist," Captain Olivetti said. "The Table of Organization requires one in each Y Team. There was a directive from Thaitan about it the other week."

"Psywar, spywar," the major said. "I don't care what he is, as long as he can type. I just wish he'd leave that damned thing alone."

There were two things about the Incident-Flow Priority Indicator that bugged Major Barker, apart from the fact that the glare from it bothered his eyes.

For one thing, he didn't understand it. The clerk-typist spent hours sifting reports of attacks, patrols, ambushes, casualties, desertions, and God knew what else; then he assigned number values to them and entered them on his Incident-Flow Chart. From this, in some mysterious fashion, came the names which were mounted on the Priority Indicator in Major Barker's office.

The second thing that bugged Major Barker was the fact that Muc Wa was Condition Yellow, making it the number-three trouble spot in his entire command.

"How can that be?" he said. "Muc Wa is nowhere."

"Yes, sir," Captain Olivetti said.

"Muc Wa doesn't help us, so how can it be hurting Charlie? How come he's trying to knock it off?"

"I don't know, sir."

"Boo Jum is Condition Orange. Mung Tau is Condition Red. Okay. I don't need any damned spywar expert to tell me *they're* in trouble." Boo Jum and Mung Tau were outposts near the border. Half the time Major Barker didn't know whether they were garrisoned by his men or by the rebels. "But Muc Wa! What's Muc Wa doing up there in Condition Yellow?"

"Why don't you ask what's-his-face?" Captain Olivetti asked, jerking his thumb at the door, beyond which the clerk-typist was pecking slowly at a typewriter.

"I did," the major said. "He just fed me this crap about parables and ratios and medium averages until it was coming out my ears." He leaned back and studied the names on the Priority Indicator—Mung Tau, Boo Jum, and Muc Wa. They were lettered in block capitals which slanted a bit to the right, very bold and self-assured. *In his heart,* the major thought, *that bespectacled fruit is the Secretary of Defense.* "What I ought to do," he said, "is send him to Muc Wa. Let him show his Condition Yellow to the rebels."

"Yes, sir," Captain Olivetti said.

The major stood up and went over to his model of the garrison at Muc Wa. *What's-his-face will be Secretary of Defense, and Lieutenant Schlitz will be his Chief of Staff. But I'll be dead by then, with luck. . . . I was kneeling right there,* he thought, moving one of the toy soldiers to a point on the east wall, midway between the gate and the southeast machinegun post. *God, that was fun! I just wish I'd known at the time that it was real.* He moved another toy soldier, a rifleman. *Lieutenant Hamilton was with me. Ackley and the general were over there. Al was . . .* "Where the hell were you, that night at Muc Wa?" he asked.

"Sir?"

"Where were you during the scrap?"

"Well, I was here and there. I was moving around, actually."

"That was a great night, wasn't it?"

"I've had better," Captain Olivetti said.

"God!" the major said, looking at the toy soldiers who were manning the defenses of Muc Wa. "I just wish I'd known it was for real."

Ackley enjoyed his first ambush so much that they let him take out another, Friday night. The patrol limped home at eight o'clock next morning. The Raiders were carrying two dead men, lashed to poles, and seven more were wounded. One man had been shot through the belly. He was making short, barking noises, like a Siamese cat. The other Raiders were embarrassed; they kept touching the wounded man, gently, then looking away.

"We got hit on the way back," Ackley said, jubilant and scared by turns. "We ran into a muh-muh-*machinegun*," he said, his teeth chattering. Then he grinned. "We blew it up. With grenades. Just like they showed us at Fort Darby. Boy, I bet Charlie's sorry he messed with *me*."

"You took damn near thirty per cent casualties," Ski said. "What did you do to Charlie?"

"Lay off, Ski," Stephen said. "Anybody can make a mistake."

"When you go out to set an ambush, there's one mistake you *don't* make," Ski said, spitting. "You don't get ambushed on the way home."

"Aw, Ski!" Ackley said, his teeth chattering again.

"Go to bed," Stephen advised him. "You can tell us about it later." He began to help Ski with the wounded men. They left the gut-shot Raider to the last, because they were afraid there was nothing they could do for him, and they were right. "From now on," Stephen said, "we'd better not move around at night with less than a platoon. Three squads aren't enough."

"The whole damn company ain't enough," Ski said, his hands stained with blood up to the knobby wrists. "Charlie's putting the pressure on."

Two days later it was Stephen's turn. He was across the river with the third platoon, clearing brush, when a sniper began pecking at them from the rain forest. They went in after him, and Charlie closed the gate behind them. Slam! Bang! Stephen found himself on the spongy forest floor with bullets zinging every which way, and the Raiders showing the whites of their eyes like scared horses. Charlie was stitching the area with two Browning automatic rifles—*whuk-whuk-whuk-whuk!*—and old reliable M-1 Garands, pride of the Springfield Arsenal. Goddamn! And the Raiders had nothing but their dinky little carbines.

I could have been in Penang this minute, Stephen thought, rolling behind a tree. *I could have been in Penang with Rebecca.* Something like a hornet bit him on the left shoulder, but he was too busy to swat it: flash of khaki between the trees. *There!* He fired, saw a man tumble to the ground, saw him roll over and struggle with his rifle. Stephen put two more bullets into him. *Jesus!* he thought, looking for something else to shoot at. *Men are sure hard to kill.* He fired a couple rounds at the nearest BAR, although he couldn't see it. The carbine jumped with every beat of his heart. *If I had any goddamn sense at all, I'd be safe in Penang with Rebecca.*

Ski came to the rescue, like the U. S. Cavalry, galloping through the rain forest and bawling at the top of his voice, while the fourth platoon skipped along somewhat nervously behind him. Charlie's men melted away.

"Was that a BAR I heard?" Ski said.

"Two of them."

"And M-1s?"

"I think so."

"Congratulations," Ski said. "That was the 507th Battalion

you just tangled ass holes with. Guerrillas don't carry no BARs."

"Yes," Stephen said, and brought his hand away from his neck. The palm was smeared with blood. "Oh, shit," he said. "I'm shot."

"Just a scratch," Ski said cheerfully, poking at the wound with his finger. "Two inches to the right, though, and you'd be one dead Raider. . . . Let's go back to camp before Charlie decides he ain't so scared as he thought he was."

Stephen found himself trembling at odd moments throughout the day. Two inches to the right! A man's life was all that he possessed, and two inches was less than the width of his hand.

If you toss a coin often enough, he thought, *sooner or later it's bound to come up tails.*

Next morning, their present-for-duty strength was one hundred and thirty-four men.

"We ain't doing so good," Ski said, looking at his duty roster. "We picked up egg-zactly five recruits since we been here, and we lost six men killed and one man deserted, not to mention ten men absent-wounded and three men absent-sick."

"Are you carrying the lieutenant as sick?"

"Yeah. Thought maybe we could get you a field commission."

"No, thanks," Stephen said. "I've got all I can handle, just being a corporal."

He went outside the command post and looked around the camp—his camp. The Raiders were marching off in squads and platoons, some to clear brush from the field across the river, others to patrol the rain forest. . . . The forest seemed closer today, somehow. The tree trunks were thick as Roman soldiers; the foliage was like a roof of broad green shields, overlapping, protecting the legion as it advanced upon Muc Wa. . . . Stephen shivered. *Two inches to the right and you'd be one dead Raider!*

He would have liked to go down to the gravesite, to sit in the sun and think about Rebecca, but it wasn't safe. His aching shoulder told him it wasn't safe.

Charlie attacked that night. It was a dull, stolid, careful attack, and when Stephen led a platoon through the east gate to take the pressure off, Charlie was waiting. The Raiders staggered and fell. The first one down was Corporal Old Man; then two more, then others uncounted. Stephen got his Raiders across the river, but then they dove under the shelter of the opposite bank and would not move. Poor bastards; he didn't blame them. So he took them back, and saw two more of them fall and vanish into the warm black water. The Raiders bolted as soon as they were safely across. They ran for the gate, and some were thrown against the barbed wire and caught, and died there when Charlie got the range. Stephen grabbed one man and turned him around. Private Bung. Together they searched for Old Man, found him, and dragged him through the gate. He was still alive, thank God.

"Thank you, Bung," Stephen said, and then to Ski, who had run up to them, a shocked look on his face: "Tell Ackley to radio for a flare ship. And a couple armed helicopters if he can get them."

Major Barker and Captain Olivetti were returning from the officers' club when they saw the flares. They parked the jeep and got out, bumping into each other in the vicinity of the tailgate; then they sheared off and went separate ways in the darkness. They came together again on the height-of-land between the schoolhouse and the commo shack. A couple of enlisted men saw them, saw that they were drunk, and scuttled away into the night.

"Some poor bastard is really getting it," Major Barker said, watching the flares drift down. He couldn't see the flare ship, of course, just the bright stars as they were born in the southeast sky and fell slowly to earth, casting a gray light on the clouds as they fell. "Some poor bastard . . ."

"Muc Wa," Captain Olivetti said.

"No!"

"Yes," Captain Olivetti said. "Don't I know? Didn't I walk there on these two goddamned feet?"

"I know, Al," the major said, reaching up to pat his executive officer on the shoulder. "I know you did."

"Well, it *is* Muc Wa."

"I know it is, Al."

"You said it wasn't."

"Who else?" the major said. "Who else but those bastards at Muc Wa?"

"Lieutenant Hamilton."

"College girl! Drank river water and got the runs."

"Corporal Courcey."

"*That* homely bastard!"

"Sergeant Oleonowski."

"Ski's got the Silver Star," the major pointed out.

"Ski's a good man," the captain agreed. "Ackley . . ."

"God!" the major said.

Friends again, they walked to the schoolhouse, where the office lights were burning uncertainly. Major Barker's office was lighted, too. He tried the door, hit an obstruction of some sort, and threw his shoulder against it. "Yow!" cried a voice from inside. Then a crash which seemed to go on forever, like the noise of Fibber McGee opening his closet door, those nights on radio when the major was a boy.

They went inside. The new clerk-typist was sprawled upon the model of Muc Wa, his head by the command post and his boots crushing the refugee camp. The model was on the floor, its legs having collapsed. There was an overturned chair nearby. "What the hell are you doing in my office?" the major thundered, just to keep the clerk-typist on the defensive. An enlisted man should never get the idea that his commanding officer owed him an apology. Otherwise, what would happen to discipline?

What's-his-face sat up and groped through the wreckage of

Muc Wa. "Please, sir," he said, "you don't see my glasses anywhere, do you?" Then he found them in the river. "I was posting the Priority Indicator when you came in, sir," he said, standing up and dusting a few pieces of the command post from his shoulder.

Major Barker reconstructed the accident: the clerk-typist standing on the chair, the door opening . . . "Jackass," he said, and looked up at the Incident-Flow Priority Indicator. Muc Wa had replaced Boo Jum in the center panel, and was now Condition Orange.

"Corporal Ackley called in two hours ago," the clerk-typist said. His spectacles were lopsided, giving him the look of an owl who had just been hit by an automobile. "The signals are on your desk, sir. Muc Wa is under attack by a force estimated at five hundred men, and that, plus a skirmish yesterday afternoon, gives it an Incident-Flow Rating of thirty-two point nine, so I thought you'd want me to make the change on the Priority Indicator. And I called the Air Force liaison office in Penang; I thought—"

"Oh, clear off," the major said.

"Yeah," said Captain Olivetti. "Let us do the thinking. That's what we're paid for."

When what's-his-face was gone, Major Barker sat down at his desk with his chin in his hands. He was burdened with that tired, defeated feeling which comes from sobering off too quickly and too soon. He looked at the wreckage of his model garrison. "That was a piece of bad luck," he said.

"Couldn't be helped," said Captain Olivetti, who remained on his feet. He was swaying slightly, looking at the wrecked garrison with unfocused eyes.

The major drummed his fingers on the desk. There was only one cure for this kind of hangover. Action! "All right," he said. "I don't know why Charlie wants Muc Wa so bad, but he's damned well not going to get it. . . . Al?"

"Sir?"

"Draw up a contingency plan for reinforcing Muc Wa."

Captain Olivetti lurched and almost fell. "But, sir," he said. "Muc Wa is a waste of time."

"Couldn't be, or Charlie wouldn't be committing five hundred men to knock it off."

"Well . . ."

"*Five hundred men,* Al!" Major Barker cracked his knuckles. "Think of it! Charlie's throwing a whole battalion against Muc Wa—would he be doing that if it wasn't important to him?"

"Well, sir, maybe he's thinking the same thing. Maybe he's throwing men in there because he thinks it's important to us."

"Nonsense!" the major said. "Charlie wouldn't be such a damn fool as that, now would he?"

"I guess not," Captain Olivetti said.

"No, goddammit! I want that place reinforced—trucks, helicopters, artillery." The major stood up, feeling better already. "Get on the hook, Al," he said. "See what we need, see what we've got, and see how fast we can get it there."

Captain Olivetti groped for the overturned chair, righted it, and sat down. "Yes, sir," he said.

Eighteen

Charlie broke off at dawn, but he didn't go very far. He hunkered out there in the rain forest and lobbed mortar shells at the camp. A shell came over every fifteen minutes or so: a flurry of air like birds exploding into flight, giving each man time to freeze or shrink into himself or drop to the ground, depending on his mood, then WHUMP-SOCK!—his ear-drums popped and his bones trembled with the earth.

"It's Loc Gia all over again," Ski said, his eyes flaming red. "It ain't fair that a man has to go through this, twice in one lifetime."

Ski hit the ground when he heard a shell coming over, while Stephen and Ackley were the freezing type. This was a nasty business. A man's face would congeal upon the expression he had just been wearing, his eyes slipped out of focus, his blood turned to slush in his veins. WHUMP-SOCK! He was better off when he came out of his trance, however. He was still standing on his feet.

"Lookit old Ski!" Ackley jeered. "He's so tuckered out he just lays down and takes himself a nap, every time one of them dinky little shells comes over. . . . Hey, Ski!"

"What?" Ski said sourly, getting up and dusting his knees and elbows.

"You want a shot of vegetable juice, to keep you awake?"

"Gor!" Ski cried. "I'll juice *you,* you little—"

Stephen jumped in between them. "We've got work to do," he said, and Ackley moved off to a safe distance, haw-hawing to himself. "He's only nineteen," Stephen added.

"Yeah?" Ski said. "Well, he's gonna be a regular comedian by the time he gets to be twenty. If he lives that long."

The worst thing about Ackley was that he didn't seem to understand the fix they were in. At sunrise Stephen had counted one hundred and fifteen men on the wall. Charlie had maybe four times as many, hunkering out there in the rain forest with nothing to do but drop an occasional mortar shell into Muc Wa, resting up for tonight. It was not a promising situation. It was positively hairy, in fact. But Ackley was having a ball: he swaggered around the camp with his carbine muzzle-down, like Dan'l Boone, and hand grenades dangling from his belt.

"Wait'll tonight!" he boasted. "I'm gonna tie a knot in old Charlie's tail, tonight."

Stephen kept all the able-bodied Raiders on the wall, paired off, with one man sleeping and the next man awake. They were safer there, anyway, since most of Charlie's shells were landing in the center of the camp. The walking wounded were assigned as hospital orderlies. The refugees handled all the heavy jobs—hauling ammunition, filling sandbags, putting out fires—under Corporal Old Man's command. Old Man's head was wrapped in a turban of bandages, and he was somewhat given to fits of bewilderment, in which he would plop down on his butt and stare at nothing with a fierce expression. He was possessed by spirits, Cowboy explained. But Ski, who had been studying Toffee's medical manuals, had a different opinion.

"Old Man's got a concussion," he said with a long face. "Lieutenant Hamilton is half dead with dysentery. We got two men gut-shot, so's I can't do nothing for 'em, and more compound fractures than I know what to do with. *She*-it," he said, rubbing his jaw with a sound like a hacksaw cutting metal. "We got to have a med-evac."

"Will helicopters land here, with mortar shells coming in like this?"

"American pilots will, if it's an American that needs evacuating."

"All right," Stephen said. "We'll tell them Lieutenant Hamilton has to go out. They can't send less than two helicopters, so we ought to be able to put four or five Raiders on board, too."

"That's the ticket," Ski said.

"What do we need for supplies?"

"Bodies," Ski said. "Tell 'em we don't care what kind of bodies, just so long as they got one eye to see with and one finger to pull a trigger. . . . Yeah, and tell 'em to send us some man-sized rifles, too, because sooner or later Charlie is gonna come over that wall, and this here war is gonna be settled with bayonets."

Stephen walked over to the commo bunker and dictated the message to Ackley. The bunker was dark, damp, smelling of earth. "Keep sending that until you get a confirmation," Stephen said.

"It sounds like we're yelling for help."

"We are."

"Hell," Ackley whined, "we don't need no help."

"Send it," Stephen told him. "Then get some sleep if you can, because it's going to be a long night."

He went outside, his shoulder aching bitterly where the bullet had grazed it, reminding him of his mortality. *I'd like to go down to the gravesite,* he thought, *but it's not safe any more. Charlie can come and go as he likes out there, and he can move right up to the gates at night. We've lost control.* He turned toward the command post, meaning to go in and say hello to the lieutenant, but then!—that god-awful flurry of wings. *Sweet Jesus not on me . . .* WHUMP! Something picked him up and slammed him to the ground. SOCK!

Rebecca's arm was around his neck, supporting him. *She has such beautiful arms,* he thought. *So warm and smooth. She must know it, too, because she wears sleeveless dresses whenever she can.* But no: the girl was Butterfly. She was holding a bowl of hot rice soup to his lips with her free hand, and giggling. The sun had moved in the sky. *Was I knocked out,* he thought, *or did I fall asleep? God! I'm getting punchy.* He drank the soup, his head cradled wonderfully in the hollow between Butterfly's arm and her breast.

"Thank you," he said then.

"Well-come," Butterfly said.

He felt better toward sundown, and he walked around the perimeter to prove it. The Raiders were watching the sunset, trying to hold it back. The light turned their faces to bronze. Whenever Stephen stopped beside one of the Raiders, the burnished face smiled up at him, not giving comfort but asking it. *Poor bastard,* Stephen thought, *you'll earn your pay this month.* He smiled back until he thought his cheeks would split.

Then it was dark, and the mortars cracked down on them. Muc Wa flamed and trembled. Stephen knelt close to the wall, at the point where he found himself when the barrage began, and gulped for air between concussions. *All right, Charlie,* he thought. *All right.* He pressed his face against the steel of his carbine until he could feel the pain. *This is the worst you can do, you son of a bitch, and I'm still alive.* He stood up, seeming to lift the entire garrison upon his shoulders. *Still alive.* He ran to the nearest mortar position, and dragged and kicked the Raiders into action, to get the star-shells up. Then he ran on to the next mortar. It was gone, wiped out, with a single leg of the tripod still slanting toward the sky.

He met Ski at the third mortar position. The Raiders were already dropping explosive rounds into the tube, while star-shells were bursting green-white across the river. "Charlie'll try to swamp us before the flare ship gets here," Ski yelled into Stephen's ear. "Ackley's on the radio now." Stephen nodded. They could have accomplished more by splitting up, but Ski didn't suggest it, so they went on together to check the machinegun bunkers.

They were in the southwest bunker when the first wave came out of the rain forest—fifty or sixty men, running with nervous, mincing steps across the field. *Jesus!* Stephen thought. *They're sure in a hurry to die.* The rebels crossed the ghost road, running dreamlike toward the west gate. *If Charlie can afford to throw away a whole platoon, just like that, he's got us by the balls.*

"Shoot!" Ski bawled at the gunners. "SHOOT, goddammit!" They fired, and Stephen clapped his hands over his ears. His teeth ached from the noise.

Another line of men had emerged from the rain forest, dressed in floppy black pajamas like the first wave, but carrying no weapons. They would scavenge rifles from the dead.

"What'd'you think?" Ski yelled.

"A hundred men," Stephen yelled back. "Charlie's going for broke."

"Yeah! Let's pull some men off the other walls."

Stephen scrambled through the tunnel after him. They were halfway around the camp, sending a squad from each platoon to the west wall, when the machineguns quit firing.

"Charlie's in the barbed wire," Stephen said.

"Yeah. Maybe he's through already."

They picked up another squad and ran to the west gate. The black pajamas had broken through. Ackley was already there, grunting and yelping and swinging his carbine like a sickle. Stephen jumped in beside him—it seemed like the safest place. Ski thought so, too, because there he was on Ackley's other side. They formed a flying wedge to push Charlie back upon the barbed wire.

A bayonet lunged at Stephen's eyes, with a bucktoothed, terrified face behind it; he smashed at the face with the butt of his carbine, and felt the bones shatter, and vomit trickled into his mouth. The machineguns were hammering again—

more men charging the wall. Then he heard the drone of airplane engines, and the worried flutter of helicopters.

"Get on the radio!" he shouted to Ackley, who only yelped and continued to swing his carbine. "*Move*, damn you!" But Ackley did not hear. His upper lip was sunk into his gums, so that his teeth seemed to be growing on the outside of his face; the whites showed clearly all around his eyes, and those mad-dog yelps kept leaping from his throat. Stephen broke out of the fight and ran to the commo bunker, where he raised the helicopter pilot on the handset radio.

"Hello, Blaze!" a cheerful voice crackled in the earphone. "This is Black Knight Five, Black Knight Five. I say: how you doing, boy, over?"

"This is Blaze," Stephen said, taking the radio outside and locating the helicopters by their flashing red navigation lights. "Charlie is on your three o'clock position."

"I see him, I see him," the pilot said, and Stephen heard the thunder of fifty-caliber machineguns on the radio before he saw the tracers pouring down, a searing red stream which wavered and steadied as the gunners found their target.

"Who's driving you, sir?" Captain Olivetti asked.

"What's-his-face," the major said.

"D'you want me to come?"

"No," the major said. "If I take an aide, Major Minh will want two aides, and then we'll sit up all night, drinking that rotgut of his." He shuddered, remembering the walking death that was a hangover in this country. "Anyhow, somebody ought to stick around and monitor the reports from Muc Wa."

Major Barker was wearing his best khaki uniform, with blouse and tie, hoping that his elegance would not cause Major Minh to lose face. These damned Orientals spent more time saving face than they did soldiering. Just to be on the safe side, Major Barker loosened the knot in his tie, so that he could quickly take it off if the province chief happened to be wearing fatigues. Then he walked over to the schoolhouse with Captain Olivetti. Across the mountains to the southeast, the flares were drifting down upon Muc Wa like burning fingers, pointing to the source of all his troubles.

In the schoolhouse they found what's-his-face on a chair in the major's office. He jumped down when he heard them coming, as if suspecting they would pitch him into the model table again if they had the chance. "It's Muc Wa, sir," he said, starting to salute but breaking it off halfway.

"Condition Red?"

"Yes, sir. The Incident-Flow Chart—"

"I'll take your word for it," the major told him.

Captain Olivetti stared up at the Priority Indicator, where Muc Wa had just moved into the place of honor, replacing Mung Tau on Condition Red. "Yep," he said. "Charlie's digging in for a siege."

"That's what I told you last night," Major Barker said. "This could go on for three or four days—a week, maybe."

"If Muc Wa can hold out that long."

Captain Olivetti made a mitt of his left hand, and punched his fist into it. "Sir?" he said then. "The qualifications for the CIB—has there been any change lately, do you know?"

"I haven't heard of any," the major said.

"It's still three consecutive days under enemy fire?"

"I believe so, Al."

"Well, well," the captain said, studying the partly restored model of Muc Wa. "Well, well, well."

Major Barker left him there, punching his palm. The major drove down the hill and through the outskirts of Penang, where kerosene lamps were sparkling in the night. Two blocks from the province chief's office, he stopped and changed places with what's-his-face. The clerk-typist drove him the rest of the way. There was a new directive from Thaitan, forbidding field-grade officers to appear in public without an enlisted driver, in order to maintain the dignity of the U. S. Advisory Command.

"Wait here," Major Barker said.

"Yes, sir," the clerk-typist said unhappily, cradling his carbine in his arms, and eyeballing the street in search of rebel terrorists.

A Chinese woman greeted the major at the door. She wore her hair in a bun, to show that she was no longer interested in men, or they in her. She had been the province chief's mistress until recently. Then he had picked something younger and sweeter from the refugees flowing into Penang.

"Major!"

"Major!"

They shook hands warmly, like brothers, while Major Barker reflected that he had been screwed again. Major Minh was flanked by not one but three aides. And he was wearing dress blues, which he must have picked up while attending Army school in the States. Sweat was rolling down his full-moon face. He was very happy.

Major Barker was drawn gently but firmly to the table, where a cloudy glass was waiting for him. One of the aides, a captain, slopped liquor into the glass from a bottle labeled Three Roses, and, in smaller letters, SAME AS U.S.A. They stood shoulders touching around the table, which was no more than two feet square. Major Barker realized that he should propose a toast. "To the Premier!" he said, forgetting which general was now in power in Thaitan. They drank, and the captain filled the glasses again.

"To the President of U.S. of A.!" Major Minh said then. They drank.

"To the Army of the Republic!" Major Barker said.

"To the U. S. Advice Command!"

"To your health, Major Minh!"

"To you likewise, Major Barker!"

This toast emptied the bottle, fortunately, and Major Barker melted into his chair. A plate appeared in front of him, filled with rice and greens and small cubes of black, nameless meat. He stirred the mess with his chopsticks, trying to bring something tasty to the surface, until the captain reached over and took the chopsticks away. "Fuck," he said, beaming at the major.

"What's that?"

The captain pressed a fork into the major's hand. "Number-one fuck," the captain assured him, pointing to the words embossed on the handle: U. S. NAVY.

"I'll use the chopsticks, thanks," Major Barker said.

"Fuck."

"But I *like* chopsticks."

"We have fuck for you," the captain said, and sat back, very pleased with himself.

So Major Barker used the fork. He lifted a cube of meat to his mouth, tasted it, and found it rather dry and tough. Dog, most likely. The fried rice grated alarmingly between his teeth. But the greens were good; Major Barker devoured the greens, trying not to remember that the fields on the hill were manured with scrapings from the Raiders' latrine. "Good greens," he told Major Minh, who nodded and seemed to expect more, so Major Barker said, "Good rice," and finally, despairingly, "Good meat." Then he slapped his belly to indicate that it had been troubling him lately, and therefore he was eating less than he would have liked.

After the meal Major Minh inquired the health of Major Barker's wife and children, his superior in Thaitan, and the President of the United States. Major Barker said they were all well, as far as he knew. Then they got down to business.

"It's Muc Wa, Major," Major Barker said.

"Yes," the province chief said.

"We need artillery support so we can bring in a relief column."

"Yes."

"The Raiders have no artillery, and the Marine howitzers are tied up with Operation Blackjack."

"Yes."

"But *you* have artillery, Major Minh," he said, sweating with excitement. He had trapped the province chief in the best Oriental manner. But Major Minh extended his hands, knuckles up, and moved them like a man parting a veil. It was a denial of some sort, but Major Barker was too foggy to decipher it. "We could provide the gunners," he said experimentally. The province chief looked hurt. "We'd prefer to use yours, of course," Major Barker said, "and naturally we'd supply the ammo." The province chief smiled. "Yes, yes," Major Barker said, "the X Team in Thaitan can send us five hundred rounds by air transport, and a thousand rounds by truck convoy."

Major Minh was glowing like the full moon in springtime. "Truck convoy take four-five days," he pointed out.

"Yes," Major Barker said.

"May get here too late."

"That's true," Major Barker said.

"In such a case, your Axe Team would desire the return of the ammo?"

"Absolutely not!" Major Barker said. "The U. S. Army doesn't give with one hand and take away with the other. Why, I don't think we *have* any forms to get things back."

The province chief spoke in dialect to the captain, who went to the kitchen and returned with another bottle of Three Roses. Major Barker winced. *God,* he thought, *I hope those bastards at Muc Wa appreciate what I'm going through for them.* "To your artillery, Major!" he said when the glasses were full. They drank.

"To your ammo, Major!" the province chief said, and they drank again. Then Major Minh leaned confidentially across the table. "It is the coups, Major," he said. "The corps commander takes all my shells away from me so he can overthrow the Premier, that funny man with the beard. Then the corps commander becomes the Premier. But he does not give us the ammo back, because he fears to be overthrown himself."

"I see," Major Barker said.

"But is not to worry!" Major Minh said. "The Air Force will throw him over with their planes, and then we will all have ammo again."

"I see," Major Barker said.

"It is politics."

"Yes."

"Now you understand me," Major Minh said. "But I do not understand this business of Muc Wa. It is a useless place."

"Yes."

"Why do you have a garrison there?"

Major Barker shrugged. "Orders from Thaitan," he said.

"Ah!—politics."

"No, no," Major Barker said. "We don't have politics in the U. S. Army."

"You do not desire this garrison, but your Axe Team tells you to build it, so you build it?"

"Well—yes."

"It is politics."

"You don't understand, Major."

"Yes, Major, I understand. It is politics. This I understand." Major Minh lifted his glass and beamed across the table. "To politics!" he said.

Cowboy was prowling like a hyena among the black pajamas, trying to find one that moved. He was not having much luck. He cursed the dead men bitterly in their own language, and prodded suspicious ones with the point of his bayonet.

"Corporal Ackley kill them all," he complained to Stephen.

"Where were you when Charlie broke through the wall?" Stephen asked.

Cowboy stood tall. "Sir!" he said. "I am the interpreter, no soldier!"

Stephen found himself looking for the smashed-in face of the man he had killed. *Three men,* he thought. *I've killed at least three men, and each time it gets worse. I damn near lost my dinner over this one.* But he did not see the face he had clobbered.

He met Ski at the wall, surveying the ruin Charlie's men had made of it before they died. "We'll fix it in the morning," Stephen told him. "Why don't you go to bed?"

"It won't be as strong as it was before."

"Neither will Charlie," Stephen said. "Get some sleep, Ski. Nothing more will happen tonight."

They walked together as far as the mess hall. The helicopters and the flare ship had departed, leaving an aching hole in the sky; occasionally this hole was filled with the rustle of a mortar shell, but they were too groggy to care. Ski plodded on toward his hooch. Stephen went into the mess hall, where Ackley and Corporal Old Man were tending the wounded. Ackley looked green around the mouth. He was going from table to table, shooting morphine into arms and legs. Old Man followed him with a saucepan swimming with herbs, from which he ladled a gray, steaming liquid into the Raiders' mouths. When they found a dead man, they shifted him to the floor. The Raiders were about equally divided now, a dozen men on the tables and a dozen beneath. Among the living, Stephen recognized Private Bung and another man from the third platoon, his favorite. He went over to say hello and to check their bandages. After a while Ski came in. "I thought you went to bed?" Stephen said.

"I did," Ski said. He drew a cup of coffee from the urn, lighted a cigarette at the chimney of the kerosene lantern, and sat down at an empty table. "Butterfly's got hot pants, with all this shooting and killing," he explained. "I'm too tired to make love tonight. I'd rather stay up and fight."

"Drink some vegetable juice," Ackley told him. "*That'll* put the lead back in your pencil."

"What the hell?" Ski said, shifting along the bench.

"Did you see me zap them gooks?" Ackley said. "We'd all be buzzard bait now if it wasn't for me and that vegetable juice."

"You're a tiger, all right," Ski said. "What the hell is under this table?"

"Corporal Tam," Old Man said. "Second platoon."

Ski jumped up, spilling his coffee. He stepped back a few paces and peered under the table. "It's Tam, all right," he said. "What's he doing under my table?"

"Him dead," Old Man said.

"So he is," Ski said, still hunkered down with his hands planted on his knees, peering into the gloom beneath the table. "I don't mind fighting," he said in a weary voice. "But the shit a man has to put up with, *between* fights, that's what bothers me." Then he slung his carbine and went outside.

At four o'clock Charlie probed the south wall, but he lost his nerve when the machineguns opened up. Half an hour later the mortarmen filled the sky with star-shells and caught the rebels flat-footed, scavenging weapons and bodies from the field. Then it was morning. The Raiders built twig fires and cooked their rice, chattering happily in the buttermilk-yellow dawn.

"The men seem to be in good spirits," Lieutenant Hamilton said when they carried him out to the landing strip, using his coffin as a stretcher.

"Sure they're in good spirits," Ski said. "They're alive, ain't they?"

Stephen sat on the foot of the coffin while they waited for the helicopter. The lieutenant's face was thin as a hatchet against the olive-green pillow; his mustache, though, was glossy and fat. Automatically his fingers crept up to stroke it, brushing it down toward the corners of his mouth.

"I'm sorry," he said.

"Nothing to be sorry about," Stephen said.

"I got you into this mess, and I can't do anything to help you out of it."

"We'll manage."

The lieutenant nodded. "I know you will," he said. "That bothers me most of all." He turned his head and coughed. Then he said, still facing the quilted side wall: "Do you remember what you told me, one time? About doing a thing well—that doing it well made all the difference?"

"Yes," Stephen said. He should be down there on the wall, patching up the damage from last night, instead of nattering here with the lieutenant. But the poor guy needed some kind of a send-off.

Ray was shaking his head. "No," he said. "That's not enough, to do the thing well. What you're doing has to be worthwhile."

"If you're talking about Muc Wa—I *made* it worthwhile, by working my ass off for it."

"That's true, you did. You're a good man, Steve."

"Oh, crap," Stephen said.

Ackley came running down from the knoll, carrying a handset radio. He pointed to the northwest. Before he could speak, the rain forest exploded with the hysterical, fluttering noise of helicopters. Then the bottle-green machines came into sight, two of them, roaring down upon Muc Wa at treetop level.

"If you see Rebecca," Stephen said, standing up, "tell her—"

"Yes. I'll tell her."

"—that I love her."

"Yes, I will." The lieutenant laughed, but ended by coughing against the side wall of the coffin. "Didn't you ever tell her yourself?"

"Sure I did."

"But did you *show* her?" Ray asked. "A girl likes to be shown that, you know, that you need her."

"I—"

The helicopters were landing now, whipping twigs and dry grass across the slope. Stephen was torn between the question his old friend had asked, and the need to see that the choppers were unloaded.

"I thought I did everything right," he said, "but I guess something was missing."

Then he stepped aside and signaled the Raiders to pick up the coffin. While they were carrying it to the nearest helicopter, he jumped aboard and helped the crewmen unload the crates of ammunition and rifles—fat, ugly M-1s, with the kick of a mule and just as hardy. "Hoo boy!" Ski cried when he saw the rifles. He pulled an M-1 from its crate and kissed it. "Gor!" he said. "I feel like a soldier again."

Stephen jumped down. "So long, Ray," he said, reaching into the coffin to shake the lieutenant's frail hand.

"You're not as coldblooded as you pretend, Steve," Ray said, lifting himself a bit. "And work wasn't all you put into Muc Wa."

"What else, then?"

"Your heart. You put your heart into this garrison, and that's what made it worthwhile for you." He grinned at Stephen. "If you'd put half as much devotion into courting Rebecca, you probably wouldn't be here now."

"*Hey!*" the helicopter pilot yelled. "We ain't got all day, you guys."

Ray sank back. "No," he said, "you're not as coldblooded as you pretend. You ought to be careful about that, Steve. It could get you into trouble."

"GET ON WITH IT!" the pilot yelled.

"What kind of trouble?" Stephen asked, but the Raiders were shoving the coffin into the helicopter.

They crammed four wounded men into the cabin before the pilot made them stop. "Where are our reinforcements?" Stephen asked then. The pilot grinned, held up one finger, and pointed it at the second helicopter, which had settled upon the hillside about fifty meters away. A rucksack tumbled from the cabin door, and after it jumped a man—Captain

Olivetti. He ran toward Stephen, his white teeth sparkling, waving a carbine in his big hand.

"Lemme at 'em!" he crowed, like a rooster greeting the sun. "All I want out of this stinking mess is the CIB!"

Nineteen

There was a riot in progress when Rebecca left the Thaitan Astor. On the hotel sidewalk the rioters were waving placards accusing the government of religious persecution; across the Avenue de la Paix, where Rebecca wanted to go, the placards announced that the hotel-siders were Communist dupes. All the placards were in English. The opposing sides met from time to time in the middle of the avenue and trampled the white-clad policemen who were trying to keep them apart. On a side street near the hotel, Rebecca saw several truckloads of paratroopers, wearing steel helmets and carrying nasty little sub-machineguns.

"Excuse me, please," she said, stepping off the sidewalk. "*Excusez-moi.*" She picked her way through the straining, shouting rioters, using her rolled-up copy of the *Liberal* as a weapon. "Thank you! *Merci!*"

Halfway across the street, she came upon a clear space, and in the center of it a praying monk, sitting cross-legged on the cobblestones. He was wearing a brilliant yellow robe, and his begging bowl was beside him. Rebecca dropped a coin into the bowl. "*De rien,*" she said, smiling brightly at him. But the monk paid no attention to her. His newly shaved head was motionless, reflecting the rays of the sun. *How serene he is,* Rebecca thought, passing through the police line and into the anti-Communist rioters. She began to compose her next dispatch: *The hope of Southeast Asia may lie in its unpolitical monks, their eyes fixed serenely on eternity while* . . . It would require a lot of research, of course.

Slightly damp from her journey, she slipped into Le Longchamps, where the air-conditioning unit was murmuring and twenty or thirty crewcut young men were drinking Cokes and reading the *Thaitan American.*

"Meddem?" said the waiter, admiring her with his caramel eyes. Rebecca turned to the French side of the menu.

"*Le poulet, s'il vous plaît,*" she said.

"South-flied chicken, yes meddem!"

"*Avec salat et—*"

"Tossed sellit, yes meddem!"

"*—pommes frites.*"

"Flench flies, yes meddem!"

"Oh, *merde,*" Rebecca said, and the waiter blinked his lovely caramel eyes and backed away. He returned a moment later with a sweating bottle of Coca-Cola. *All right,* Rebecca thought. *So I'm an American. But I'll bet my French is better than yours.* She filled her glass, sipped from it, and solaced her pride by opening the *Liberal* at page sixteen:

"ALL I WANT IS THE CIB!"

BY REBECCA SHAW

Surrounded by barbed wire, Coca-Cola, and complaisant native women, the U. S. Army Raiders have turned this mountain paradise into one great concentration camp. . . .

The magazine had arrived that morning, and she had read her article six or seven times since breakfast. With each reading, her words had gained in grace, authority, and worth, until now they had the timeless force of inscriptions in stone. Petrel McMurphy had also sent her a check for sixty-five dollars. She had put the check into another envelope and mailed it to her father, as part payment on the two thousand dollars he had loaned her for this trip. She did not send him a copy of the magazine, however. Daddy was a Jew, but he was also a Cadillac-Oldsmobile dealer, and Rebecca suspected that he voted Republican as often as not.

"Mind if I join you, young lady?" a voice bawled in her ear. Rebecca looked up and saw General Hardnetz. "Seems to be the only empty chair in the house," he said. Then he recognized her, and his meaty, smiling face lost most of its cheer. "Ah," he said. "It's the correspondent." He looked around, as if tempted to flee, then he squared his shoulders and lowered himself into the chair. Rebecca rerolled her magazine and sat on it. "Lovely day," the general said, shaking out a copy of the *Thaitan American.*

"There seems to be a riot," Rebecca said.

"Yes," the general said. "Students."

"Oh," Rebecca said.

"Draft the lot of 'em!" General Hardnetz said. "Send 'em to fight the Commies—that'll cure their egghead notions." He glared meaningfully at Rebecca, then lifted the *Thaitan American* as a shield between them. "Draft the women, too, if I had my way," the general growled behind his newspaper.

Rebecca tried not to read the front page which General Hardnetz was holding up to her, but she couldn't help it. She skimmed the headlines about rebel atrocities and government aid programs and how many guerrillas had Rallied to the National Cause and—*dear God!*—a little one which announced: INCIDENT AT MUC WA. Rebecca moved the Coke bottle to one side, leaned forward, and read:

> Communist rebels in battalion strength last night failed in an attempt to capture a government outpost at Muc Wa, 200 miles north of Thaitan. The rebels were driven back with heavy losses, a military spokesman said.
>
> The spokesman described government casualties as "moderate." Muc Wa is garrisoned by a company of native Raiders and a small U.S. advisory team.
>
> The garrison will be reinforced against the possibility of further Communist attacks, the spokesman said.

Even before she finished the last paragraph (*Stephen is there*) Rebecca knew that she was going to squeal (*perhaps he is wounded, perhaps he is dead*). She struggled against the squeal, as she had so often struggled against stupid female impulses in the past, and lost. "NNNNNH!" she said, hating herself. The newspaper collapsed; she was gazing into General Hardnetz's eyes across a distance of twelve inches. *He's nearsighted, too*, Rebecca thought, and said: "I was reading about Muc Wa." The general nodded. Then, like embarrassed turtles, they withdrew their heads.

"Yes," the general said cheerfully. "They're having a bit of trouble at Muc Wa. Well, that's what comes of building these dinky little outposts around the countryside."

"What's wrong with outposts?"

"If you build an outpost, young lady, you've got to defend it," the general said, raising his newspaper again. "That's what the French did, and you know what happened to the French. They got the, um, stuffing kicked out of them." The story about Muc Wa came into view again as the general disappeared.

"What do they mean by 'moderate casualties'?" Rebecca asked.

"Means they weren't wiped out," the general said. "Yet."

"But the reinforcements—"

"Don't believe everything you read in the papers, young lady," the general said on the other side of the page. "They're full of lies. If you want to know something about Muc Wa, read the Hardnetz Report."

"What's that?"

"Can't discuss it," the general said. "It's classified."

Rebecca turned away, and through the plate-glass window she saw a flame, boiling yellow and black from the cobblestones of the avenue. *What?* she thought. *What's happening?* The straining, sweating rioters had vanished. The avenue was deserted, except for that boiling, incredible flame, like the burning bush in which Moses had seen the Lord. *I've lost my mind,* Rebecca thought. But there were people on the opposite sidewalk, and they saw the miracle, too. They were kneeling on the cement, their hands clasped, their faces turned toward the flame.

Then she recognized, at the heart of the flame, the black shadow of a man. He was still sitting cross-legged on the cobblestones. *It's my monk,* she thought. *He's set fire to himself, and I . . . I . . . I . . . I GAVE HIM TEN PIASTERS!*

A photographer ran up and began taking pictures, dancing around the flame with a camera glued to his face.

Rebecca could smell the charred flesh. *Oh, I wish I were home,* she thought. She looked at the table, where a plate had been set before her, and saw golden skin, delicately blackened at the edges.

"South-flied chicken, meddem!" the waiter said.

Outside the plate-glass window, the burning monk had fallen back upon the cobblestones, his legs still folded. The paratroopers had arrived. They knocked the photographer down, and two of them clubbed him with their sub-machine-guns, while the others threw buckets of sand upon the burning monk.

Twenty

"The relief column will be here Friday," Captain Olivetti said.

"Friday?" Stephen said, ready to collapse on the spot. "But that's three days."

"So it is," Captain Olivetti said. "Three days exactly."

"Why don't they wait three weeks while they're at it?"

"Don't get your balls into an uproar, Corporal," Captain Olivetti said firmly. "The convoy will be here Friday. We'll hold out."

It was the firmness that convinced Stephen. *What the hell!* he thought. *Let him take over. He knows what he's doing; he's a professional. And he slept last night, and the night before that. Let him take over, if he wants the CIB so badly. I'll keep an eye on him, though. These are my men, after all. This is my camp.*

Captain Olivetti led them on a tour of the garrison, tossing orders over his shoulder at Ski. Stephen walked on his right side, Cowboy on his left. When the captain smiled, Cowboy smiled, and they looked like identical twins. Captain Olivetti was head-and-shoulders taller and maybe fifty pounds heavier than the interpreter—but they had the same flashing smile, the same olive-brown skin, the same dark, cruel eyes.

"All right," Captain Olivetti said when they finished the tour. "The first thing we've got to do is fortify that little hill yonder, to give us someplace to fall back on. How are we fixed for bob-wire?"

"Just what's on the wall," Ski said.

"Cannibalize it."

"But, Cap'n, my wall—"

"Your wall, my ass. Take two squads and cannibalize it. . . . Courcey?"

"Here," Stephen said.

"Take two squads and dig a line of trenches around the command post. Dig 'em deep. . . . Cowboy?"

"Yes, sir!"

"Tell the refugees we want a thousand bamboo stakes. *Stakes,* got it? Two feet long, pointed at both ends, fire-hardened, dipped in shit. Tell 'em we want those stakes by fifteen hundred hours, and if they don't deliver we'll turn 'em over to Charlie Romeo. Got it?" Cowboy rubbed his palms together and ran off to terrorize the refugees. Captain Olivetti began shouting for Ackley.

"He sounds like he's calling a square dance," Ski grumbled. "Do this, do-see-do; do that, and ALL promenade!"

"He's right, though," Stephen said.

"I know he's right, goddammit. I just don't like the idea of some son-of-a-bitch flying in here from Penang and telling us how to run our camp."

"We'll keep an eye on him," Stephen said, putting his hand on Ski's shoulder.

By sundown Captain Olivetti was installed in his fortress with a handset radio, giving orders every ten minutes to Stephen and Ski on the perimeter. The Raiders were more cheerful, now that they had someplace to run to. They kept turning around to admire it in the last golden light of the sunset—bristling with stakes and barbed wire, slashed by trenches, and crowned with a five-foot wall of sandbags. The sandbagged wall was shaped like a dumbbell. It enclosed the command post and the commo bunker, where the Raiders would make their final stand, if things came to that.

I hope it doesn't come to that, Stephen thought. And then: *I should have fortified that knoll long ago. The trouble is, I've fallen in love with* Muc Wa. *A man loses his professional status when he falls in love. Captain Olivetti is doing a better job of defending Muc Wa than I was able to do, yet all he wants from this place is a silver rifle on a blue field, with a silver wreath around it—the Combat Infantryman's Badge. He is a professional, and I'm still an amateur.*

Charlie came with the darkness. He moved about two platoons of riflemen up to the river, where they dug in and began to shoot, stitching a three-foot ceiling of bullets over Muc Wa. Stephen, talking to Captain Olivetti on the handset radio, could hear the bullets pecking at the sandbagged walls of the command post.

"When will Charlie come over?" Captain Olivetti asked.

"I don't know," Stephen said, hugging the wall and listening to the bullets singing overhead, on their way to the command post. "He sounds pretty content, just as he is."

"Ackley?" the captain said, and the radioman came on. "Get us a flare ship," Captain Olivetti told him. Stephen moved along the wall to the northeast bunker and said hello to the Raiders inside. Then Ackley came on again. No aircraft tonight: the Americans were grounded and the locals were on red alert. "Another coup," Captain Olivetti said. "Goddamn these goddamned gooks." He sounded a bit anxious. "Corporal Courcey," he said then, "pull two squads off the west wall and replace them with the walking wounded."

Stephen picked the two smallest squads, because there was always the possibility that Charlie was suckering them, and the assault would come from the west. Corporal Old Man came back to duty with the walking wounded. He was very pleased to be commanding a platoon again, even a ghost platoon. Stephen could see him halfway across the camp, patrolling the west wall beneath his turban of bandages.

Toward ten o'clock Old Man sent a runner to Stephen. "Charlie there," he said when Stephen arrived. "Make hole." He went into a pantomime of soldiers digging a trench.

"Boom!" he said, and showed how Muc Wa would be blown up by dynamiters.

It was possible. Stephen listened, and sometimes between the cascades of rifle fire he thought he heard the clink of a shovel. He called Captain Olivetti on the radio and asked for star-shells over the west wall.

"Negative," the captain replied. "We don't have any to spare. Wasn't that old buzzard wounded in the head?"

"Yes," Stephen said.

"He's hearing things," Captain Olivetti said. "He's spooked."

That was possible, too.

All night, Captain Olivetti waited for an assault from the river, and Corporal Old Man waited for dynamiters to blow them up from the west, and Stephen moved from wall to wall. And nothing happened except the endless pecking of bullets against sandbags, trees, and human bodies.

Charlie's wearing us down, Stephen decided in the chill gray watch of morning. *Forty-eight more hours of this, and he'll be able to walk through the gate and find us all asleep.*

Ski loomed up in front of him, like a dead man emerging from the sea. "Well, Steve," he said—tonelessly, like a dead man. "What'd'you think of combat?"

"It's hard work," Stephen said.

"None harder," Ski said, and they walked on together.

Then the sun was up. It revealed an L-shaped earth wall, confronting the southwest bunker.

"Hot damn," Ski said. "Trench warfare." He raked his scalp with his fingernails. "Wednesday," he said in a thoughtful voice. "Two more days of this shit—if we live that long."

Charlie's earthworks were about twenty-five meters from the machinegun bunker, and ran for about twice that distance along the south and west walls. Every ten or fifteen minutes, a man popped up beneath a toadstool helmet and threw a grenade at the camp. Captain Olivetti took an M-79 grenade launcher down to the bunker and showed the machinegunners how to use it. Neither side did much damage, but the competition gave the Raiders something to do, to while away the hours. They cheered when the machinegun crew dropped a missile into the enemy trench. They also cheered when one of Charlie's grenades exploded on top of the bunker, and the machinegunners came boiling out of the sally port, covered with dirt. After a while the Raiders formed two teams. They took turns on the wall, trying to guess where Charlie's grenadier would pop up next, and to shoot him.

"I bet there's a whole damn company lying doggo in those trenches," Captain Olivetti said. "Just think what a couple of napalm bombs would do for them—*whoosh!*"

"The stink would be something awful," Ski said.

Captain Olivetti said no, that jellied gasoline burned too hot, that even a gook wouldn't smell when it was done with him. Stephen agreed with Ski. The captain called Ackley down from the commo bunker, to side with him, and they kept the argument going for an hour or so, knowing all the time that it was nonsense. There were no planes to drop the napalm. The local pilots were overthrowing the Premier in Thaitan, and the Americans were grounded, for fear some loyalist antiaircraft battery would mistake them for locals and shoot them down.

The sunset was splendid, red and purple, and the night was a repeat of the night before, with a fury of bullets from the east and the sound of digging from the west. They put up a few star-shells, but saw nothing. Then, at midnight, the southwest bunker exploded. The explosion was nothing spectacular: the logs and sandbags jumped a few feet into the air, then fell back, burying the dynamite's pale yellow flash, and the men and the machinegun inside. Then Charlie's men came through the gap.

"Jesus," Captain Olivetti said.

Ackley ran forward, swinging an M-1 rifle by the muzzle. "Watch me, Cap'n!" he shouted. In the light from a burning hooch they saw him tear into the rebels, swinging his rifle in the grand old Ackley manner, grunting and barking as he clubbed them down.

"The goddamn fool," Captain Olivetti said. He fired short bursts to the right and left of Ackley. Stephen did the same, but he was hollow inside, like a Confederate statue, condemned to fight forever in a hopeless cause. *First Toffee,* he thought. *Now Ackley.* The radioman was standing off twenty or thirty men, and more of them were swarming across the ruined bunker. *I wonder who's next,* Stephen thought.

Then Ackley went down. One moment he was standing tall above Charlie's men, then he disappeared, and the rebels surged across the ground he had been defending. "Silly damn fool," Captain Olivetti said. He changed magazines and fired into the center of the swarm, and Stephen did the same. Once, briefly, there was an eruption in the center, as if Ackley had succeeded in rising again. Then the swarm broke up and became a skirmish line, charging the Raiders with wild little yells.

They abandoned the southern half of the camp, pulling the machinegun out of the southeast bunker and mounting it on the knoll. Charlie did not press them. He was too busy digging in.

At dawn on Thursday three T-28s came down from Penang and looked them over. The planes carried U. S. Air Force markings. Stephen ran to the commo bunker and raised the flight commander on the radio.

"I got it, Blaze," the pilot said, when Stephen explained which part of Muc Wa belonged to the Raiders, and which to Charlie. "I got it. . . . How close d'you want me to come, over?"

"Stay the hell away from us," Stephen said. "Over."

"I can't get Charlie's forward position without hitting yours, Blaze. Request permission to drop it right on you, over."

"If you hurt one of my men, just one," Stephen said into the microphone, "I'll tell them to shoot you down. Over."

"There's no heroism left in this world," the flight commander said. "Over and out."

The T-28s came in one by one and dropped their bombs, four apiece, filling the air with noise and bits of earth, wood, metal, and flesh. Each blast seemed to tear a hole in Stephen's side. Then the planes came back to strafe the wreckage. Each T-28 was armed with pairs of fifty-caliber machineguns which fired at a leisurely pace: BRAK-BRAK-BRAK-BRAK.

"Training planes!" Captain Olivetti said. "What a way to fight a war."

But the Raiders were delighted. They stood up and waved at the pilots, until the T-28s dipped their wings and flew away, and Charlie began shooting again.

"One more day," Ski said. "One more lousy day, and that relief column will be here."

"That's right," Captain Olivetti said, smiling handsomely at them out of his mask of stubble and powder burns and dirt. "Just one more day."

Major Barker inspected his convoy—eight boxy deuce-and-a-half trucks, crammed with Raiders, and a little three-quarter-ton out in front—and felt so good about it that even Miss Shaw did not trouble him. "Don't be silly," he told her.

"But I flew all the way from Thaitan just to go on this convoy," she said. "Give me one good reason why I can't."

"One reason?" Major Barker said. He looked at her. *Cute little thing,* he thought. *I wonder if Olivetti was able to knock off a piece of that?* He searched for the world's best reason, the one that would vindicate him, the U. S. Army, and all masculine endeavors to the end of time. "All right," he said. "One reason—there's no filling station from here to the South China Sea."

"I don't quite see—"

"No ladies' room, Miss Shaw," the major told her. "I know what my Raiders will do when they hear nature calling.

They'll stand up in the trucks and fire over the side. What would you do?"

She opened her mouth, waggled it for a moment, closed it. Major Barker nodded politely and mounted the first troop carrier, beside Captain Jellison, who was going along for the ride and because he knew the lay of the land around Muc Wa. The major raised his right hand. The driver of the three-quarter-ton truck pulled his goggles down over his eyes, let out his clutch, and gave Major Barker an agonized smile. If the road had been mined, he would be the first to know it.

"Miss Shaw!" the major shouted. "Any message you'd like delivered to Captain Olivetti?"

Miss Shaw stuck out her tongue at him.

The convoy rolled down the hill to Penang. They swept through the outskirts of town, where bare-ass children ran out to squat in the dust and stare at them. Then they were hightailing down a twisty dirty road. The road followed a river, turning when the river turned; little mountain villages were scattered along it at intervals of three or four kilometers.

Captain Jellison asked about the operations plan. Major Barker drew a map on the dashboard, in the soft white dust which the three-quarter-ton truck was laying down on them: the Raiders would spend the night *here*, Major Minh's artillery was moving into position *there*. . . . Then he inquired about the progress of Operation Blackjack, which the Marines had launched in the western highlands.

"They broke and ran," Captain Jellison said. "One of my sergeants busted an artery in his neck, trying to keep up with them."

"Oh," Major Barker said. "Sorry about that."

"When I think what we could do with a couple divisions of U. S. Marines—"

"Or GIs."

"—we'd push old Charlie into the sea."

"Chase him all the way to Burma," Major Barker agreed.

"You're right, Jelly. We won't win this war until we bring in American combat troops. But it'll never happen."

"Wait until the elections," Captain Jellison said. "Things will be different then."

But Major Barker didn't want things to be any different. Not really. He was enjoying himself as he hadn't done since the last Commander's Conference in Thaitan.

By noontime the convoy had left the river and was climbing a mountain pass. The road looped like Christmas candy, on switchbacks supported by rotten timbers. The trucks groaned in their lowest gear. The men in the three-quarter-ton crouched behind their machinegun, waiting for Charlie to jump out of the bushes. Sweat trickled through the dust on Major Barker's face.

Then they were rushing downhill with the motors screaming. At the bottom, Major Barker saw a small white tombstone beside the road, and the rusted, weed-grown carcass of a French armored car. This was Checkpoint Alpha.

"A thousand men," Captain Jellison said, looking at the ambush site. "The French really did things in the grand style, didn't they?"

Major Barker checked his watch: thirteen hundred hours. He noted the time on the operations plan. The trucks would put them down at fourteen hundred hours, and the Raiders would strike south on a forced march that should bring them to Muc Wa before dawn, when Major Minh's howitzers would begin to fire. There was nothing grand about this operation. Major Barker felt a twinge of envy for the French, who could throw away a thousand men in a single gallant gesture. Lacking this flair, American officers had to settle for victories.

"Chopper!" Captain Jellison shouted.

"What the hell?" Major Barker said. "The Op Order doesn't call for any aircraft."

But the helicopter was after them, all right, buzzing the convoy like a motorcycle cop after a line of speeders. Then it settled into the field on the right side of the road. Major

Barker and Captain Jellison jumped down from the truck as soon as it stopped, and ran toward the helicopter.

The first person to step down from the aircraft was Miss Shaw, and right behind her was what's-his-face, the Y Team clerk-typist.

"Did she kidnap you?" Major Barker asked the clerk-typist, who was terribly anxious behind his dark-rimmed spectacles. "You'd better have a good explanation for this," the major told him. "A damned good explanation, or I'll have you shot."

"Sir, this message came for you at ten o'clock—"

"Ten hundred hours."

"Yes, sir, ten hundred hours, just after you left. I knew you'd want to see it, sir, so I took it upon myself to request a helicopter in your name—"

"SHOOT HIM!" Major Barker cried at the Raiders, who had dismounted from the trucks.

"Sir!" the clerk-typist said, going gray.

The Raiders didn't seem to understand. "Are you language-trained?" the major asked.

"Yes, sir," the clerk-typist said.

"Then tell these men to shoot you."

What's-his-face drew himself up to his best height. "Sir," he said, "the Uniform Code of Military Justice expressly forbids summary executions."

"I'm afraid that's right, Major," Captain Jellison said.

"Took it!" Major Barker cried, struck by a vision of the U. S. Army ruled by bespectacled, nameless clerks, all of them college graduates, all knowing the Uniform Code of Military Justice by heart. "Took it *upon* himself! To order a *helicopter!* In MY NAME!"

"And I took it upon myself to come along," Miss Shaw said.

"The message, sir," what's-his-face said, and pressed a radiogram into the major's hand. It read:

TO THE COMMANDER
Y TEAM (PENANG)
US ARMY RAIDER GROUP AIRBORNE

1. PENDING FURTHER ANALYSIS OF HARDNETZ REPORT RELATIVE TO STRATEGIC VALUE OF OUTLYING GARRISONS, YOU WILL NOT REPEAT NOT COMMIT ADDITIONAL PERSONNEL TO THE SUPPORT OF MUC WA.

2. PREVIOUS SOPS WILL APPLY.

FOR THE COMMANDER
X TEAM (THAITAN) USARGA

"My God," Major Barker said.

"What's up?" Captain Jellison asked.

Major Barker gave him the radiogram. "They want us to cut and run," he said. "I told them Muc Wa was nowhere, but they made me garrison it anyway, and now the silly bastards want us to cut and run."

"Sorry about that," Captain Jellison said.

"The Hardnetz Report. What the hell is the Hardnetz Report?"

"I asked them about that, sir," the clerk-typist said. "They wouldn't tell me. It's classified."

Miss Shaw cleared her throat. "I know," she said.

"You know? *You?*"

"Well, all my clothes were in the laundry and I had to borrow some underthings, you know, so I could fly back to Penang this morning—"

"Miss Shaw!"

"—so I went to see Beverly Ames, the *Tribune* correspondent? She told me."

"Miss Shaw," the major said, taking a deep breath. "We are standing in the middle of hostile territory. We could come under attack at any minute. *What* is the Hardnetz Report?"

"Well, it seems that General Hardnetz has proved that it's more expensive in the long run to scatter troops here and there around the countryside, as advisors. He wants to bring in American soldiers. You know—divisions and things."

"Hallelujah!" Captain Jellison said. "We're escalating!"

"What about the Raiders?" Major Barker said. *And what about me? I guess it's the old soldiers' home for me.*

"Can't they break out?" Captain Jellison asked.

"Sure they can break out," the major told him. *The old soldiers' home,* he thought. *The old soldiers' home for me.* "One hundred men carrying their wounded. How many d'you think would make it back to Penang?"

"Well . . ."

"And my Exec is there," the major said. "I don't want Al to get zapped."

"True," Captain Jellison said. "Al's a good man. Ambitious."

"We'll have to write off Muc Wa," the major said. "That's all we can do—write it off."

"Sorry about that."

"Right!" the major said, cheerful again. He put his hand on Captain Jellison's shoulder. "You've been to Muc Wa," he said. "You went in there with Al's section when we garrisoned the goddamned place. Can you show that helicopter jockey the way?"

"Sure."

"Tell Cap'n Olivetti that all American personnel will exfiltrate with you. Tell the Raiders . . ." *I should have been French,* he thought. "Tell them I wish I were with them in their last stand." He turned to Miss Shaw and the clerk-typist. "You two will ride back to Penang with me," he said. As he glared at them, he remembered what General Hardnetz had said, and wondered if this whole thing wasn't a Communist plot to discredit the Raiders, with Miss Shaw as their agent.

"You needn't worry about me, Major," she told him with a saucy smile.

"What's that?"

"I said: don't worry about me. I went to the bathroom before we left."

When he heard the helicopter, Stephen ignited a yellow smoke grenade just below the commo bunker, which was now the most sheltered spot in the camp. Then he told the machinegunners to stitch the fields to the west, north, and east, to encourage Charlie to keep his head down. Then he crossed his fingers.

The helicopter plumped against the hillside like a weary sow, and Captain Jellison and Captain Olivetti had a great reunion while the crewmen looked for bullet holes. They found three, and a small but determined flow of green oil. The crew chief looked at the pilot and pulled a long mouth. The pilot said: "How many Americans here?"

"Four," Captain Jellison said.

"Three," Captain Olivetti said. "The radioman was killed last night."

"That's a piece of good luck," the pilot said. "I can take three men and their sidearms and not a damned thing else. I'm losing my hydraulic fluid."

"So that's the way of it, huh?" Captain Olivetti said. He began to count on his fingers. "Well," he said when he was done. "It was only two nights, but it was three days, sure as hell." He flashed a big beautiful smile. "What're we waiting for?" he said. "Let's go home!"

The Raiders were getting the picture. They looked at the helicopter, then at the officers, then at the rain forest where Charlie was waiting. Then they looked at Stephen. *Time to come back from vacation,* he thought, and went over to confront the officers. "What's up?" he said.

"The relief column was called back," Captain Jellison told him. "Orders from Thaitan."

"So now we're supposed to bug out?"

"HEY!" Captain Olivetti said in his command voice. "The word is *exfiltrate*. You know the SOPs, Corporal."

"Why can't we bust out?" Stephen said. "Why can't we put the wounded men on the helicopter, and the rest of us bust out of here tonight?"

"We've already talked about that, Corporal," Captain Jellison said, soothing him. "Major Barker doesn't want to take the chance of losing you men on a breakout."

"What about the Raiders?" Stephen said. "We brought them here; we can't run out on them."

"Don't get into a sweat, son. It's not your country. They're not your men."

"The hell they're not!" Stephen said.

The crowd around the helicopter was growing larger, as the refugees and the walking wounded pressed in, and even some of the Raiders who were supposed to be on the wall. The pilot nodded to the gunner and the crew chief. They climbed inside the helicopter and casually took up their automatic rifles. "Let's get a move on," the pilot said to Captain Olivetti. "A buddy of mine got the ass this way, over on the border. The friendlies swamped his chopper and he couldn't get off the ground."

"Yeah!" Captain Olivetti said. "Where's that goddamned interpreter?"

Cowboy burst through the circle of Raiders. "Here, sir!" he said, grabbing the captain's sleeve.

Captain Olivetti shook him off. "Tell the Raiders to get away from that helicopter," he said. "Tell 'em the gunners will shoot any man that comes closer than ten meters."

"Yes, sir," Cowboy said. "You take me with you, sir?"

"TELL 'EM!"

"Please, sir! I am the interpreter, number-one interpreter."

Captain Olivetti made a fist and shook it in front of Cowboy's nose. Stephen walked between them, forcing the captain to stand back. "Tell the men, Cowboy," Stephen said.

"You don't forget me, sir?"

"No," Stephen said. "I won't forget you."

Cowboy looked at them. Then, his face twitching with doubt, he went off to shout at the Raiders.

Captain Olivetti laughed. "Well, goddamn!" he said. "You've really got a way with these gooks, Courcey."

"They trust me," Stephen said, a great hollow where his guts should have been.

Then there was Butterfly, very definitely pregnant beneath her camouflage shirt—Stephen's shirt. She was following three paces behind Ski. Her pretty nut-brown face was made up to refusal in advance. Ski led her up to the pilot and said: "This here is my wife. She don't weigh more than a hundred pounds. For Christ's sake, sir, can't you throw out a radio or something and take her along?" The pilot opened his mouth to object, but Ski beat him to it. "I'll pay for the goddamn radio," he said.

Captain Olivetti grew two or three inches. "Sergeant Oleonowski," he said. "Cut this shit out."

"But she's my wife, Cap'n."

"You don't have any wife."

"We was married by a priest," Ski told him.

"Your Form Twenty says you're single."

Ski's face was donkey-stubborn. "I slept with Butterfly every night for four months," he said. "She cooked for me. That's my kid in her belly. She's my *wife*, goddammit."

"Never mind, Ski," Stephen said, the hollow growing until it emptied his chest as well. "Butterfly can take my place. I'm . . ." He had to clear his throat, to keep the emptiness down. "I'm not going," he said.

Captain Olivetti lifted his big hands and shook them. "What the hell is this?" he demanded.

"Aw, Steve," Ski said. "I couldn't let you do that."

"You don't have anything to say about it. I'm not going."

"Well, Jesus," Ski said, scratching his head. "Thanks, Steve. If we have a boy we'll name him after you."

"Courcey," Captain Olivetti said. "I give you a legal order to get on that aircraft."

"You can wipe your ass with your legal order, Cap'n," Stephen told him, every bit as solemn.

They glared at each other for a moment, then Captain Olivetti gave a barking laugh. "The trouble with you, Corporal," he said, "you're a sentimental goddamn fool. You think with your balls instead of your brains. . . . But all right! I understand you to say that you're volunteering to lead the native personnel on a breakout."

"Understand me any way you want," Stephen said. *Captain Olivetti is the man I wanted to be,* he thought. *The efficient man. The engineer who does his job and gets out.*

"Very commendable, too," the captain said. "I'll put you in for the Bronze Star—if you make it. Don't forget to destroy the files, by the way."

I'm glad I failed, Stephen thought.

"Mortar!" Ski yelled, and the Raiders hit the dirt. The shell rustled down on them—WHUMP!—and carved a shambles of flesh where three of them had been crouching. The helicopter pilot went ghost-white.

"Load up!" he shouted. "Let's get the hell out of here!"

They buckled themselves in—Ski and Butterfly sitting against the firewall, between the gunner and the crew chief, and the two captains in the jump seats—and the jet turbine screamed. Another mortar shell exploded on the hillside, rocking the helicopter where it sat. The rotor blades blurred and screeched, the landing skids lifted . . . and then it was away.

Ray was right, Stephen thought. *He really learned something in that Unitarian Sunday School, in Michigan or Minnesota or wherever it was. . . . I'm not as coldblooded as I thought; Ray was right about that. I wonder if he was right about the rest of it.*

He ran up to the knoll to see the last of them. As the helicopter flew across Charlie's trenches, Captain Olivetti leaned perilously from the doorway and emptied his carbine at the rebels below. Then he waved the empty weapon at Stephen.

When I fell in love with Muc Wa, Stephen thought, *it seemed like a pretty good joke on the U. S. Army Raiders. And all the while . . .*

They made it, bucketing across the field until they reached the rain forest, then scrambling for altitude, and safety. They dwindled to a speck on the horizon, moving north-northwest. Then they were gone.

All the while, Stephen thought, as the silence closed down upon Muc Wa, *the joke was on me.*

Twenty-one

The convoy reached Penang at three o'clock. Major Barker refused to take her out to the airport, now or later, so Rebecca jumped down and hailed a pedicab. The trucks rattled to a halt just beyond her, and the major began shouting something about White Women Alone on the Streets. "Airport," Rebecca said, climbing into the cab, which was a little two-wheeled trailer slung behind a bicycle. There were motorized pedicabs, too, but she didn't trust them.

I wished him dead one time, Rebecca thought as the driver towed her at a great clip across the cobblestones. *But I didn't really mean it.*

The pedicab went into the main American compound and stopped in front of the officers' club. Rebecca got out. "No," she said, stamping her foot on the wooden sidewalk. "*Pas au* officers' club. *Je voudrais aller à l'aéroport.*" She stretched out her arms and swayed from side to side, making bumblebee noises. The driver nodded vigorously, she climbed back into the cab, and they were off again.

Let him be unhurt, she prayed. *Just let him be unhurt. I'll take it from there.*

After stopping at the PX, the Marine Corps compound, and the American Baptist Mission, they finally reached the airport at four o'clock. Rebecca paid the driver and ran into the stucco administration building. "The helicopter from Muc Wa," she said, her heart bumping anxiously against her ribs. "Has it landed yet?"

"Muc Wa?" said the airman behind the counter. "We got no traffic for Muc Wa today."

"Maybe it was the C-and-L ship," a sergeant said, coming up and leaning his elbows on the counter. "Was it the C-and-L ship, lady?"

"That's White Knight Six," a captain said from the row of desks beyond the counter.

"White Knight Six is on a round robin to Ambush Alley," the airman said, looking at a large blackboard with mysterious chalk marks upon it.

"They were diverted," the captain told him. "You don't have the revised manifest yet."

They all looked expectantly at Rebecca. "But where *is* it?" she asked.

The captain grew a sly and stubborn look. "Why do you want to know?" he said, and the airman and the sergeant drifted away. "Do you have authorization to be on U. S. Air Force property? Who are you, anyway?"

Rebecca gave him her iciest stare. "Where is your commanding officer?" she asked.

The captain pointed to a row of doors at the other end of the waiting room. Rebecca walked briskly toward them, then ducked outside, where she found a fat sergeant with a walrus mustache, sitting on a pile of canvas mail bags. He told her that White Knight Six was due in twenty minutes. "They had to stop and plug some bullet holes," he explained, fanning himself with his broad-brimmed hat.

Bullet holes, Rebecca thought. *Dear God!* And then: *I should have gone back to the Raider compound and put on fresh lipstick.*

She slipped into the administration building and found an airman to investigate the latrine for her, and to stand guard while she went inside. *Just let Stephen be unhurt,* she prayed. *Oh, I'm covered with dust!* She scrubbed her face with wet paper towels, while her nostrils quivered, assailed by the randy goat smell of the urinal. *I don't care if he is a soldier, I don't care if he did make love to Butterfly. I don't want him to be hurt.*

When she left the latrine, she saw . . . Ray Hamilton! He was dragging his duffel bag across the waiting-room floor. "Ray!" she cried. "Where did you come from?"

"I've been at the Baptist hospital," he told her, dreadfully pale and sad beneath his mustache. "Now they're evacuating me."

"Poor Ray! Were you wounded?"

"No," he said. "Malnutrition." He dragged his duffel bag to the doorway and paused there, gasping. "That's my ride," he said, pointing to a dowdy cargo plane, a twin of the one which had brought Rebecca to Penang. It was parked far down the field.

"Oh, please," she said to her fat friend, who was now loading mail bags into the back of a jeep. "This man is a casualty. Can you drive him to the plane?"

"Rebecca!" Ray said.

"Aw, sure," the fat sergeant said. "Where'd you get hit, sir?"

"Well, I—"

"At Muc Wa," Rebecca said.

"Lemme do that," the sergeant said, taking the duffel bag from Ray. "Everybody's talking about the fight you put up at Muc Wa, sir."

Rebecca made Ray sit in front while the sergeant finished loading the jeep. "When did you see Stephen last?" she asked, almost unable to breathe.

"The day before yesterday."

"Was he . . . all right?"

"Sure. He was hit in the shoulder, a week or so ago, but it wasn't anything serious."

"Wounded?"

"Just a scratch . . . Why, Rebecca! You're sweet on him, aren't you?"

"Of course not," she said, while her heart pounded with

delight. "But he's a man, after all, and there's enough suffering in the world already."

"Well, I'm glad," Ray said, looking sadder than ever. "The last thing Stephen said to me was how much he loved you."

"He didn't!"

"Sure he did."

"Stephen said that?" Rebecca felt as though she were floating. "Muc Wa has been good for him," she said. "He's learned something there."

"Yes," Ray said. "Only—"

"Only what?" she said, and thought: *He's going to tell me about Butterfly.*

"Well, it's not a good idea to fall in love with a country that isn't your own."

Yes, he means Butterfly, Rebecca decided. "It'll work out," she said.

"Sure it will," Ray said.

Rebecca rode out to the plane with them, sitting in the back of the jeep with the mail bags. "Good-by, Ray," she said, while the sun burned into her eyes. "Will I see you in North Carolina?"

"No," he said. "I'm planning to resign my commission."

"Good."

Ray touched his mustache. "It's not good to fail," he said.

"But to fail at something evil!"

"It didn't have to be evil. It wasn't for Stephen."

Rebecca wanted to object, but she couldn't. *If it's so terribly wrong to be a soldier,* she thought, *why do I want to see Stephen again?* So she hugged Ray's skinny body, and planted a kiss on his neck. *Please bring Stephen back to me. Please give us another chance.*

Then she saw the helicopter, a fat green beast, settling to the runway. It landed heavily, bounced once upon its landing skids, and came to rest. Rebecca ran toward it, her boots ringing on the perforated metal plates from which the runway was made. She was conscious that others were running, too, running to see the heroes of Muc Wa.

The first man down was Captain Olivetti, bristling with whiskers and pride; then that darling popeyed sergeant; then pretty Butterfly, wearing Stephen Courcey's shirt. *Ouch!* Rebecca thought. But still she strained to recognize the fourth passenger, and almost died when he proved to be the Marine Corps captain from Major Barker's convoy.

"But where's Stephen?" she asked. Sergeant Oleonowski stared at her with his pale, startled eyes. Then he jerked his thumb in the direction from which they had come. "Dead?" Rebecca asked.

"Well, well!" Captain Olivetti said. "Look at the reception committee!"

"Corporal Courcey," Rebecca said. "Is he—"

The captain slung the carbine over his shoulder, tugged the baseball cap down to his eyebrows, and gave her a long, appraising look. "In the Army," he said, "we count the living, not the dead. Be glad that two of us made it back, sweetheart. Forget about the two that didn't."

"Oh," she said. "Corporal Ackley, too."

"Died like a Raider!" Captain Olivetti said.

Rebecca was aware that Butterfly, wide-eyed as a frightened doe, was holding her hand, and that they were walking back to the administration building with a crowd of soldiers and airmen. A truck appeared from somewhere. She sat in front, between Butterfly and Captain Olivetti. The captain smelled of sweat, and gunpowder, and probably blood. *Stephen would have smelled like this,* Rebecca thought, accepting the massive arm that went around her shoulders. *Like flesh that has marched through hell . . . Stephen! Oh! You wanted to make love to me, and I was otherwise engaged, and now you're sleeping with the worms.* The truck rattled away from the airport and down the dusty dirt road to Penang. Rebecca felt that she was weeping, but the tears were internal, washing her heart instead of her cheeks. *The Army counts the living,* she thought. *Women count the dead.*

The truck stopped, and Captain Olivetti helped her down. They were standing in front of the Hôtel de Paris, a low, grim place with a roof of corrugated tin. Rebecca allowed him to lead her inside, and waited while he signed the register. *He's giving me a place to be weak in,* she decided. *He's kinder than I gave him credit for being. Or maybe he just understands women better.* She followed him up the worn wooden staircase. Two women in purple tunics were playing cards at the head of the stairs. One of them glanced up and gave Rebecca a hard, whore's smile, then returned to the game.

They went down a long creaky corridor, with jungle boots and high-heeled sandals outside some of the doors. Captain Olivetti stopped in front of number twelve, where there were no shoes. He opened the door and gently pushed her inside.

The room was dark. A great, sagging bed filled half the floor, and a toilet was running somewhere. Rebecca sat down in a cane-bottomed chair while Captain Olivetti drew back the mosquito netting and fluffed up the pillows; she glanced at the wall and found herself gazing into the inquisitive eyes of a reptile, larger than her hand. "Ooo!" she cried, jumping up.

"Just a lizard," Captain Olivetti said, drawing her to the bed. "Harmless. They catch mosquitoes and things."

She was sitting on the bed, then lying on it, and the captain's great sweat-smelling, gunpowder-scorched body pressed down on her.

Oh, dear God, Rebecca thought, going weak in all her joints, *he wasn't being thoughtful, after all. He means to make love to me.* Heavy lips smothered her, and a big hand fumbled at her belt. *I can't fight him—he's too strong. I've never known a man so strong.* The belt buckle came undone, and great, blunt fingers probed at her belly. *Scream? Who'd care if I screamed? And anyhow . . .*

I'll pretend he's Stephen, Rebecca decided, when the big hands lifted her up to get at the snap fastener on her bra. *I'll do it for Stephen.*

"Charlie will bust in here tonight," Stephen said.

"Okay," Old Man said, patting his bayonet. At some point in the past few days he had appropriated one of the M-1 rifles brought in by Captain Olivetti. "Me ready."

"Well, I hate to disappoint you, old buddy," Stephen told him, "but we're going to bust out before Charlie can make his move."

Old Man grinned toothlessly. "A-okay," he said, and they set to work.

Nothing had changed since morning. They still held the northern half of the camp, including the command post knoll, the latrine, and Toffee's vegetable garden. The parade field—where Stephen had turned out the Raiders every morning for four months—was now a no man's land. Beyond it, Charlie had slapped up his own defense perimeter, using the wreckage of the Raiders' sleeping huts, and barbed wire and sandbags from the south wall. And, of course, the main force of rebels was still hunkering out there in the rain forest, waiting for the big push tonight.

Old Man issued three kilos of rice to each man, and dumped the rest into the latrine. Cowboy smashed and burned the command post. Stephen went on a tour of the machinegun and mortar posts, showing the Raiders how to spike their weapons when the time came.

Toward sundown, while he was in the northwest bunker, five men appeared at the edge of the rain forest. Stephen checked them through his binoculars. They were running laboriously toward the camp, carrying no weapons, but with bulky packages tied around their waists. Dynamite. Charlie had worked out his plan of attack, apparently, and it called for a hole in the west wall. The machinegunner looked at Stephen. "Wait," Stephen said, holding up his hand, "wait

. . . wait . . . NOW!" The gunner fired, while his partner lay curled up on the sandbags beside him, asleep. Stephen fed the belts. *I can save the best part of Muc Wa,* he thought, watching a fly alight on the sleeping Raider's nose. *I can save the men who built the camp with me.* The sleeping Raider twitched his nose, then raised his hand to brush away the fly.

Three of the dynamiters managed to cross the ghost road, and one of them made it into the barbed wire. He lay there, wounded and gasping, while his buddies sniped at him from the rain forest. Eventually they hit him, and he vanished, together with twenty or thirty square meters of barbed wire. Stephen sighted the machinegun on this point, and made the gunner memorize the coordinates, in case Charlie moved first tonight.

Old Man's work crew had shifted most of the camp's hardware to the north slope. It made an impressive pile—jungle boots, bales of uniforms, thirty or forty carbines, cases of C-rations and sardines, and even a couple of General Hardnetz's Fiberglas coffins. Stephen mined the heap with thermite. He gave the trip wire to Old Man, who smoked a pipe until one of Charlie's mortar shells came rustling down. Then he pulled the wire. The heap burst into stinking flames, and Charlie would never know that his own shell had not started the blaze.

Seven o'clock. Stephen went into the commo bunker and told Ackley's assistant to warm up the generator. The codebook was on the counter. Stephen had a hell of a time finding the Morse alphabet, but finally he did, and he picked out THUNDERHEAD, THIS IS BLAZE on the telegraph key. He repeated it until the loudspeaker began to spit dots and dashes at him. He waited for a pause, then picked out the rest of his message: AS OF TWENTY-ONE HUNDRED HOURS, YOU MAY CONSIDER MUC WA ENEMY TERRITORY. Then he smashed the radio and the generator, and went outside, where the sun was a golden disc beyond the mountains.

And here was Angel, running toward him in her brilliant, electric-orange dress, made from parachute silk like the rest of her clothes. She jumped before she reached him, and Stephen caught her, supporting her with an arm beneath her bony little butt.

"You can't wear that dress tonight," he told her. "It'll show up in the dark."

"Okay," she said, locking onto him with her arms and legs.

"Don't you have anything else to wear?" he asked, but Angel only pressed her warm face against his neck.

Cowboy was sitting glumly in the shelter of the command post. Stephen squatted down beside him, still holding the little girl.

"Cowboy," he said, "why don't you hunker like the rest of us?"

"I am half-French, sir," Cowboy said in an unhappy voice.

"So what?"

"Frenchmen sit on the ground, sir. This is the white way."

"It's not my way," Stephen pointed out.

"Yes, sir," Cowboy said. "But I think you are more Buru than me . . . sir."

Stephen unhooked Angel and stood her on the ground. He lifted the electric-orange dress and pulled it over her head, managing to get it caught in her hair. Angel was enchanted. She helped him to untangle the garment, smiling at him out of her dark, delicate face, as if she knew all about men, women, and silk dresses. "You're too young, scamp," Stephen told her. "Why don't you look me up in five years or so?"

"Okay," Angel said.

He took off his fatigue shirt and buttoned her into it. With the sleeves rolled up, it made a pretty serviceable johnny. Angel held out the tails and turned around, admiring herself. *Between them,* Stephen thought, *these refugee girls have just about cleaned me out.*

Seven-thirty. The sun was down, and dusk was flooding the rain forest and the field.

"Cowboy!" Stephen said, slapping the interpreter's shoulder. "How'd you like to lead the breakout with me?"

"I am no soldier, sir," Cowboy said.

"Would you rather go with the refugees?"

"Oh yes, sir!"

"All right," Stephen said. "You can go with the refugees—on one condition. You'll take care of Angel. You'll carry her if you have to, but you won't let her out of your sight. Got it?"

"Yes, sir."

"If she's missing when we regroup," Stephen told him, "you'll wish Charlie had gotten to you first."

"You trust me, sir," Cowboy said.

Stephen kissed the little girl good-by. Then he went looking for Corporal Old Man, his lips tasting of the sardines which had been Angel's last meal at Muc Wa. *Here I go,* he thought. *Into combat with a white T shirt, like a goddamn fool.* He stopped at the lister bag and daubed the T shirt with mud. This was an improvement, but not much of a one.

Seven forty-five. The darkness was almost complete.

Following their orders, the gunners spiked their weapons and fell back on the knoll, where the burning supplies still gave some light. There were about twenty fighting men in each platoon. Corporal Old Man formed the platoons into a diamond, with the wounded men and the refugees in the hollow center. He would command the rear guard. Stephen would take the point. They would punch out through the north gate, which was the only one they still controlled.

Eight o'clock.

"All right," Stephen said. "Let's go."

As soon as he was clear of the gate, Charlie's men sprang

up from the ground at his feet. The night winked with muzzle flashes. Somewhere a machinegun was hammering. Stephen felt desperately lonesome, knowing there was no haven at his back, no reserve platoon, no Ski to come hollering to the rescue. He clubbed down a shadow that appeared in his path, ran on a few paces, swung his carbine at another shadow. The platoon was still with him, and still seemed in pretty good shape. They were halfway down the slope, halfway between the camp and the gravesite. The wet grass swished under Stephen's boots. . . . Great flurry of shooting behind him: Charlie must be swarming over the knoll and biting at Old Man's heels. *The second and fourth platoons are through the gate,* Stephen thought. *I can't push too hard now or I'll lose the wounded.* . . . There was the gravesite, the French cross looming gray in the darkness. Stephen went on at a hard walk, firing the carbine single-shot from the hip. *It's all a matter of statistics now,* he thought. *So many men, so many cubic meters of air, so many bullets flying across . . . There's not a damned thing I can do to better my chances.* The carbine clicked empty, and he turned the taped-together magazines end for end, and fired again.

He saw the rain forest, a black line between the sky and the ground, and a crazy winking of flame that meant Charlie was waiting for him there. *Sweet Jesus,* Stephen thought. *I wish I was wearing my camouflage shirt.*

THUNK-THUNK! of carbines, just behind him. The second and fourth platoons had closed the gap.

"Move out!" Stephen said. He slapped the shoulder of the man beside him, and set off at a jog trot to the forest's edge. *So many bullets, so many cubic meters of air for them to travel through* . . . A shadow reared up, a thunderous weight fell upon his shoulder, he staggered against a tree. The shadow disappeared; the Raiders were moving past him into the rain forest. Stephen ran on. Thorns tore his fatigue trousers, branches whipped his face. *We're through!* he thought, and then the bullet struck him. It exploded like a star-shell in the flesh and muscle at his waist, lifted him on a ballooning, crimson wave of pain, and finally dropped him from a great height upon the forest floor.

Rebecca sat up in bed. She felt a vague sense of unease, as if the roof were about to be torn from the world, leaving her naked to eternity. Of course, she *was* naked; maybe that was it. She heaved at Captain Olivetti's mighty arm until the luminous dial of his wristwatch came into view. Nine-thirty. "Wha?" the captain said in his sleep. "Wha?" Rebecca let the arm drop. Even then, Captain Olivetti slept on.

She was bone-chilly, but she was damned if she would snuggle up to *him* for warmth. So she searched the floor until she found the blanket, which she wrapped around herself, still sitting up in bed. The sense of unease did not go away. It wasn't caused by the sex business, either. She was a bit sore around the chest, but otherwise she felt fine, at peace with her body if not her soul.

"Oh, hell," she said, and got out of bed. Her toes curled on the cold floor. She moved the cane-bottomed chair to the window and sat down, overlooking the corrugated rooftops of Penang.

"Wha?" Captain Olivetti asked from the bed.

Beyond the town, far in the mountains, a white light was playing against the clouds. Rebecca held her breath and listened. Across the night she heard a low, distant grumble, like the faraway passage of a train. "Oh, that's it," she said. "It's a storm. The monsoon is beginning."

"WHA?" The bed creaked, and Rebecca saw the captain's ghost-gray form, lurching upright.

"It's a storm," she said, pleased that she had awakened him.

Captain Olivetti stumbled out of bed. He groped toward the window, clearing his throat and whacking his chest. "*Pagh!*" he said. He leaned through the window and spat.

Then he turned his great head, studying the stars. "Howitzers," he said.

"What?"

"One-five-five howitzers. Looks like Muc Wa's fallen, and Major Minh is blowing it to hell."

Rebecca shivered. "Poor Stephen," she said.

The captain hitched his butt upon the windowsill. "Hell," he said. "Don't worry about him. He's a Raider."

"But why?" Rebecca said. "That's what I've never been able to understand."

"Why what?"

"Why Stephen was a Raider."

"Sweetheart," Captain Olivetti said, "Raiders are the roughest, toughest, goddamnedest soldiers in the U. S. Army, as I plan to demonstrate in about five minutes." He spread his hand across the nape of her neck. "I guess Courcey just wanted to prove he was good enough to belong to the best." His fingers closed. The awful thing, the unforgivable thing, was that her neck thrilled to the grip, her whole body thrilled, as if it wanted to curl up in a warm, pulsating ball and be clenched forever in the captain's hand. "But!" he said. "He didn't quite make it."

"Why do you say that?" Rebecca asked. *Squeeze harder!* she thought. "What do you know about Stephen Courcey, anyway?"

"He got too involved with the gooks, I know that. He wasn't a pro."

"Professional killer?" But while her mind kept him off, her body ached to be overwhelmed by him. "Professional *murderer*," she said, hunching her shoulders beneath his great, massaging fingers.

"Professional anything," he said. "A professional knows when to quit. . . . But what's all this crap about Courcey, anyway? He's only an enlisted man."

"Damn you!" Rebecca said, jumping up. The blanket fell away. "You snob," she said. "You . . . you . . . you TURD!"

The captain laughed. "Anyhow," he said, "if you're so all-fired interested, why don't you ask him?"

"How?"

"Well, if he got out of Muc Wa before the howitzers opened up—"

"But—"

"—I'll bet he comes walking down out of those hills with most of his company intact. He's a hard-assed Yankee. I think he'll make it, if he uses his head and doesn't pull any more damn-fool tricks."

"But you told me—"

"Soldiering isn't as dangerous as it's cracked up to be," Captain Olivetti said. "If a soldier remembers what he's been taught, he'll be all right. The main thing is—"

"You told me—"

"The main thing," Captain Olivetti told her, "is not to get involved. A man loses his cool when he gets involved."

"You told me he was dead!"

"Not me."

"You told me—"

"I said Ackley was dead. Not Courcey."

Rebecca balled her fists and advanced upon him. He backed off. "Just tell me clearly," she said, "was Stephen Courcey alive when you left Muc Wa, or was he dead?"

"Alive," the captain said, backing toward the bed.

"But why did you leave him behind?"

"He volunteered to stay, so the Raiders wouldn't stampede. Hell, he insisted on staying. That's what I was telling you: he got involved with the place, and all for nothing."

"But it's a good thing, to be involved."

"Not if you want to stay alive."

"What kind of a life is *that?*"

"Better than no life at all," Captain Olivetti said. He had reached the bed, and they both stopped.

"You're wrong," Rebecca said. "Wrong, wrong, wrong!" And then the tears came. They flooded her eyes and poured down her cheeks—sweet, easeful tears. There seemed to be no end to them. Through them, she saw the lights dancing against the clouds, dancing above Muc Wa, dancing over the grave that had suddenly been opened. "Do you really think," she said, "there's a chance that Stephen will come back?"

"Sure," Captain Olivetti said. "If he uses his head for a change." He grabbed at her, but she was too quick for him. She hammered his face and chest with her fists, pounded him as hard as she could, and he fell back on the mattress without her.

I did the same thing to Stephen, Rebecca thought. *The very same thing.* She had a sudden vision of the world as a place where men and women tripped over each other's feet, endlessly. *Dear God,* she thought, picking up the scattered pieces of her clothing. *How will I ever look Stephen in the face again?*

Twenty-two

Stephen was half out of his skin all night, and for a while he left it altogether. He saw himself as a frozen, muddied tramp in a marshaling yard. Sometimes the boxcars were slamming together, shaking the earth with their SLAM-SLAM-SLAM, and at other times he heard the ghostly freights, highballing in the distance. The tramp's body—his body—was sprawled on its back with an arm across its face and one leg drawn up. A fox was tearing at its guts. Every now and again the fox would stop, clean the blood and the scraps of flesh from his muzzle, and look up at Stephen with bright, friendly eyes. Stephen was floating on a glistening silver cord, fifteen or twenty feet above the body. Sometimes the fox disturbed this cord, and Stephen bobbed up and down like a kid's balloon, and the tramp moaned: *It hurts it hurts O Christ it hurts.* And the boxcars shook the earth:

SLAM—*shrrr—sh—sh—shrrrrrrr*—SLAM . . . SLAM!

Toward dawn, however, he returned to himself and understood that he was listening to 155-millimeter howitzer shells passing overhead. The guns were four or five miles beyond him. The target was a mile or so behind. First he heard the guns going off, then the shells rustling and rumbling on their invisible tracks, then the explosion, and finally the echoes as they crashed back from the hills.

I've been left behind, he thought. *My boys ran out on me. Or they missed me in the dark. Yes, that was it: darkness, and Charlie all around. I don't remember yelling when I was hit. Maybe I didn't make a sound, so how would the*

Raiders know I was down? Sure. They just kept on going. That's what I taught them to do: keep moving, no matter what. Yes. I bet Old Man is kicking himself right now. I bet he's on his way back to get me, the old buzzard. Yes.

He slept for a while, and awoke to morning, and silence. But the fox was still gnawing at his side. He explored the pain with his fingers, expecting to find his guts bagging out, but there was only a small, neat puncture and a lot of blood. So he was in pretty good shape, except for the pain. Sometimes it was larger than he was, and nearly drove the soul from his body. He clenched his teeth and held it in.

Toward midday he got his feet underneath him and managed to stand. He seemed ten feet high, six feet wide across the shoulders. His knees could barely support the great bulk of him.

I'm nowhere near Muc Wa, he thought. *I must have crawled into the rain forest after I was hit. I'd better get the hell back there, back to Muc Wa, or Old Man will never find me.*

He had a hellish job of it, steering his great body through the rain forest. Every few minutes he had to stop and rest against a tree. The sunlight came dappled through the branches, not much, but enough to give him a rough compass, so he could pick out the next tree between him and Muc Wa.

Once he heard voices. They were rebel voices, must have been rebel voices, because the Raiders knew better than to talk when they were moving through the rain forest. Stephen rested against his tree with his eyes closed, and after a while the voices went away. He picked another tree and steered toward it. He could see blood on his T shirt, where thorns had snagged him, but he could not feel the pain. There was no more room in his body for pain.

I gave my shirt away, he thought. *I should have been more careful.* He reached the tree and leaned against it. *Life is a funny business,* he thought. *It keeps throwing these choices at a man, so the damn fool thinks he's free as a bird; but all the time he's just a man walking down a road, making his own road as he goes along, and he can never go back and take one of those forks over again. . . . A man ought to be careful about that,* he thought. *A man should be mighty careful.*

Like that business with Rebecca. I decided it would be a great thing to get Rebecca into bed, and before I knew where I was—I was in love with her. And that brought me to Muc Wa. I fought for it, the best way I knew how, just as I had fought for Rebecca, and so I fell in love with Muc Wa, too. And it has killed me. Yes. Because Old Man won't come back for me, not unless he has forgotten everything I taught him.

But he kept moving from tree to tree, steering his clumsy, bloated body in the direction of Muc Wa. There was nowhere else for him to go.

Late in the afternoon he broke through to the sunlight. For a moment he thought he had come to the wrong place. Even the trees were gone, torn to yellow splinters, and the earth had been plowed by a madman's plow. But of course it was Muc Wa. Not even a madman would have gone to so much trouble to destroy an empty field.

You have to admire efficiency like that, he thought, looking across the shattered field, at the garrison he had built. The wall—Ski's wall—had disappeared. The bunkers were gone, and the gates. The command-post knoll had been scalped clean, and only the red-black earth remained, like drying blood. *All our work!* Stephen thought. *All our barbed wire, sandbags, logs, canvas; all our planning and our digging; all those months of sweat—they smashed it in an hour with their howitzers. Men are clever dogs.*

He steered across the field, from shell hole to shell hole, knowing that if he fell into one he would never get out. Then, halfway across, he was challenged. The voice came from a thicket of broken trees. Stephen peered into the thicket, and saw that it was the old French gravesite—earth, wood, and stone now mingled together. *Toffee's grave,* he thought. *They've smashed that, too, the bastards.*

A rebel soldier was hunkering there in the shade. He was Buru, like the Raiders; he had the same flaring cheekbones and gentle eyes. His black pajama shirt glistened with blood. *He's been wounded, too,* Stephen thought. *We have been wounded by the same enemy.*

An M-1 was cradled in Charlie's delicate arms, looking more like an antitank gun than an infantry rifle. The rack number of some basic training outfit—G-74—was stenciled near the butt. Charlie brought the rifle around until it was aimed at Stephen. But his eyes were still gentle. They looked at Stephen across the blade front sight, then they hardened a bit, like fudge cooling in the pan. Stephen held out his hand. "Don't shoot," he said. "There's no reason to shoot." Too late: he was spitted on the muzzle flash. The M-1 rang in his ears like a baseball bat—WHUCK!—and he was lifted off his feet. *Of course,* he thought. *Charlie fought for Muc Wa, too.*

He was on his back, and Charlie was tugging at his boots, pulling them off. *Silly bastard,* Stephen thought. *They'll never fit you.* Then he was alone, looking up at the sky. He saw what he had never seen before—that the blue dome had veins in it, tiny hairline cracks, and that these cracks were now widening.

A *man ought to be careful,* he thought, as the blue dome came apart like a jigsaw puzzle, revealing the blackness which had always lurked behind it. A *man should be mighty careful what he chooses to love, what he chooses to fight for,* Stephen thought. *Because life will damned well make the choice stick.*

1. Vietnamese Conflict, 1961- —Fiction. I. Title.

PZ4.F6929In 67-12876